CLOSE CALL

*J. M. Gregson titles avilable from
Severn House Large Print*

Dusty Death
Just Desserts
Too Much of Water
Wages of Sin
Witch's Sabbath

CLOSE CALL

J. M. Gregson

Severn House Large Print
London & New York

This first large print edition published in Great Britain 2007 by
SEVERN HOUSE LARGE PRINT BOOKS LTD of
9-15 High Street, Sutton, Surrey, SM1 1DF.
First world regular print edition published 2006 by
Severn House Publishers, London and New York.
This first large print edition published in the USA 2007 by
SEVERN HOUSE PUBLISHERS INC., of
595 Madison Avenue, New York, NY 10022.

British Library Cataloguing in Publication Data

Gregson, J. M.
    Close call. - Large print ed. - (A Lambert and Hook
    mystery)
    1. Lambert, John (Fictitious character) - Fiction 2. Hook,
    Bert (Fictitious character) - Fiction 3. Detective and
    mystery stories 4. Large type books
    I. Title
    823.9'14[F]

    ISBN-13: 9780727876058

Printed and bound in Great Britain by
MPG Books Ltd, Bodmin, Cornwall.

This, my thirtieth detective novel, is dedicated to the memory of my parents, Harry and Elizabeth Gregson, who died before the first one was published but encouraged me mightily in everything I ever attempted.

One

It was not the sort of place where anything dramatic should happen.

Gurney Close was a small new cul-de-sac of modern houses, completed in the late spring of 2005. Few of the residents knew much about the man after whom their little road was named. Ivor Gurney was a tragic participant in that war to end wars which ravaged Europe from 1914 to 1918. He survived the slaughterhouse, half genius, half madman, after the shells had shattered the fragile control which directs the human brain.

Ivor Gurney's poetry and music are remembered with affection and reverence by a few devotees in his native Gloucestershire, so that, almost a century after the war which had at once formed him and destroyed him, this little close of detached residences in pink-red brick was named after him. It was a well-meant but rather desperate sort of homage.

Apart from its name, Gurney Close was an unremarkable place. These were excellent dwellings, erected by a local builder of good repute. There were only four residences, three detached houses and the bungalow at the far end of the development, which the planning committee said should be included to provide a proper balance and take account of the needs of the elderly.

The new residents were a diverse group, but they found themselves united by that camaraderie which comes from a common experience: in this case, that of establishing themselves in brand-new homes on what had formerly been rough pasture land. The uneven ground, crudely levelled into building plots by the builder's bulldozer, ran down to within sixty yards of the banks of the Wye, one of England's loveliest rivers. But none of the houses had a view of its waters, though the tall oaks between the close and the river provided a pleasant enough backdrop to the little group of new buildings.

The new owners went into each other's homes to study the plastering and the plumbing, to deplore the mistakes the architect had made and which any sensible mortal would have avoided. They shook their heads sadly over the work confronting them as they strove to carve out their small new gardens, and moaned their ritual moans about the way the builder had removed the topsoil and left them to contend with clay and stones.

They met each other in the supermarket in Ross-on-Wye, as they stocked their new built-in fridge-freezers. They came across each other again in the garden centres as they bought roses and bedding plants and strove for some immediate colour in front of the raw new walls. They deliberated together over the shrubs in pots, and then bought flowering cherries and robinias which would soon grow too tall for their modest modern plots.

They called cheerfully to each other across the fences of their gardens, as they filled their new wheelbarrows with stones, buoying each other with a horticultural optimism which was mostly destined for disappointment. They even drank cans of beer and bottles of wine together at the end of the long June days, when their limbs ached and their bodies filled with a not unpleasant lassitude.

It was all predictable and acceptable. It was even, if the truth were told, a little boring, to those not involved. Gurney Close would probably have disappeared quietly into an unchronicled suburbia, if it had not been for those startling events at the beginning of July.

Two

Ronald Lennox fancied himself as an observer of people. He had retired from teaching eight months earlier. This was a relief to him: he had felt out of touch with modern youth for a decade and more, and found control of his pupils increasingly onerous. But with time on his hands after forty years in schools, Ronald found his life unexpectedly empty at first. Then, during the dark months of his first winter of retirement, he had taken much care over the purchase of the new bungalow at the end of Gurney Close. After much heart-searching, he had disposed of most of the furniture in his big semi-detached house in Ross-on-Wye, and moved into his spruce new residence during a heatwave in the first week of June. Ronald Lennox thought he had taken all of these decisions himself, but his grown-up son and anyone else acquainted with the couple knew that they had in fact been taken by his very capable wife, Rosemary.

Ronald's fair hair was silvering and

thinning now, a little easier to control than it had been in his youth, but it still usually looked in need of a comb, even when he had just attended to it. He was one of those men upon whom even well-tailored clothes never sit easily. His suits crumpled when they would have settled smoothly upon others; his sweaters always seemed to need a hitch at the top to make them sit properly upon his thin shoulders.

Lennox remained cheerful in spite of these trials heaped upon him by a hostile fate. Nevertheless, he usually appeared rather surprised when events followed the course he had envisaged for them. He was well-informed about most things, though he had never been able to carry his learning lightly. He looked well-meaning, and he generally was well-meaning, but things rarely turned out exactly as Ronald Lennox had planned them.

Rosemary Lennox was as neat and well-organized in her life as Ronald was erratic in his. It seemed that there was never a hair in her neatly coiffured grey locks which dared to stray out of place, however vigorous the activities she undertook. And her head, with its small, pretty features, seemed to set the tone for the body beneath it. Rosemary's once-tiny waist had thickened a little with the years, as was only fitting, but she retained a neat and well-defined figure.

She had been an excellent tennis player in her youth, the reliable partner everyone had wanted in doubles, whether women's or mixed. 'Neat but never gaudy,' her favourite partner had called her, at the dinner to celebrate her retirement from the county tennis scene. Rosemary played a sturdy game still at her local club, and was much in demand on various committees for her common sense and efficiency. She organized the rota which ran the aged and the infirm to hospitals, and helped to staff other medical and day centres.

It was Rosemary Lennox who suggested the street party.

It was ten days after the last of the new residents had moved into Gurney Close. At nine forty on a perfect June evening, they were exchanging notes across their embryo front gardens in the last light of the long day. Rosemary thought afterwards that she had made the suggestion as much to distract Phil Smart as for any merits of its own.

Phil was fifty-one, florid, and with an excellent head of rather unruly grey hair. He was already threatening to become the roué of the new little community. He was eyeing the rear of his next-door neighbour, Alison Durkin, when Rosemary made her suggestion about a party.

It was, Rosemary was forced to admit, a splendidly rounded rear, and the flimsiness of the cotton skirt which the thirty-two-year-old Ally was wearing was entirely appropriate to the heat wave. But Philip Smart's eyes were getting more bulbous by the moment, and the lecherous attention he was bestowing upon Ally's flanks suggested fantasies which were anything but honourable. Rosemary decided that in a man who had a largely sedentary occupation and was running a little to fat, a prolonged attempt to clarify the mysteries beneath his neighbour's skirt might lead to all sorts of cardiac dangers.

And the randy sod must learn to control himself, if Gurney Close was going to be a pleasant place to live.

So Rosemary Lennox said, 'I think we should have a street party.'

'A street party?' Phil Smart wrenched his attention unwillingly away from Alison Durkin's buttocks to his neighbour on the other side.

'A street party,' said Rosemary firmly. It had been a spur-of-the-moment idea, but she spoke now as if it had been the product of many hours of mature consideration. 'We had them to celebrate the end of the war, when I was a small child.'

'A very small child indeed, you must have been,' said Phil Smart, with automatic and highly suspect gallantry.

'I think I was three. So I can't remember

13

the details. But I know we all sat round tables in the street, and had sandwiches and cakes and lemonade.'

'And you're suggesting we should do that?' This was Robin Durkin, who had appeared round the side of his house at the sound of this conversation. He patted his wife's splendid rear absent-mindedly as he passed her, and she straightened up and came to stand beside him. Robin Durkin tried to smile at his worthy older neighbour, but his square face showed his horror at the thought of sandwiches and lemonade. 'To be honest, Rosemary, it doesn't sound like much fun, this street party.'

Robin was a coarse-featured, cheerful man, who had started doing car repairs behind his house in Gloucester nine years ago and now, at the age of thirty-three, employed two mechanics in his own garage. He was swinging a plastic pack on his fingers, and he now passed tins of beer from his fridge to a grateful Phil Smart and Ron Lennox. Rosemary Lennox refused his offer with a smile, but Ally Durkin accepted one readily, pulled the ring-pull, and took a long, appreciative drink directly from the can, like the men beside her. 'Hits the spot, that,' she said, and wiped the froth from her lips with the back of her hand.

Phil Smart found this a captivating perfor-mance. The idea of a woman shaped like Ally

Durkin who could also drink like one of the boys was a new and beguiling concept to him. Women like that hadn't been around in his young day: Phil was left feeling, as he often did, that he had been born a generation too early. He ran a hand through his abundant hair and gave Ally a broad smile of approval.

Then he dragged his mind back to the notion of intelligent comment. 'I can't say that the idea of sandwiches in the street and lemonade has much appeal for me either, frankly, Rosemary.' He'd just stopped himself from saying 'old girl'. It must be his natural gallantry which made him so sensitive, he supposed.

Rosemary Lennox shrugged. 'Just a suggestion. Thought it would be nice to have a little get-together of some kind, that's all. And we needn't have sandwiches and cakes. We could have beer and wine. And sausages and pork pies, if we felt that was more appropriate.' She tried not to stare at the portion of Philip Smart's stomach which bulged over his belt.

'Now you're talking!' Like many men who exude a professional bonhomie, Phil Smart was not really very sure of himself, and constantly checked other people's reactions, anxious to make certain that he was voicing the general opinion. 'A bit of nosh and a decent booze-up sounds a better idea altogether. Might even develop into the first Gurney Close orgy, with enough alcohol and a following wind.' He laughed rather nervously and looked away from everyone and towards the fresh green leaves of the oaks at the end of the close, fearing that he might be pushing things too far and too fast.

'I can get us a discount on a couple of cases of wine and a few cans,' said Robin Durkin, warming to the idea as he saw a way to assert his importance to this new community. His rather scanty educational qualifications had left him feeling at a secret disadvantage, but he was well aware that he could buy and sell most of the people in this little group. When you were in the garage trade, there were always people who were looking for reciprocal favours. And it would get him off on the right foot with his new neighbours here; there was nothing wrong with letting everyone know that he was a man of influence when it came to getting hold of things.

'We'd better all be honest about this. We shouldn't arrange a communal celebration without being sure that everyone approves of the idea.' This was Carol Smart, who had come out through the open front door of the house and watched her husband's performance with a resigned air. She had forced herself to speak: she had so far found it difficult to join in the communal sharing of troubles, to enjoy the small hilarities which were part of the inevitable consequences of moving into the new houses.

Carol Smart was eight years younger than her husband. She was a doctor's receptionist at a surgery in Hereford, who spent most of her time dealing with the general public. Perhaps that had given her a jaundiced outlook on life, which she treated with suspicion, as if it were constantly trying to waylay her. She was forty-three and still very attractive in her buxom and busy persona, when she allowed herself to be. But she professed herself to be happier with records than with people, and so far she had not found it easy either to relax with her new neighbours or to respond spontaneously to them.

But Rosemary Lennox was already seeing Carol as a challenge. She knew her a little already, because they had been on the governing board of the same primary school for the last year. In that context, she had found Carol both intelligent and perceptive. She had no doubt that Carol Smart should be centrally involved in any celebration involving the occupants of the new residences. For one thing, it was axiomatic to Rosemary that any such occasion should involve everyone; diversity in personalities should be a strength of any community, not a weakness, in her view.

And for another, she was sure that Carol

17

Smart would prove to be naturally retiring, perhaps even a little shy, rather than stand-offish, as the Durkins had already hinted to her that she was. Rosemary said firmly, 'I'm sure you'd enjoy it, Carol. And we'd certainly need you to be involved, if we decide to have the street party. We'd need one of the excellent home-made quiches which Phil says you're so good at, to get the thing off to a good start.'

'And I'm told I do quite a good cheese-cake,' said Alison Durkin with a modest smile.

'And of course we must include Lisa,' said Phil Smart cheerfully. They all looked automatically towards the first house in the close, secure in the knowledge that there was no one there at the moment to look back at them.

Lisa Holt had just completed her divorce. This move into a new house was intended to be tangible evidence, to herself and to others, of her determination to make a fresh start in life. The traumas of separation and marriage break-up seemed to have had little visible physical effect upon her. Lisa was a very well preserved thirty-nine-year-old. Ms Holt's newly-divorced status would no doubt always have attracted an enthusiastic and conventional libertine like Philip Smart, but her trim figure and shining blonde hair were more immediate attractions for him.

And suddenly, as if riding into a film on a cue, Lisa Holt was with them. In the silence and the heavy heat of the June evening, the sound of the car engine was audible long before the vehicle came into sight. The noise, seeming at first to come faintly through the trees to them from some higher reach of the river, grew steadily in volume, and the little group which had assembled by their new garden gates fell foolishly silent. It was as if the noise held a mysterious significance for them, and was stilling their tongues with some ridiculous spell.

The silence gave the car's driver the entrance of a distinguished visitor. The small, dark-blue Vauxhall Corsa seemed to have been expected for a lengthy period by the time it turned into the close, and one or two of the spectators had to resist an impulse to applaud. Lisa Holt must have been conscious of her audience, but she was in no hurry to acknowledge it. She parked the car carefully near her new front door and made sure the handbrake was firmly on before she undid her seat belt. Then she slid from the car, gathered the various plastic bags containing her purchases, and turned towards the entrance to her house.

Only when she was almost there did she call a cheerful 'Good evening!' to acknowledge the attention of her new neighbours.

It was Ron Lennox who responded. 'Have

you got a minute, Mrs Holt?' he said. It sounded a stiff form of greeting, but he was not sure what the correct address was for a newly-divorced woman. And Lisa made him a little nervous in any case, as an older man; Ron found his mind leaping back over half a century, to the days when his father had taught him to raise his cap automatically to any adult female. Indeed, his hand moved a little towards his thinly-covered pate, then, as if it were disconcerted to find no hat there, dropped foolishly back to his side.

Lisa came back down the drive and stood at her own gate, only a few yards from the rest of them. They all stood close together but carefully just inside their own boundaries, as if these demarcation lines were a protection against an intimacy which might be embarrassing, either to them or to the people they addressed.

It is an odd relationship, that of neighbours; you are not automatically friends, but you certainly cannot remain strangers. Lisa Holt was more determined than any of them to preserve the barriers, until she decided just how far she wanted to venture out beyond them. She forced a smile, tried not to sound too brusque and dismissive as she said, 'You look almost like some sort of committee waiting for me. What was it that you wanted?'

Phil Smart looked appreciatively at her

dark-blue trousers and her red kitten-heeled shoes and decided this was a moment for gallantry. 'Only your excellent presence, Lisa. A presence which would of course grace any occasion, formal or informal.'

'We were just discussing some sort of gathering to mark our arrivals here,' said his wife hastily. 'We thought something quite informal. And we might even manage something outdoors, at this time of year. Rosemary has just put up the idea of a street party.' Carol's nervousness made her speak a little too quickly, so that the information came tumbling out like a collapsing house of cards.

'It was only a suggestion,' said Rosemary Lennox. 'I just thought that with all the trials of moving in, none of us wants to be making formal meals yet.' Or inviting any of these relative strangers into our houses for dinner parties, she thought. Let's keep it all outdoors and informal, so that we can all of us back away from anything closer if we choose to; there's at least one person whom I shan't be inviting round for dinner.

'A gathering like that sounds a good idea to me. It could be quite a lot of fun, if we get the right weather!' said Lisa Holt. There was a collective but silent sigh of relief, and the other women wondered why it seemed that it was Lisa who was being asked to give final approval to their suggestions.

'Robin has already offered to get us booze at a discount,' said Phil Smart. 'And his lovely wife has already offered to rustle up one of her splendid cheesecakes for us.'

Carol Smart threw her husband a look which was neither loving nor domestic, and Rosemary Lennox said hastily, 'We could discuss that nearer the time. I'm sure we could all provide some simple food. It's just a matter of co-ordinating what we do, so that we don't duplicate each other's efforts.'

'In about a fortnight, we thought,' said Robin Durkin. No one had suggested a time, so he thought he'd nip in and secure a Saturday which was convenient for him. He was often busy on Saturdays, with activities which he couldn't discuss with anyone here. 'And of course, we wouldn't expect you to prepare anything elaborate, Lisa. After all, the rest of us are couples, whereas there's only one of you, and—'

'But an excellent one. One who more than makes up for the absence of a significant other,' said Phil Smart unctuously.

Lisa Holt looked at him coolly. Her calm grey eyes sank his lechery suddenly down to the soles of his well-worn sandals. 'Oh, you can put me down as a pair,' she said with a smile at the company. 'I'm sure I shall have someone with me on the evening in question.'

Three

They eventually agreed that the street party should be on Saturday the ninth of July. That was a little later than they had originally intended, but the first date which suited all of them.

It was agreed after a short debate that children would not be present on this first celebratory occasion. That was no problem for the Smarts, whose daughters were working in the north of England, or for the Lennoxes, whose single son was now at Cambridge university. Lisa Holt had suggested this Saturday for the party because this was one of the weekends when her nine-year-old son was spending the weekend with his grandparents.

The Durkins had no children; it was generally the opinion among the parents who inhabited the rest of the close that they would have enjoyed a much fuller existence if their union had been blessed with offspring. But people who undergo the more extreme trials of this life are normally anxious that others should have a taste of suffering.

The British weather is much maligned. It does not exhibit the extremes which cause such havoc in the rest of the world. Earthquakes are not a problem; hurricanes and floods are rare and not usually as destructive as elsewhere on the planet. But one undisputed fact is that no one can arrange an outdoor function in Britain and be certain that the day will be fine. So it surprised not a single occupant of Gurney Close that, as soon as they had set a date for the street party, the weather broke.

The new residents had some heavy rain, and even some unseasonably chilly days, in the three weeks between the setting of the date and the event itself. Rosemary Lennox said they must make contingency plans to take account of whatever the elements might throw at them. All the residents gallantly offered to use their new living rooms if necessary, but it was eventually agreed that in an emergency, they would use that of the Durkins, since they were awaiting the delivery of a new three-piece lounge suite and would thus have much empty space.

'If necessary, we'll all move in with our glasses and our garden chairs, but hopefully it won't be,' said Rosemary Lennox.

It wasn't. The weather was unusually co-operative. It took up again a week before the party, and on the evening of Saturday the

24

ninth of July, there was not a cloud in the bright blue sky, and but a zephyr of a wind from the Wye to rustle the fresh green leaves of the oaks at the end of the close.

The tasks of the evening were resolved along traditional gender lines. The men set up two long tables in the Durkins's back garden, one with the copious supplies of drink which Robin Durkin had obtained at wholesale prices, the other with the food which the women had prepared, covered with linen and wire at the beginning of the evening to protect it from the unwanted attentions of insects and birds. The participants arrived together, carrying with them a variety of garden furniture to supplement the expensive wooden set which Alison Durkin had just purchased for the small patio beside the newly-laid lawn.

It was a small group, and one which did not seem to promise a lively party. It was composed almost entirely from the people who had moved into the three new houses and the single bungalow between three and five weeks ago, rather than from old friends with many previous occasions to recall. Admittedly, they now felt that they knew each other quite well after exchanging notes on the various deficiencies of builders, water boards, electricity providers and local councils.

There was just one person who was not a

resident of the close. Or, as Carol Smart suggested darkly, not an official resident. Jason Ritchie's physique had been much in evidence around the house of Lisa Holt during the last three weeks. He had a splendid torso, which had become increasingly bronzed in the very warm June sunshine of the last few days. The tattoos on the upper arms were no doubt not to everyone's taste, but they were a phenomenon as modern as the bearer himself.

Jason Ritchie was twenty-three years old. As far as Gurney Close was concerned, he was a gardener. It was not clear how knowledgeable or experienced he was in the field of horticulture, but he had toiled with some success towards the establishment of a garden in what had been the building plot of Lisa Holt's house. His arrival and his activities had been observed closely by the other women in the new development, and with considerable dismay by Philip Smart, who had been indulging lascivious ideas of his own about the glamorous divorcee of Gurney Close.

Jason had worked long and hard, full of the energy and enthusiasm which went with his years. He had unearthed a bewildering variety of broken concrete, rusting metal strips, lengths of wire and other unwelcome constructional detritus, and taken them away to the tip in his battered white van. On several evenings, he had laboured with pick, spade and fork into the last of the summer light. And when his work was over, he had enjoyed a well-earned beer with his employer. And perhaps other rewards as well.

Phil Smart peered from behind the new curtains hung by his efficient wife and speculated darkly about the activities of this young stud. Jason was in his view the classic 'bit of rough' which educated women of Lisa Holt's age and background were rumoured to find attractive. Phil feared the worst, which was that Lisa had not only taken this brawny young man into her bed, but would as a result find what he himself could offer her in that department lacking in both vigour and imagination. This breezy young ruffian had cast Phil Smart into an unwonted gloom.

And now Lisa had insisted upon inviting him to the party. 'He's almost one of us, really,' she said cheerfully, running her eyes appreciatively over his shining biceps. 'And you must admit, he's done more to knock our new environment into a manageable shape than any one of us.'

The others looked at the front gardens of the new close and admitted glumly that Lisa was probably right. Of the little patches at the front of the houses, Lisa's was the one which was nearest to a garden. There were still some ugly lumps of intractable clay evident, but the ground had been cleared of builders' rubble and battered into something like submission. Where the rest of them were still laboriously unearthing half-bricks and bits of electric cable from earth which the long days of sun seemed determined to turn into concrete, Ms Holt's little rectangle already had turf, installed two days earlier, and the shapes of flower borders were now clearly defined. Indeed, a couple of pot-grown roses had already been transported from the garden centre in Jason Ritchie's white van; they now blazed defiantly crimson and yellow in the evening of the perfect day.

All of them had been working hard during the day, but they had disappeared into their residences for an hour before the party began, to shower and prepare for this evening of pleasant celebration. The women, at least, showed the benefits of forethought and effort. They emerged in a variety of colourful and becoming summer dresses, estimating each other carefully, even among the compliments they flung out cheerfully as they arrived in the Durkins's back garden at around eight o'clock.

The men were chivalrous in exactly the sort of way that was expected of them. There was not too much variation in their leisure shirts and chinos and sandals, the male uniform where al fresco informality was determined to be the order of the day. Philip Smart, startlingly vivid in a bright green shirt and sage trousers, was very complimentary about Rosemary Lennox's newly-shaped hair and her dark-blue dress, singling out the oldest woman at the party for his attention with uncharacteristic tact.

Robin Durkin fondled his wife's bare shoulders in a display of uxorious attention which bordered upon the embarrassing, as she told him sharply when she had had enough of it.

Ron Lennox felt emboldened to assure Alison Durkin that her dark hair looked very splendid. He had not seen it done before in this loose and carefully informal style, which she had chosen for the party. The normally boisterous Ally seemed rather muted at the beginning of the evening, and Ron was rewarded with something very like an unexpected blush on her rather pale face.

Phil Smart took a huge breath and plunged in at the deep end. 'You light up the whole close,' he assured Lisa Holt. 'I don't know how you manage to work so hard in your new house and still come out here looking like something out of *Vogue*.'

'I don't think *Vogue* deals much with Marks and Spencer's summer dresses and sandals from the seconds shop,' said Lisa dryly. 'But thanks for the thought all the same, Phil.'

'And don't kid yourself she works that

hard.' Jason Ritchie came round the side of the Durkin house, an immaculate white tee shirt stretched tight over his muscular chest, the barbed wire tattoo winding its way impressively around his biceps to disappear beneath the cotton. 'There's only one person does the work around Lisa's place, and that ain't the owner.' He bathed the divorcee in a look that seemed to Phil Smart altogether too proprietorial; it roamed unhurriedly from her blonde head to the well-pedicured feet upon the grass. Jason's labours, the look seemed to say, extended far beyond the garden. And the way in which Lisa Holt grinned back at him implied that the work he delivered in every different area was accounted wholly satisfactory.

The two men, with almost thirty years and a ton of resentment between them, stared hard at each other, hostility hardening in this least appropriate of contexts. But Carol Smart, with a world-weary expertise born of long practice, thrust a beer can into Jason's hand and a glass of wine into her husband's, and said, 'I'm sure we all wish we were making the rapid progress you are in Lisa's garden, Jason. But then you have youth and strength on your side. I suppose I can't expect the same rate of progress from Philip.'

Jason looked at the attractive forty-three-year-old appreciatively. It suited him sometimes to play the young stud with more brawn than brains, but he understood exactly the sort of diplomacy which Carol Smart was attempting here. He smiled, looked deliberately away from the panting Phil Smart, and said, 'My dad always says that you can't rush gardening. You make mistakes if you try to rush it.'

The moment passed. It had been a tricky one, the kind which could easily have got the evening off to a bad start. But once the drink began to flow, the strange dynamics of this diverse little group of people took over and things bowled along happily, even hilariously. The only common factor they had was that of beginning life anew in the close, but it was a surprisingly helpful one. The fact that they had moved in at this time of year, when the days were longest and the weather at its best, meant that they had seen a lot of each other as they moved their possessions into their houses and began the struggle to create gardens out of a building site. They had spent hours of digging, tugging and cursing in equal measure, commiserating over aching limbs and backs which seized up after hours of abuse.

Now they exchanged stories and recalled the more entertaining disasters of the last month, which were already being embellished with the hyperbole of nostalgia, as alcohol assisted imagination and the participants relaxed into a perfect English summer

31

evening. The food was excellent, and Rosemary Lennox's organizational skills had ensured that the selection of dishes they had brought to the trestle table in the Durkins's garden was both varied and complementary. And the drink flowed, loosening tongues and weakening inhibitions.

The laughter became more genuine and more prolonged over two hours of recollected disasters and plans for the future; the decibel level rose higher and higher, until any listener from a hundred yards away would have thought that there were far more than eight people involved in the party. But there were no near neighbours for them to disturb. The fishermen a mile away down the river wondered about the source of this noise and laughter as the evening moved into dusk, but they were too busy with their own concerns to have any real interest in such speculation.

Robin Durkin had paid the builder to construct a small, unofficial gate in the back fence of his garden, to give him access to the land behind. He smiled and tapped the side of his nose when the others asked him about it. 'All strictly speaking illegal, I'm sure,' he said airily, in answer to their queries. 'There's no official footpath until you get to the banks of the river, but it's only pasture land and I shouldn't think anyone's going to bother about it.'

Emboldened by drink and the courage which comes from being in a group, they went out together and walked for a few minutes beside the river, admiring the deep crimson sky where the sun had disappeared over the Welsh hills, watching the numerous rings disturbing the still surface of the water as the trout rose towards the invisible flies. There was no one about here, but the occupants of Gurney Close found themselves whispering, perhaps because they felt themselves conspirators in this minor trespass, more probably because they did not want to disturb the peace of these magical moments by the river.

And then they were back, lounging in their garden chairs with glasses refilled, full of good humour and relaxed reminiscence as dusk moved into darkness. The last of the breeze had disappeared with the sunset, and the night retained its summer warmth. There were not many better places in the world to be than the heart of England on an evening like this, Ronald Lennox announced appreciatively, and the others nodded sage agreement and sipped contentedly.

It was at this time that Philip Smart made an unexpectedly graceful and well-turned speech about the excellence of the food, the quantity of the drink, and the brilliance of Rosemary Lennox's original concept of an evening of celebration like this. It reminded all of them that he could be more than a lecherous bore when he chose to be: Phil caught the mood of the moment; the sense of general bonhomie; the pleasant, uncritical, alcoholic lassitude which seemed to be overtaking all of them.

No one wanted to be the first to move, to break up the atmosphere which felt so relaxed and so right. Robin Durkin burrowed into a cardboard box he and Ally had still not unpacked and found balloon brandy glasses. 'Time for a nightcap,' he said, and went round the company with the cognac bottle. The last remaining signs of the caution some of his guests had displayed towards him seemed to drop away with the brandy. The talk grew more quiet and sporadic, the thoughts expressed more sentimental than they would have been in daylight and sobriety.

The warmth of the night and the effects of alcohol meant that no one felt cold. It was almost another hour before the woman who had suggested this party drew it to a close. 'Time us oldies were in bed,' Rosemary Lennox said with a smile, and stood up with a resolution which none of the others could muster.

Her husband took the hand she held out to help him and levered himself rather stiffly and reluctantly to his feet. 'It's been great!' he said, untypically enthusiastic. 'Perhaps we should agree now to make this an annual event.'

There was general assent to that. But with two of the company on their feet, everyone suddenly realized that it was now almost one o'clock and time to break up the party. There were token offers to help with tidying up, an assurance from Ally Durkin that she would leave everything until the morning, when those who wished could come and help to clear the tables of debris.

There was a final burst of animation as they all took leave of each other, much self-congratulation and laughter about the shortness of the journey home for all of them. The Lennoxes picked up their garden chairs and the remnants of the bowl of strawberries which Rosemary had prepared for the feast, and stepped away into the darkness. Phil Smart put his arm loyally around the shoulders of his wife and held her lightly against him in readiness for the thirty-yard journey to their front door; brandy was having a considerable, if temporary, effect upon him. He couldn't be sure, but he thought Lisa Holt showed a fleeting embarrassment as she departed quietly with Jason Ritchie to the first house in the close.

Lights flashed on in the four homes of the new settlement, and at one a.m. the place seemed a blaze of light compared with what it had been a little earlier. But within half an hour, all was in darkness, and silence reigned, more profound after the boisterous conviviality which had preceded it.

The dawn chorus of the birds began at four thirty on a perfect summer's day, and was exuberant and sustained. But there was no human sound to intrude upon the avian exultation. It was another three hours before that came.

The screaming was piercing and prolonged. No one could have slept through it for more than a second or two. They stumbled from their houses in their dressing gowns, all drowsiness banished by the urgency and agony in the voice. They hurried to the house they had left so happily a few hours earlier, then to the back garden whence came this imperative and primitive clamour.

Ally Durkin stood screaming at the empty sky, surrounded by the pathetic debris of the party. The women went and put arms round her, turned her forcibly away from the sight which had set her shrieking so frantically, pulled her back into the house and away from what had been her husband.

Robin Durkin lay on his back, with his legs splayed and one arm crushed unnaturally beneath him. The cord had cut so deeply into his bull-like neck that it was almost invisible. His eyes bulged out so far that it seemed they would leave his face at any moment. They stared glassily at the sun as it climbed the eastern sky. But those eyes would never see light again.

Four

Gurney Close was suddenly full of vehicles. Scarcely a square foot of its newly laid tarmac was visible when Superintendent John Lambert drove his ageing Vauxhall Senator into the tiny cul-de-sac. It was twenty past nine on the morning of Sunday, the tenth of July.

He had been about to start a round of golf at Ross Golf Club when the call had come through to him. He had made the ritual noises of resentment about pleasure interrupted, but in truth his pulses had quickened and his senses been made more alert by this news of what seemed almost certainly a murder. John Lambert was in his fifties now, heavy with achievement and reputation. He was familiar with the slightly guilty excitement he felt now. The hunting instinct always takes over the CID man when there is the prospect of a serious crime to be solved. As he crossed the River Wye and drove through the lanes to the crime scene, Lambert was metaphorically sniffing the air and anticipating the challenges to come.

There was no mistaking the house he wanted. The blue and white ribbons defining the limits of the crime scene were already in place, the uniformed constable already looking bored at the prospect of long hours of policing a quiet area with no interlopers in sight. But the unwelcome sightseers would come, no doubt, even to this quiet place, when the sensational news got around. There were always those who wanted to get as close as they could to the scenes of shocking events. And even in an age which was far more violent than the one Lambert had entered as a policeman thirty years ago, murder retained its unique, grisly glamour.

The police surgeon had already been and gone, fulfilling his formal function of confirming that there was no life remaining in the body of Robin Arthur Durkin. But the pathologist was still on site, moving among the civilians who nowadays made up most of the Scene of Crime team. Lambert pulled the plastic bags over his shoes and slipped the thin white overalls reluctantly over his clothes; the day was already hot, and growing hotter by the minute under a cloudless sky. He picked his way carefully between the female photographer and the fingerprint man and watched the pathologist recording the reading from his thermometer.

The medical man glanced at the Chief Investigating Officer: he knew him quite well after several meetings over the last few years. 'I've only taken the ambient temperature. I won't disturb the clothing until he's in the mortuary and the forensic boys have taken the clothing.'

Lambert nodded, glancing at the big windows of the new house's sitting room, scarcely ten yards behind him. Someone had drawn the curtains, shutting away the sight of what was going on out here from the widow inside. She would have to get used to that word: at thirty-two, she could scarcely have expected to carry the label of widow for many years yet. Unless, of course, this Mrs Durkin was the one who had committed or engineered this death: Lambert made the CID officer's automatic caveat to himself. The spouse was always the leading suspect until he or she could be eliminated from the enquiry.

He went and stared down impassively at the grossly distorted face, with its darkening flesh and bulging eyes. He was glad the curtains had shut it away from the widow, but he had seen much worse sights among murder victims. 'Time of death?' he said, without taking his eyes away from the face.

'Several hours ago. The flesh is cold.'

'Last night, then.' He was thinking aloud

rather than looking for information; the pathologist wouldn't give him anything more accurate without rectal temperatures and some estimation of the extent of rigor mortis. He picked his way carefully along the line the Scene of Crime Officer indicated until he reached the small gate in the fence at the back of the new garden, then looked out to where the grass had been trodden outside. One of the team was working his way alongside the tracks in the grass made by human feet, searching for any tiny clue which might have fallen from someone fleeing this way after the killing.

The SOCA investigation is by far the most important part of the early investigation of any murder. The theory is that there is always an 'exchange' between the murderer and his or her victim at the scene of the death. However carefully the killer plans his crime, however warily he covers his tracks, he will leave behind something of himself. With a sex crime, it will be something obvious: semen or saliva. With a killing like this, it might be something as tiny and unnoticed as a falling hair or a fibre from clothing. The man on his hands and knees already had a collection of small items in the plastic container beside him; only time and forensic examination would tell whether they had come from some entirely innocent source, or from the killer of the man who lay on his back behind them.

Lambert watched the man use his tweezers to lift the tipped end of a cigarette from amongst the blades of grass. Now that so many fewer people smoked, at least among the middle classes, tobacco evidence was more easy to pin down to a suspect than it had once been. But this particular item, squashed flat and grubby, looked as if it had probably been here for some time – perhaps since the builders had erected the fence beside it to mark the boundary of the property.

The civilian head of the SOCA team came over and stood by Lambert, watching his man working his way methodically along the ground towards the oak trees outside the fence. 'This gate was open when we got here,' he said.

'So our man might have come in this way. Or left this way. Or both.' The perpetrator of violence was always male until there was definite evidence to the contrary. The superintendent was not surprised, but certainly not pleased. This entrance and the tracks beyond it introduced the possibility of the wide world outside to the list of suspects, which might otherwise have been confined to the tight little world of Gurney Close. They might have hoped for a result within a few hours, with the killer emerging from within the family, as it did in sixty per cent

41

of cases.

The man on all fours looked up. 'There's been someone along here quite recently. More than one person, though.'

Lambert nodded. The dew from a still, warm dawn was still present out here, where the tall oaks threw their shade over the open area outside the new garden fences. No one save the SOCA member, picking his way carefully alongside the previous flattening of the grass, had passed this way since the morning dew. He looked back towards the raw brick of the new houses, catching the twitch of a curtain at an upstairs window as someone observed the police activity. Some-one who would need to be questioned, in due course.

In the small back garden where the corpse lay, the photographs had all been taken, the evidence from the immediate vicinity gather-ed. The body was being carefully rolled on to the sheet of polythene and wrapped to contain all remaining evidence for examina-tion by the forensic scientists. The van police officers call the 'meat wagon' had reversed into the drive; its rear doors were open, and the plastic 'shell' inside was ready to receive the corpse.

Lambert waited until the van had eased its way quietly, almost apologetically, out of the close. Then he went and knocked at the front door of the house. A squat woman with a drawn face opened the door and he said 'Mrs Durkin?'

'No. I'm her sister. She's not fit to talk to anyone. Not at the moment.'

He caught a glimpse of a ravaged, tear-stained face before the door of the kitchen shut at the other end of the hall. 'I understand that. But I'll need to speak to her. Just a brief preliminary interview to confirm a few of the facts of the case. We need to get our investigation under way quickly, if we're going to find out who did this terrible thing.'

Sentiments he had voiced dozens of times before, but the fact that this was routine for him didn't make things any less harrowing for the recipients of his demands. For a moment he thought she was going to refuse him, to shout at him for his insensitivity. But all she said was 'When?'

'Some time later today would be best. This afternoon, perhaps.'

'All right. I'll tell her. She'll understand, will Ally. She'll want to nail the bastard who did this.'

John Lambert nodded and went back round the back of the house to check whether the SOCA team had turned up anything they thought significant.

In the first house of Gurney Close, Jason Ritchie had been watching the activity of the last two hours with increasing apprehension. Now he watched the tall figure of the superintendent disappearing round the back of the murder house and took his decision. He moved swiftly out to the battered white van in the drive. It started at the second turn of the ignition switch and he revved the engine fiercely, then lurched out of the drive and away from the place. He felt the relief growing with each yard he put between himself and the place where Robin Durkin had fallen.

Five

Detective Sergeant Bert Hook was enjoying Sunday lunch with his wife Eleanor and his two boisterous sons when the call came.

'How much golf did you get in?' asked Lambert.

'A full round. I was off early. I heard you'd been called away without ever getting on to the course when I got back to the club-house.'

'All right for some! We have a murder on our hands, Bert.' Lambert rapped out the bare essentials of what had happened at Gurney Close as rapidly and dispassionately as if he had been delivering a railway timetable. They were professionals to the bone, these two, in their very different ways. They had worked together for over ten years, and each knew and respected the other's strengths.

Hook's sturdy common sense was a counterpoint to Lambert's intensity, his impatience to find a solution to even the most impenetrable of crimes. Each relied on the other to provide the necessary counterbalance when interviews became tricky, when the strains of police bureaucracy or the cynicism of the public at large became particularly trying. Their understanding, both of each other and the criminal world they fought against, was such that much was left unsaid between them which would have had to be voiced between officers less confident of each other.

'You'll want to see the victim's wife. Have we heard anything about how she's taking it?' said Hook. He did not need to voice the thought that until they knew otherwise the widow, however grief-stricken she might appear, was a leading suspect.

'I spoke to her sister this morning. She says Alison Durkin is upset, but will see the need to get on with the investigation as fast as we can. We'll see her later this afternoon, if you can make it.'

'I'll be there.' And Hook had a name, now. The first small step in making human sense of what seemed at first a lurid, unbelievable story.

Bert watched his boys getting out their cricket gear. He had been a doughty Minor Counties cricketer himself for many years, a pillar of the Herefordshire side, opening the bowling at a brisk military medium and providing big hitting lower down the batting order. 'Finished your homework, have you?' It was the parent's reflex check on a thirteen-year-old. Bert had married relatively late for a copper, at twenty-nine, and very happily.

'Finished mine. What about yours?' Jack grinned up cheekily at his father. Bert was nearing the completion of an Open University degree, which had given him much satisfaction, but been difficult to squeeze in amidst the irregular hours of CID work. The boy put his bat and his gloves into the battered bag his father had once carried around the dressing rooms of the area.

'Where's Luke?'

'I don't know. He usually can't wait to get out.'

The younger boy came into the room as he spoke. He was normally the noisier and cheekier of the two, but today he scarcely managed a grin. 'You'd better go on your own, Jack. I don't feel so good.'

He looked very white. He had had his hair cut on the previous day, and his scalp seemed to show through, making his head look out of proportion to his body.

Bert looked at the white face. 'You sound as if you might have a bug. You'd better get yourself some paracetamol and lie down for a while. Your mum will know where the tablets are.'

At the time, Bert Hook thought no more about it than that. He had other, more professional concerns on that Sunday afternoon.

Alison Durkin looked bad. The carefully informal hairstyle she had chosen for last night's celebration had disintegrated into turmoil. Her black hair now hung lank and disordered, like that of a swimmer emerging from dank water. There was a button undone on her white shirt. Her face was without make-up and channelled with weeping; despite her relative youth, she looked haggard.

Lambert and Hook noted it all, even as they prepared themselves to be as tactful as the situation would allow them to be. CID work demands a professional cynicism, a capacity to assess how far grief is genuine in those closest to a suspicious death. But they would not place too much reliance on appearances. Even those who have committed violent crimes can be in genuine rather than simulated shock, as the consequences of what they have perpetrated in a moment of madness become clear to them.

Lambert made his ritual noises about the necessity of their intrusion at a time like this, and she nodded, almost impatiently, saying before he had quite finished, 'What is it you need to know?'

Lambert gave her a small smile, a tiny token of his recognition of the awful situation in which she found herself. 'I understand that it was you who found the body of your husband.'

'Yes. He was just lying there. But I could tell by the way he had fallen that there was something wrong. And then I saw his face. And I knew that – that someone had...' Her voice tailed away. There were no words for the image of that face, which was with her still.

'What time was this?'

'Just after twenty to eight this morning. Seven forty-one.' She gave a little, unexpected, bitter smile, as if amused by the irony of this precision. 'I'd looked at the clock beside the bed before I went out, you see.'

'And you got out of bed and went straight out into the garden?'

'Yes.'

'And why was that?'

'Because I knew that something was wrong. Because Robin never came to bed last night.'

'You're sure of that?'

'Yes. His side of the bed hadn't been disturbed. He's an untidy sleeper, Rob. He messes the sheets up.' She had got her tenses wrong, as the newly bereaved often do, and the tears sprang anew to her cheeks at the realization of it.

'This is a help to us, you see. Because the first indications are that your husband died last night. The first step towards finding who did something like this is usually establishing the exact time of death.'

'Robin never came to bed.' She repeated the words carefully, as if clarity would be the key to discovery.

'And what time did you go to bed yourself?'

Her brow furrowed. In that instant, she was like a child anxious to give precisely the right information to an adult. 'We'd had this party. It was just the people who'd moved in here during the last few weeks. To Gurney Close, I mean.' She spoke wonderingly, as if she could not believe that it was only so recently that there had been laughter and noisy enjoyment around her in this place.

'Tell me a little about it, if you feel that you can. Remember that we know nothing as yet about the people who live here, or about what went on last night. It might be quite important to remember in some detail what happened amongst you all, in the hours before this happened.'

She shook her head hopelessly at the impossibility of that. She said dully, 'There was a lot of drinking. We were all enjoying ourselves. Or at least I thought we were, at the time.'

'How many people were involved?'

'Just the people from the close. There were only eight of us, though we made a great deal of noise, at times.' She looked up at them, realized they were waiting for more, and furrowed her brow again in that concentration that was almost that of a dazed child. 'There were the Lennoxes, from the bungalow at the end. Ron and Rosemary. It was Rosemary's idea, the party. To celebrate our arrival here. A street party, she called it. Like they had when she was a little girl of three at the end of the war, she said.'

Hook made a careful note of the name of the woman who had suggested this celebration which had ended in murder. He gave her a smile of encouragement and said, 'We need the names of everyone who was there. We'll be talking to all of them, before very long, but you can help by giving us their names and whatever you can recall of the evening.'

She smiled back into his earnest, village-bobby face. She had thought this would be an ordeal, but it was almost a relief to be talking to these quiet, vigilant, sympathetic men. 'The other people were our next-door neighbours. Philip and Carol Smart, who live in the house between us and the Lennoxes' bungalow, and Lisa Holt, who lives on the other side, in the first house as you turn into the close. She's divorced, is Lisa. Not long ago. The lawyers are still sorting out the details, I think.' Alison Durkin looked up nervously at them, feeling that such tittle-tattle must surely be out of place here.

But Hook just gave her his reassuring smile again and said, 'You said eight people were at your little party, I believe.'

'Yes.' For a moment she looked embarrassed. Then, realizing how inappropriate embarrassment was in the face of murder, she said, 'The eighth member was Lisa Holt's gardener. A young chap called Jason. Jason Ritchie, I think it is. Robin knew him, I think, but I hadn't met him until he came here – except that I'd seen him working on Lisa's garden.'

'And this Jason was at the party, even though he wasn't a resident?'

A small smile, as if she now felt the relief of triviality, even gossip, in this context. 'Jason has been here a lot in the last three weeks. Pretty well full-time. Lisa said that he almost qualified as a resident, and no one seemed to have any objection to his attending the street party.'

Well, some of the men probably had reservations. Alison thought of Jason's burnished

51

torso, with the barbed wire tattoo disappearing beneath the white sleeve of his tee shirt, and was threatened with an inappropriate smile. But she wouldn't go into that here. She put her hands together on her lap, watched them shaking a little above the blue of her jeans.

Hook said gently, as if they were conspirators here, with Lambert at a further remove from them, 'And do you think that this Jason Ritchie is providing Mrs Holt with a little more than gardening services?'

'He might be. I won't pretend we haven't discussed the possibility. The other three women in the close, I mean.' She gave Hook a nod of confirmation and then, as if feeling such intimacies were out of place here, said firmly, 'But we shouldn't be talking about rubbish like that, should we? Not now, I mean.'

This time it was Lambert who spoke, his long, lined face relaxing its gravity as he said, 'On the contrary, we need to know everything you can tell us, Mrs Durkin. Most of it will eventually prove to be irrelevant to our investigation, as you imply, but at this stage we have no idea what may have a bearing on this death. So please tell us everything you can.'

She nodded, then felt a great lassitude stealing suddenly upon her, after the emotional switchback of the day. 'You'll need to give me some guidance, then. I'm feeling very confused.'

'You say you enjoyed your little gathering last night. Can you give us some of the details? Times and places, for a start.'

'Well, we met up at about eight o'clock, or perhaps a few minutes after that. Everyone arrived at more or less the same time. And we met here. On our back lawn. If you can call it that. It's only been laid for two weeks, and we have to keep watering it until it's taken hold, the man said.'

'And you were outside for most of the evening?'

'Almost all of it. People brought their own garden chairs to supplement our new garden set, and we stayed outside. We got noisier and noisier, I'm afraid, but there was no one to disturb. It was a beautiful warm night, if you remember.' It seemed to her now quite remote; she couldn't believe that it was less than twenty-four hours earlier that they had all been enjoying themselves so innocently.

'And all this took place in and around your house?'

'In our back garden, for the most part. We set out two trestle tables there, one with the drink on – Robin had got most of that at discount rates – and the other with the food which the women had brought. Rosemary Lennox organized us on that, so that we didn't duplicate things. She's very good at organizing things, is Rosemary.'

Lambert thought he caught a little resentment in that last phrase. He said, 'I noticed that you have a gate cut into your back fence.'

Alison nodded. 'Robin got the builders to put that in. He said that it was a shame to be so near to the river and not have access to it.'

And possibly thus engineered the entrance which brought a murderer to him. Lambert said gently, 'And did you use the gate last night?'

'Yes. We all went out through the gate and walked down to the banks of the Wye.'

So the SOCO was right. There had been eight pairs of feet over that grass behind the houses. Quite enough to obfuscate any signs of a single, more vicious, entrance or exit. 'What time was this?'

Again that furrowing of the brow, as if it were important to her to get this as right as she could. 'It must have been somewhere around ten o'clock. The sun had gone down some time earlier, but we could still see the deep red sky over the Welsh hills. "Red sky at night, shepherd's delight," someone said. But someone always says that, doesn't he?' She almost apologized for being so trivial, when they had more important things to consider.

'Was the gate left open when you all went out?'

'I think it was, yes. Robin led the way, and I wasn't at the end of the line.' She suddenly saw what she thought was the point of the question. 'Someone could have come in that way whilst we were out walking by the river, couldn't he? He could have hidden in the garage or our new garden shed, and just waited until everyone had gone.'

She was animated by the thought. Like most people near to a murder victim, she found it more acceptable that he should have been felled by some stranger's hand than by that of someone she had known and trusted. Lambert said, 'It's a possibility, no more than that. It's also possible that someone came in that way much later in the night, when your party was over and people had gone home.'

'But Robin wouldn't have been out there then.'

'He might. If he had heard someone moving out there. Or if he had arranged to meet someone.'

He was watching her closely, to see how she reacted to the suggestion. She said, 'I think I'd have known about that. We didn't have many secrets from each other.'

Lambert was sceptical about that thought. She hadn't spoken with any great certainty. In any case, one thing which murder investigations had taught him over the years was that couples who thought they had no secrets from each other were often deceiving themselves. He said, 'It's a possibility, that's all. I'm not saying it's probable, but we have to keep our minds open to all possibilities at this stage. If someone just came in here at random, we'd have to ask ourselves what he was after, what there was here which could make him commit murder. There's no evidence of any attempt at burglary.'

'No. Your men who were here this morning asked me to check my jewellery. There's nothing missing.'

'So tell us what happened during the rest of the evening, when you came back from your stroll by the river.'

'We stayed in the garden. It was still very warm, even when it went completely dark. And I think all of us had drunk quite a lot, by then, so we weren't feeling any chill. We sat and chatted and drank a little more. It got quieter, but everyone was very happy. Mellow, someone called it – I think it was Phil Smart who used that word.'

'So you sat for maybe an hour or so, like that? Just chatting.'

'Longer than that, I should think. We'd been there for some time when Robin decided to go round with the brandy bottle. We'd all had quite enough to drink already, I think, but I think most of us accepted a nightcap when he pressed us.'

Except, perhaps, one person, who was

keeping himself alert for what followed. 'Can you remember any disagreements during the evening, anything which seemed to rankle between people?'

'No. I thought about that when I found him. But I can't remember any fallings-out during the evening. Not even any mild disagreements.'

'And what time did you finally break up?'

'It must have been about one. I think Rosemary Lennox said that it was time for the oldies to get to bed, and within two minutes everyone was on their feet and leaving.'

'So everyone left together? You're sure of that?'

'Yes. There were only three couples, you know.' It seemed fair enough to call Lisa Holt and Jason Ritchie a couple, in this context. 'Everyone was very light-hearted about not having to drive and being close to home, and everyone left together.'

'And this was about one a.m.?'

'Yes, it must have been. I remember looking at the clock as I got into bed and it was twenty past one. And it hadn't taken me long to get to bed; we'd agreed to leave all the clearing up until the morning.'

'But your husband didn't get ready for bed when you did?'

'I thought he was following on behind me. He said he'd just put the drink away and put the scraps of food into the rubbish bin. I heard him flushing the toilet in the down-stairs cloakroom before I got into bed. But he never came up, did he?' She was suddenly near to tears again.

'But you didn't realize that until this morning.'

'No. I'm afraid looking at the time on that bedside clock is the last thing I remember. As soon as my head hit the pillow, I was away. As I said, we'd all had quite a lot to drink. I certainly had. It was after half past seven this morning when I woke up and found that Robin wasn't there. That he'd never been there.' The tears ran silently down her cheeks. There was no great sobbing; it was as though she had no energy left for that.

'And a few minutes later, you found him in the garden.'

'Yes. He'd been there all night, hadn't he? Since some bastard put a cord around his neck and strangled him.'

'That seems very likely, yes. Do you know of anyone who had a grievance against Robin?'

'No.'

'And you're sure you saw no disagreements during the evening?'

'No. The men were cautious, but they eventually all seemed pretty easy with each other. I remember thinking how well they were all getting on. What a good thing that was going to be for Gurney Close.'

Lambert nodded, then said quietly, 'It isn't just the men we have to consider. The method of killing indicates that this crime could just as easily have been committed by a woman.'

She looked shocked by that. Perhaps it was a reminder to her that she had not yet been ruled out as a candidate for murder. Or perhaps she just found the idea of a woman killer more shocking, as many people did. She said dully, 'But none of the women had words with Robin, either. We all got on very well last night. It couldn't possibly have gone better.'

And of course there might have been one person there who wanted to achieve exactly that impression. On the other hand, their killer might be miles away from this tight little group of residents. Lambert said, 'Thank you. You've been very clear and helpful, in very trying circumstances. I know it won't bring him back, but we shall get the person who killed Robin. If anything which might be significant occurs to you, however trivial it might seem, please get in touch with me or Detective Inspector Rushton at Oldford CID. DI Rushton is the man who will be co-ordinating the evidence as the enquiry proceeds.'

She stood on the steps of her new house, clutching the card with the telephone numbers which Bert Hook had left with her, and watched them as they drove away.

It was ironic that Lambert had mentioned DI Rushton to her. For Chris Rushton was at that moment recording some interesting findings about Alison Durkin.

Six

'Ronald, come away from the window. You're like a little old lady watching from behind her lace curtains.' Rosemary Lennox smiled indulgently and pulled at her husband's sleeve.

Ron Lennox started a little; he had not realized that she was watching him. Then he smiled back at her and sat down. 'I read somewhere that they can be very useful to the police, observant old ladies. They see things that other people miss.'

'Except that in this case, it's the police you were observing.' She watched DS Hook's silver Ford Focus following the superintendent's big old Vauxhall out of the close.

'They weren't in there very long, really. Twenty-seven minutes, I make it.' Ron checked the time on his watch, looking for a moment as if he might record it in his notes.

60

'Quite long enough for poor Ally, I should think. That wretched girl's had quite a day.' When you were sixty-three, every woman under forty seemed a girl, especially if you rather liked her. Rosemary didn't feel she had a lot in common with Ally Durkin, from what little she had seen of her so far, but she had admired her energy, her cheerfulness and her spirit in their early weeks as neighbours. And now this awful thing had happened to her.

Ron said, 'They'll have given her quite a grilling, I expect, even though she's in shock. Come to think of it, they were probably glad to get to her whilst she was still in shock. The wife is always a leading suspect when there's a violent death like this, you know.'

'I do, actually, yes.' Rosemary was always resentful of her husband when he went into his instructional vein. She looked at him curiously. He was still staring at the blank windows of the Durkin house, forty yards away. 'If I didn't think it a shocking idea, I'd say you were actually quite enjoying this.'

Ron Lennox dragged his gaze away from the front door of the new house and back to his wife, forcing an ironic little smile at himself and his weaknesses. He said impishly, 'Well, it is a new experience for us, isn't it? Being involved in a murder enquiry, I mean. You have to treasure new experiences when you get to our age. All the articles about retirement tell you that.'

'A murder enquiry? Are you sure it's that?'

'Suspicious death, they said on Radio Gloucester. That means they think it wasn't natural causes and it wasn't suicide. Murder, it means.'

She had never known Ron listen to local radio before: she was surprised that he even knew where the wavelength was on the tuning dial. And now he was gazing at the Durkin house again, as if he had only to look hard enough for the areas of raw new brick to reveal their secrets.

His curiosity was understandable, she supposed. As a teacher for forty years, Ron had no doubt had his highs and lows, and various crises to deal with. He hadn't usually brought his troubles home with him, and she was grateful for that. When their son Andy had been at the comprehensive, she'd learned more about what happened in the school from him than she'd ever picked up from her husband. But Ron certainly hadn't had much melodrama in his life, so it was probably natural enough that he should be fascinated when it hit him like this.

All the same, Rosemary Lennox wasn't certain that her husband's interest in this was entirely healthy.

Detective Inspector Christopher Rushton was a meticulous man. He liked order in his life. In the world of crime, chaos often seems to be the predominating force; Chris Rushton regarded it as a challenge to impose some sort of order on the police reactions to it.

He delighted in keeping himself up to date with the latest technology. He was an enthusiast for computers and everything which went with the digital age. And somewhat unusually in the modern police service, DI Rushton had found himself a job niche which exactly suited him.

Most twenty-first century superintendents ran murder and other serious crime investigations from behind their desks, deploying their extensive teams without leaving headquarters very often themselves. Superintendent John Lambert was a determined exception to the rule, a self-confessed dinosaur among senior CID officers. He insisted upon conducting many interviews himself, on maintaining direct contact with the prominent figures in any investigation as it evolved. It was undoubtedly eccentric, but he got results. And in the police service, if your 'clear-up rates' are good, you are given latitude.

The man left in the CID section to co-ordinate the vast amount of information gathered by the team of around thirty officers assigned to most murder cases was DI Rushton. He willingly undertook the filing and cross-referencing of the welter of information gathered from house-to-house enquiries, in-depth follow-up interviews by senior officers, information volunteered by members of the public, data from previous crimes which might or might not be relevant, and the host of miscellaneous contributions which characterize any prolonged serious crime investigation.

Chris Rushton was not only highly efficient in this work. He got great satisfaction from it. He saw himself as the champion of modern technology against older reactionaries such as Lambert and Hook. The pair played up willingly enough to his image of them, pretending to more ignorance of electronic technology than was in fact the case, gently teasing the slightly humourless Rushton about his preference for machines over people.

But Rushton's task was important, and Lambert knew that better than anyone. If computer technology had been fully available at the time of the Yorkshire Ripper, and Christopher Rushton had been in charge of it, the lives of many of the man's later victims would have been saved.

Even at five o'clock on a sweltering Sunday afternoon, in an almost deserted CID section at Oldford police station, Chris Rushton had already set to work with his usual enthusiasm. Already he had an extensive file system on the Robin Durkin murder and those involved in it. And he had news for Lambert and Hook, when they came into the station after their meeting with Alison Durkin.

'We'll have the full post-mortem findings some time tomorrow,' he said to Lambert as they came into CID.

'It won't tell us much beyond what we know now,' said Lambert, a little sourly.

'And what did you make of the grieving widow?' Chris Rushton asked.

Lambert glanced at Bert Hook, who said, 'Genuinely affected and shocked by this death, as far as we could tell. If she's acting, she's in the Judi Dench class. But even if she'd killed him, she'd be in deep shock now, perhaps. However, it was useful seeing her today: she gave us a pretty cogent account of what happened last night, before the killing. We'll need to check it against other people's impressions, of course, but her version of the party they had in the close before this murder rang true, to me.'

'In that case, you'll be interested in the first entry I've made into her file,' said Rushton. He was trying not to sound too pleased with himself. And failing.

He looked as if he was about to produce a printout for them, but Lambert said a little wearily, 'Just tell us, Chris. Has Mrs Alison Durkin got a history as a multiple poisoner?'

Chris frowned at this levity. John Lambert had a record second to none as a taker of villains: that is why the Home Office had recently extended his service by two years, in response to the Chief Constable's special request. But as well as being slow to recognize the importance of the new technology, he sometimes displayed too much levity for Chris's taste. 'I've nothing as dramatic as that to report. I merely thought you might be interested to know that the dead man's widow has a criminal record.'

'For petty thieving?'

'For criminal violence. For Actual Bodily Harm. For attacking her partner with an offensive weapon: to whit, scissors. Sounds as if she was lucky it wasn't an even more serious charge.' Chris Rushton tried not to sound self-satisfied about his information. And failed again.

It was almost seven o'clock by the time Bert Hook got home. The house seemed unnaturally quiet.

Eleanor was preparing a salad in the kitchen. Salad was always a good bet for police wives in hot weather; you could never be sure when your man would come home, and salad didn't deteriorate as quickly as other things.

Bert watched her busy, expert hands slicing cucumber and hard-boiled eggs and preparing dressings. He marvelled again at the casual dexterity and the versatility of the female of his species. 'Jack not back yet?'

His wife smiled. 'No. He rang on his mobile between the innings, though. He got forty-one. And a dodgy lbw decision, he said.'

Bert grinned, trying not to look too proud, even here, where showing pride wouldn't matter. 'That's batsmen for you. They never ever get a good lbw decision, even when it would have knocked all three stumps over. It's a good score, that, though. Forty-one's a lot, for a thirteen-year-old.'

'Jack seemed to think so. He was trying hard not to sound too excited about his score to his ignorant mum. He was trying to be blasé, but thirteen-year-olds can't do blasé very well.'

'Where's Luke?'

'He's in bed, I think. He's not very well. He had a bit of a temperature, so I gave him paracetamol and suggested he went to bed for a while. He actually went, without any argument, so he must be feeling rough. Have a look in at him, but don't disturb him if he's asleep.'

Bert went up to their bedroom and changed into shorts and a tee shirt: it was still hot and airless. He went along the landing and cautiously opened the door into his younger son's room.

He was back in the kitchen with Eleanor within thirty seconds. 'Luke's got a fever of some kind. I think we need a doctor.'

Seventy miles north of Gurney Close, in a leafy suburb of Birmingham, there was even less breeze than in Herefordshire. Even at ten o'clock on that Sunday night, with darkness dropping in fast over the second city in the land, the temperature was still in the seventies. Or to be more modern and precise, it was exactly twenty-three degrees centigrade.

This man prided himself on his precision. And he was certainly a modern man, if modernity can be measured by occupation. He had the windows open tonight, as he tried to engineer a small, cooling current of air and get it to blow through the flat. He didn't favour open windows, as a rule. They made him uneasy. He was intensely conscious of security. He also felt much safer when the windows and doors around him were locked and barred.

He was an inch above what the latest surveys said was now the height of the average Briton. He wore dark-blue trousers and a lighter blue leisure shirt, with grey suede slip-on shoes. He had his hair cut short, but not shaved to the scalp in the way some men affected. He would be forty next month, but with his lean figure and his thin, rather intense, face he looked rather younger than that. He had a small scar on his left temple, which he still inspected from time to time in the mirror; it had grown shallower and less white with the passing years, but was still quite noticeable in photographs.

This man did not care to be noticeable. Every adjustment he made to his appearance was designed to make him more average, more unremarkable in the world in which he moved.

He looked at the electronic clock on top of his television set. Ten fourteen. Another sixteen minutes before he could ring. He had never enjoyed waiting. Not like this. He should have been used to it by now, he told himself wryly. His life contained a lot of waiting; it was ironic that when everyone thought of you as a man of action, you should do so much more waiting than acting.

He found himself thinking unexpectedly of his wife and his two children. He wasn't mawkish. It was only very rarely that he indulged his emotions at all, so it must have been the waiting that turned his thoughts this way now. He hadn't seen either his wife or his children for seven years, and he didn't miss them. He had never cared much for children, and never met a woman who didn't want commitment from him. Well, there were plenty of women available for money;

women who were there when you wanted them, not when they wanted you. Much better that way.

He much preferred a life without complications. It enabled him to concentrate. And concentration was an absolute necessity in the occupation he had chosen for himself. Or which had chosen him: he was never quite sure how he had arrived here.

He enjoyed a good book. Never went anywhere without one. There were plenty of hours to kill, plenty of time for reading, in his work. People found it strange that he always had a book with him among the tools of his trade, but it seemed to him perfectly logical. Time which could have been extremely boring passed much more quickly if you had a good book.

But tonight he hadn't been able to read. It was perhaps just the excessive heat, but he thought it was more likely the unexpected complication which had cropped up in his work. One of those complications which upset him, which disturbed the beautiful simplicity of his schedule; it was a thing you couldn't possibly have foreseen.

He'd never been one for television. He switched off the film he'd long since ceased to follow. The time was almost at hand. He would phone precisely at the moment arranged, timing it to the very second. Precision. Probably the man waiting for his call couldn't care less about absolute precision, and any time around ten thirty would have been acceptable to him. But precision mattered a lot to the man waiting by the open window in the Birmingham flat.

He had to nerve himself to use the agreed sentence. He could see the necessity for it: you never knew who was listening to phone conversations these days. But the phrasing seemed ridiculous: probably the man who had arranged the call had a taste for the melodramatic. Whereas to his mind, melodrama was best avoided. The more cold and clinical you could be, the less you allowed any sort of emotion into your life, the more efficient you were likely to be. And efficiency was a *sine qua non*. Without it, you wouldn't survive a week in this game.

Game! His lips wrinkled in silent derision at the absurdity of that word. But it was coming up to ten thirty. He walked over to the phone as he watched the seconds tick towards the half hour. Then he tapped in the number and took a deep breath, preparing himself to voice the absurd mantra in a flat voice, without the inflexion which might convey his disdain for such tactics.

The phone was picked up at the other end of the line. He said with perfect clarity, 'The River Wye is a beautiful river.'

He heard breathing at the other end of the line, but no words of acknowledgement came back to him. There was a clink, which might have been glass, or might have been something else entirely. Then there was a sharp click, as the phone was replaced and the contact was broken.

Seven

Carol Smart said, 'We should really agree what we're going to say before we talk to them, you know.'

Her husband was immersed as usual in the morning paper. Philip Smart said absently, 'Yes, I suppose we should.' Then what she had said got through to his brain and he looked up at her over the top of his *Telegraph*. 'Why do you say that?'

Carol turned away from him, fiddling with the flex of the toaster, trying to sound casual. 'I don't know, really. I was just thinking that neither of us is used to dealing with the police. So it would be sensible for us to be careful about it, wouldn't it?'

Philip laid his paper down on the table and looked at her seriously. 'Got things to hide from the fuzz, have you, darling?' He decided that he would tease her a little about this. Too often the boot was on the other foot in their marital dealings, with him defending himself after some sexual peccadillo. No sense of proportion, women. Well, wives, anyway.

'Of course I haven't got things to hide!' She had come in too vehemently. She realized that immediately. What chance was she going to have with the police, if she couldn't even carry things off with Phil? 'If you're not going to be serious, there's no point in us talking about this.'

Phil thought how attractive Carol was when she was a little flushed. She was eight years younger than him, pleasantly plump rather than running to fat. She looked to him wholly bedworthy this morning in the pink blouse and filmy scarf she had adopted for the police. Sometimes, as in moments of sudden tenderness like this, Philip Smart knew what a fool he was for playing the field as he did.

He said a little ponderously, 'But I *am* serious. Perfectly serious, my dear. Each of us is quite innocent in this, so neither of us has anything to worry about, surely? Unless you're about to tell me that you slung a cord around Robin's neck and throttled the life out of him!' Phil laughed, knowing that was in bad taste. He never meant to show bad taste, but his tongue often ran away with him.

'How do you know that he died like that?'

'I don't know. I was talking to Ron Lennox and Lisa this morning, whilst we were all still so shocked. When all those police cars were around. One of them must have told me. I expect Ally Durkin's sister must have told them: I think they'd been talking to her before I spoke to them. What a funny question to ask me, Carol Smart!'

He used her full name when he was trying to make jokes with her, as if by invoking that formula he could go back to the early, happy days of their marriage. She brushed a strand of fair hair which had fallen across her face angrily away, as if like him it was trying to divert her. 'It's not a funny question at all! It's the kind of question the police will ask, isn't it? They wouldn't have asked us to put off going on to work if they didn't think we were important, would they? You're very naïve at times, Phil.'

'I don't believe we live in a police state, if that's what you mean. I don't believe we'll be woken in the middle of the night and dragged away to prison!' Phil looked out at the golden morning in Gurney Close and smiled a superior smile at the absurdity of the thought.

'And we don't live in some Peter Pan Never-Never land either.' That's what he was, her husband. The worst kind of Peter Pan, who never grew up and recognized his responsibilities as an adult. Who thought he could chase any woman in sight without there being any consequences for him. A man with a stupid, superior smile above a white polo-necked shirt which emphasized his florid complexion and was surely too young for him. A tiresome fifty-one-year-old who hadn't the sense of some twenty-year-olds.

Carol Smart tried to control her irritation with him. It might be important to get her point across to Phil. 'Let's consider this from the police point of view. Let's assume for the moment that they don't know who did this, any more than we do.' She glanced up at him to see what he made of that, but he was still looking at her with that amused, superior expression. At least she had his attention. 'They're going to be looking for a culprit. If we make silly mistakes – if we say things like you just said about the way Robin died, for instance – they'll be on to it right away. And they'll be looking for someone to pin this crime on. We could land ourselves in a lot of trouble if we don't give a little thought to what we're doing.'

Phil looked at her, still with the little smile at the corners of his mouth which he knew was annoying her. He didn't disagree with what she was saying. Indeed, he might have been counselling her on similar lines himself, if his dear wife hadn't got in first. But he was enjoying feeling superior. And in the long series of conversational skirmishes which was their marriage, he couldn't easily let that feeling go. 'You really think they're going to arrest us for a brutal murder when we haven't done anything?'

She stood opposite his comfortably-seated figure, gripping the back of the chair, recognizing the sense of what he was saying. 'You're right, I suppose. I suppose I'm over-reacting because I'm not used to the police and they make me nervous. No, I don't believe these policemen will want to arrest and convict innocent people, once I stop to think about it. But I do believe that they could cause us a lot of embarrassment if we're careless in what we say to them. I do believe that it behoves us to be careful.'

'Behoves! I like that word. It has a solemn and archaic ring to it, don't you think, dear?' Phil made a show of changing from his humorous mode to his earnest and caring mode, as he dropped his smile and gave her a grave little frown. 'But you're right, my dear, of course you are. As you usually are, if I'm honest. We shall be careful, as you suggest. Now, what exactly is it that you advise?'

But it was too late. The grey Ford Focus was turning into their drive. The tall, gaunt man was levering himself rather stiffly from the passenger seat, whilst the driver was locking the car and turning to gaze at the front of their house. Carol Smart felt a blazing resentment at her husband's nonsense, a fury out of all proportion to his failings.

It was his mistaken humour and ponderous teasing which had taken away the chance for them to prepare themselves for this meeting.

Ten miles further down the River Wye, just over the border into Wales, Jason Ritchie was building a fence in the pleasant little town of Monmouth. The flimsy panels the builder had put up when he built these houses ten years earlier had finally disintegrated. Jason was putting in new concrete posts and much stouter wooden panels between them.

'I'd have done it myself at one time, you know.' The elderly man gave him a smile and shook his head, as though he were apologizing for employing him. Old people were always saying things like that, Jason thought. Telling you they'd been as strong as you, as skilful as you, in their heyday. Always looking back to the years which were gone.

The old were almost a closed book to Jason. When his parents had divorced, it had meant that grandparents had disappeared from his life whilst he was still quite small. And he was as yet too young to have any conception of how quickly life would pass, how close this youth they kept talking about still seemed to the elderly. Nor had he any old people close enough to him to remind him with unamusing persistence about that idea.

'Be finished this afternoon,' he said. He lifted one of the heavy concrete posts and dropped it into the hole he had made for it, exulting in his physical strength, delighted with the little gasp of admiration the performance elicited from his elderly patron. He shovelled some of the concrete he had just mixed into the hole and reached for his spirit level to check that the pole was vertical: best to show the old codger that there was skill and craftsmanship in this, and not just brute strength. That would help to justify his price. It was a fair one, as the old man had no doubt found out when he got other quotations for the job, but old people never kept up with inflation. They always thought that labour should cost less than it did.

'I'll get this border back into some sort of order when you've finished the fence,' said the old man.

Jason looked at the scrubby perennials and shrubs, covered with dust after the hot weather and his efforts with the fence. There were seedlings of ash and sycamore growing among the lesser weeds. 'Take a bit of shifting, that lot. I'll give you a bit of help, if you like. Get the rough work out of the way for you. Turn it over and leave it ready for planting.'

It was a tempting picture, the old man thought. His wife would tell him to jump at the offer, to spend his money and protect his back. But he said cautiously, 'I'll have to see if I can afford it. We hadn't budgeted for replacing the fence, you see. It's not easy, when you're on the pension.'

Jason Ritchie was saved from any reply by Mrs Old Codger, who called him from the house and offered him a big mug of tea and a seat in the shade. 'It's got the two sugars in, the way you said,' she said as he sat down. 'Neither of us takes sugar, these days.'

Jason gave her a grateful smile and sampled a mouthful of her tea. 'Just the way I like it, that, Mrs Williams.' It was actually a little weak for his taste, but she was looking anxious and he wanted to please her. He looked round the garden, then over towards the field beyond it to where the Wye ran out of Monmouth. 'Nice spot, this,' he said appreciatively.

Old people always liked it when you said that about where they lived. But at that moment, he meant it. It was certainly good to be as far away as possible from Gurney Close.

'We want to get your account of the events of Saturday night.' Bert Hook opened his notebook after Lambert's introductions.

'Surely you already know all about it. You've talked to Ally Durkin already. You were in there yesterday afternoon.' Carol Smart came in too quickly, her nervousness making her unnaturally aggressive.

Lambert smiled. Nervousness, even aggression, wasn't unwelcome to him. Tetchiness, like any other emotion, could make people reveal more of themselves than calmness did. 'That's a natural reaction, I suppose, Mrs Smart. I presume that you've never been involved in a murder enquiry before. Let me explain how we proceed. We speak to everyone who was close to the victim, asking them to recall what they can remember of the time—'

'We weren't particularly close to this victim. We didn't know the Durkins at all until we moved in here a month ago and they became neighbours.'

She had interrupted him, challenging what he said as if they were in the midst of some petty domestic argument. Interesting. Yet John Lambert was at his most urbane. He said patiently, 'But you were physically close to Robin Durkin, in the hours before his death. What we shall do is get recollections of those hours from everyone who was present during them.'

'Why? You know what went on, if you've talked to Ally. Why waste your time talking to the rest of us, when you know what happened? Why don't you leave us alone and spend your time and your expensive resources on trying to catch the person who killed Robin Durkin?' Carol's hand reached up and gave a needless, nervous tug at the chiffon scarf at her neck.

'We may be doing just that in beginning our investigation here, Mrs Smart. It must surely have occurred to you that one of the people present at the party on Saturday night may in fact have killed Mr Durkin.'

'That's absurd!' She felt the colour rising to her face, lifted her hand involuntarily and set the back of her fingers against her cheek for a moment, testing the temperature. She was glad she had thought to cover her neck with the scarf; bare necks could flush far too easily.

'It's not absurd, Mrs Smart. Not by any means. It may be an unwelcome thought to you that someone you knew, whether intimately or just as a neighbour, killed Robin Durkin, but it's perfectly possible. Indeed, statistically, CID figures would say that it is probable.'

'Not in this case, it isn't.'

Lambert pursed his lips, taking his time, pointing up the contrast to her haste. 'Your confidence in that is interesting. You may be right, of course. In your position, I should probably be feeling the same sort of loyalty to my neighbours. But I can assure you that this is where we have to begin. We have a large team, and it may reassure you to know that enquiries are going on in other places as well at this very moment. But we shall talk to everyone who was with Mr Durkin on Saturday night, and then put together their impressions of the evening. Where people's recollections coincide, we shall feel that we are getting an accurate picture of a murder victim's last hours. Where they do not coincide, that will obviously be of interest to us.'

He managed to make it sound like a threat, and was quite pleased to do so, if threats would make this spiky woman more co-operative. Carol Smart shook her head sharply, her fair, slightly frizzy hair bobbing with the movement. She looked at Lambert hard for a moment, unwilling to give ground to him. 'I can understand that. But you should bear in mind that you won't be talking to the person who killed Robin. He came in from outside, after our party was over.'

'Have you any grounds for saying that?'

'Knowledge of people. I'm certain that no one from Gurney Close killed Robin. That's all.'

'In that case, perhaps you will now give us your account of the hours between eight o'clock and one o'clock on Saturday evening.'

Her mouth set in a hard line, and it looked for a moment as if she would refuse. It was at this point that Philip Smart uncrossed his legs and said, 'Come on, old girl, these chaps are only trying to do their job, you know.'

Carol glared at him. She knew she had been unreasonable. She didn't need this fool of a husband to call her to order. If he hadn't pratted about before they came and got her annoyed, she'd have been properly prepared for this exchange. She wanted to snarl at Philip that she wasn't his 'old girl'. But this grim-faced superintendent and his lumpish sergeant would no doubt enjoy that. So instead she said, 'I'm only trying to defend people who have become my friends.' Then she turned back to Lambert and forced a smile. 'All right, Superintendent. I can see the sense of what you're telling me. Perhaps everyone in the close is still a little tense and shocked, after what happened.'

She then proceeded to give an account of the Saturday night celebration which co-incided so exactly with that they had had on the previous day from Alison Durkin that they were left wondering whether the two of them had got together on this. Lambert listened carefully; Hook asked her one or two small questions as he made his notes, then answered the queries she made of him. He explained that the body couldn't be released yet, that a defence lawyer, when they eventually made an arrest and the case came to trial, had the right to a second, independent, post-mortem examination, in case he wanted to challenge the findings of the one already conducted.

Carol Smart shuddered a little at the thought, then asked whether she and Philip would be required to give evidence in the Coroner's Court. Lambert said, 'Almost certainly not. The inquest will be formally opened, but then adjourned, under Section Twenty of the Coroners' Act. When we have made an arrest, there will be a Crown Court trial; this replaces the inquest.'

She nodded, digesting this. Then, unable to resist a little barb, she said, 'You seem very certain you are going to make this arrest.'

Lambert smiled. 'I am, Mrs Smart.' Then, without varying his even tone, he said, 'Who do *you* think killed Mr Durkin?'

'That's a preposterous question!'

'Direct, perhaps, but not preposterous. You must surely have given some thought to the matter since this startling death occurred. I'm assuming you did find it startling, of course. What about you, Mr Smart?'

Philip Smart's florid and revealing face registered his surprise at this sudden switch of police attention; Lambert registered the fact that he seemed to be a man who could not easily conceal his thoughts. 'I can't think that anyone at that party would have killed

Robin Durkin. We all got on so well during the evening. We've already told you that.'

'Yes, you have. Let me put my question in another, rather more diplomatic way. Are you aware that anyone who was at your street party had any reason to dislike Robin Durkin?'

Phil pretended to give the matter some thought; he was trying to show this lanky, intense superintendent that he wasn't the only one who could be diplomatic. 'No. Robin had got us most of the booze at discount rates.' Phil spoke as if that clinched the dead man's friendship with all of them.

Lambert said impatiently, 'That's hardly a guarantee of safety, is it? Had he seduced anyone's wife? Had he done the dirty on anyone in his business? Sold someone a dodgy car, for instance?'

'No. Not that I know of, anyway. Carol told you, we haven't known the Durkins for long. Only since we all moved into the close.' He could hear himself sounding defensive, so he said, 'His wife's quite a dish, you know. I wouldn't put it past some man to have had a go at Ally. Might have set up a confrontation with Robin, that, mightn't it? Perhaps Robin was going after him and the man fought back.' He caught his wife's movement beside him and said hastily. 'That's all just speculation, of course. I'm just trying to be helpful, the way you asked us to be.' Phil

85

Smart tried to dismiss the vision of Ally Durkin's shapely rear which thrust itself embarrassingly into his mind's eye.

'I see. And what about Mr Durkin? Was he in the habit of pursuing other women? Is it possible that a jealous husband or partner might have been looking to do him harm?'

'I don't know, I'm afraid.' Phil was already wishing he hadn't raised such matters. He wouldn't want his own track record in such things put under the police microscope.

'What about you, Mrs Smart? Are you aware of any sexual liaisons being conducted by either Mr or Mrs Durkin?'

Carol was furious that a husband who couldn't keep it in his trousers should be throwing out these thoughts about other people. She gave Phil a blistering look and said to Lambert, 'No. And I wouldn't tell you if I did.'

'That would be a most unwise decision, Mrs Smart. Withholding information in a murder enquiry would be viewed as a serious instance of obstructing the police in the course of their duties.' Lambert was pleased to convey the impression that he would be delighted to arrest her for it. 'If either of you think of anything which you consider might have a bearing on this crime, it is your duty to get in touch with us immediately. Your confidences will of course be respected, unless they later prove to be needed as evidence in a murder trial. Have you anything further to contribute before we leave?'

The Smarts glanced at each other, then shook their heads simultaneously. It was the only sign of unity they had given in the entire exchange.

'We shall probably want to speak to you separately at a later stage, when we have a more detailed picture of the events of Saturday night. For the moment, thank you for your help.'

Carol Smart didn't like that last bit at all. She had always assumed that they would be together for any police questioning. The thought of what that dolt of a husband might say without her watchful presence at his side filled her with trepidation.

Eight

The full post-mortem report was in when Lambert and Hook returned to Oldford police station.

'There's nothing you wouldn't have been expecting,' said DI Rushton gloomily when they entered the CID section. Lambert scanned the print-out of the report. Robin Durkin had been strangled with a piece of electric cable three feet seven inches long, which had bitten deeply into his neck, breaking his windpipe and killing him in seconds. In effect, he had been garrotted.

There were a few scratches on the neck around the line where the cable had bitten into the flesh, but as they had feared, they had been made by the dead man himself, struggling desperately and ineffectively to remove the instrument of his death in his last seconds on earth. There was skin and a little dirt under the dead man's nails, but they were his own skin and dirt, accumulated there in those last moments as he fought for his life.

Lambert said dully, 'The cable is relatively new, but there are soil particles on it, the pH of which suggests that it had come from the area where it was used. In other words the cable was probably picked up on the building site which has now been transformed into Gurney Close.'

Rushton said, 'I haven't been out there. Presumably there are lots of bits of cable and other builders' detritus still lying around.'

'Yes. The Durkins's garden has been pretty well cleared. And so has Mrs Holt's plot, the first one as you enter the close: she's had this young man Jason Ritchie working pretty well full time at her place. But the others haven't progressed quite as far as that. In any case, the four owners have hired a skip jointly, and have been dumping builders' rubbish in there for the last two or three weeks as they began the work of clearing their plots and establishing gardens. I had a look into it. It's almost full of broken bricks and broken strips of wood and bits of copper and plastic piping.'

'And pieces of electric cable, no doubt,' said Rushton sourly. It was what they had expected, but you always hoped against hope that the murder weapon would lead you straight to your killer.

Hook was trying to picture a murderer's movements in those minutes of warm darkness thirty-six hours earlier. He said slowly, 'So anyone looking for mischief on Saturday night could have picked up this piece of wire easily enough, either from this skip or from somewhere else around. I noticed plenty of lush long grass and nettles in those gardens which hadn't been cleared; they've been growing like mad in this hot weather, after all the rain we had ten days ago.'

Lambert pointed out, 'Anyone wanting us to think that this was a random killing could have picked up the wire days or even weeks beforehand, and waited for his moment. And there are no prints on the cable, so either the killer wore gloves or wiped it clean.'

Rushton said, 'The Scene of Crime boys found bits of wire and other builders' leavings outside the fences at the rear of the gardens behind the new houses, too. So anyone coming in from the path by the river could easily have picked up this length of wire as he moved in. SOCO stresses that we shouldn't confine our enquiries to people living in Gurney Close.'

Lambert was still looking at the written PM report. 'We also can't assume the killer was male. It looks as if Durkin was taken by surprise, as if this cord was thrown over his head from behind. The neck was savagely damaged, but no great physical strength was required to do this. It could have been a woman who was tightening that cable round his neck.'

Rushton nodded glumly. 'There's nothing remarkable in the analysis of the stomach contents, which is what you'd expect. They bear out what we've heard about the evening from those who were there. Quiche, ham, strawberries, ice cream. And a fair amount of alcohol over the evening. What we were told to expect by those who were with him on Saturday night.'

Lambert was still studying the detail of the report. 'Not quite, Chris. The alcohol blood count is seventy millilitres. That's less than I would expect. A very modest amount for a man who's been drinking throughout the evening and has no worries about driving home.'

Bert Hook said, 'His drinking was spread

90

out over five hours. Perhaps he'd urinated copiously and drunk pints of water before retiring for the night, the thing we're all told to do and which most of us forget.'

Rushton took the report from Lambert and looked again at the figure, annoyed that he had previously just noted the expected presence of alcohol and not the relatively low amount. 'Or maybe he was just more abstemious than the rest of them. Maybe he felt that as it was on his own patch he should act the host and stay more sober than his guests.'

'Both of those are feasible explanations. And so is the possibility that Robin Durkin was anticipating a meeting at the end of the evening and making sure that he was sober enough to handle it,' said Lambert.

'You planning to come over to the house today? You've been conspicuous by your absence, so far.' Lisa Holt tried not to make it sound like a criticism.

'I've been working in Monmouth. Job I promised to do for a pensioner weeks ago. Nice old couple. You'd like them, I think.' Jason Ritchie was conscious that he was forcing out the phrases, not speaking freely and naturally as he had grown used to doing with Lisa. He stopped and waited for her to fill the pause. When she didn't, he said defensively, 'Anyway, it's a Monday, and

91

you're out at work all day yourself, aren't you?'

'I went home for a bit of lunch. Made myself a sandwich. I rather expected to find you there, that's all.' She could have bitten her tongue off as soon as she'd said it. It was just the kind of wimpish thing she'd told herself she'd never say again; it made it sound as though her life revolved around him. She'd told herself when her marriage ended that she'd never whine like this again. She said hastily, 'Not that it matters, of course. I just had a bit of a hiatus in my working afternoon, so I thought I'd see how your day was going.'

'Well, it's going quite well.' Jason was wondering what to say. He'd never had to do that with her before. 'Well, I suppose I'd better get back to work. I've got concrete mixed, you see. It has to be used, once you've mixed it.'

'Right. It's just that I thought we'd said that we'd carry on as normally as possible. So that the police wouldn't get suspicious, I think you said. And I thought that as you've been working at my place every day for the last three weeks, that would be classed as normal.'

She knew she should have let it go, not tried to explain away her action in ringing him. She was behaving like a gauche teenager, not a thirty-nine-year-old woman and mother. 'Anyway, I'll see you some time, no doubt. Bye for now.' She had tried to ring off briskly and cheerfully, but she knew she had got even that wrong: she had made it sound like a querulous rebuke.

Jason Ritchie looked down at the mobile phone thoughtfully before he put it back into his rucksack. He had enough to think about with the police coming after him, without Lisa Holt getting all possessive.

Bert Hook didn't normally get home for lunch, especially when there was a murder investigation in progress. But today was a special day. Luke's birthday.

When you have waited a long time for children, you tend to make more of these things. Luke was twelve today, and Bert felt childhood passing away from his sons. The boys couldn't wait to be rid of it, whilst he and Eleanor cherished every scrap of infancy which was left in their progeny. That was one of family life's many puzzling paradoxes.

Luke had insisted on new football boots for his present, despite his father's preference for cricket and his insistence that football was out of season. But the boots were still in their box on the living-room floor. It would normally have been difficult to prize their soccer-mad son out of them, even in the house. But they gleamed softly in their lidless box as Bert went into the room, their pristine state a sinister symbol that something was wrong.

'The doctor's coming back this afternoon,' said Eleanor, her normally cheerful face grey with anxiety. 'He left some more pills this morning and told me to ring back if Luke's temperature didn't come down. It hasn't and I did. He'll be here in half an hour or so.'

Bert Hook went into the boy's bedroom. Luke lay very still on the bed, his eyes closed. For a moment of horror, Bert had the illusion that he was not breathing. Then the thin, almost bloodless lips moved, almost imperceptibly, and Luke gave a tiny groan. He looked very small and frail beneath the single sheet. Bert's mind flashed back to a time he thought he had forgotten, when the boy had been only five or six and laid low with a childish chill.

Bert knew without any diagnosis that this was something much more serious. He put his hand softly on the boy's forehead, withdrawing it in horror as he felt how hot and dry the skin was. The eyelids fluttered open, the head turned just a little, and the blue eyes looked at him as if they were trying to recognize a stranger.

'Happy birthday, son,' said Bert softly.

He fancied he caught the beginnings of a smile on the ashen lips. Then the eyes clouded and shut again.

★ ★ ★

'You must know everything that happened on Saturday night by now. At the party, I mean.' Lisa Holt added that hasty qualification. They surely couldn't know who had killed Robin Durkin.

'We have a good idea. We need your account of it. It may differ from what other people remember, you see,' said Lambert. He contrived to make the information seem like a threat.

They had come to see her in the office where she operated as a solicitors' clerk. One of the partners and the girl who usually worked alongside her were both away on summer holidays, so that the place was quiet. The boss had given her the room of his absent partner for this meeting with the police. She was glad to be away from her house in the close, which was so near to the spot where Robin had died, but also glad to be on familiar ground. And she was confident that she wouldn't be overheard; she knew from experience that this room was soundproof, that nothing she said to this observant superintendent and his stolid-looking sergeant would pass beyond its thick oak door.

She gave them a measured account of the street party which had preceded this death, trying to prevent it from sounding like the prepared statement that in fact it was. She had been over this many times to herself in the last day and a half, knowing she would be asked for her story, rehearsing it many times, because she knew she must be careful about how much of herself she revealed to these observant men.

She delivered her words evenly, answering Lambert's occasional questions calmly enough, watching the sergeant making notes on what she said in his round, rather childish hand, with the tip of his tongue protruding occasionally at the corner of his mouth. It was a surprise when Hook looked up at the end of her story and said, 'And you left at the same time as everyone else?'

'Yes. I think it was the Lennoxes who made the first move, but once they had done so, we all stood up and left together. I collected most of the crockery I had brought and walked the few yards back to my own house.'

'With Mr Ritchie.'

It was the first time she had ever heard Jason called that: the title sounded strange. She felt that Jason should be older and more responsible to justify it. She resented the question, even though she understood the reason for it. 'Yes. And to save you the next question, he stayed the night at my place.'

'You were together for the whole of the night?' If Hook was embarrassed to put the question, he disguised it very well.

Lisa took a deep breath, telling herself that there was no point in getting annoyed about this, that to do so would merely play into their hands. 'Yes. We made violent love to each other, and then fell asleep. In the same bed. Does that tell you everything you need to know?' She felt the annoyance in her voice, even though she had been determined not to show it.

Lambert smiled at her, trying to defuse the situation. 'Everything and a little more, I think. You are telling us that neither of you could have left the house without the other one knowing it. That neither of you could have gone out to the back garden of the house next door and garrotted Mr Durkin.'

She swallowed hard at the word, making herself take her time before she said, 'Is that how he died?'

'Yes. There will be a brief press release this afternoon, which will indicate that. It will use the term strangulation rather than garrotting. As a person closely involved, I thought you deserved the extra detail.' In fact, he had wanted to see how she would react to the harshness of the word, to the brutal frankness of this description of the death.

Lisa Holt had flinched just a little, and just for a moment. He said suddenly, 'How soundly did you sleep, Mrs Holt?'

She made herself smile. She was not going to give this man the satisfaction of embarrassment. 'We'd eaten plenty, and drunk more. Both of us. To be honest, we were pleasantly pissed, Superintendent. And then, as I told you, we made violent and very satisfying love. I'd say we slept very soundly indeed.'

'So if Mr Ritchie had got up and moved around, even left the house, you would probably not have been aware of his movements.' Lambert made it a statement, and she was irritated to see Hook flicking to a new page in his notebook and recording the fact.

'Both of us were sleeping the sleep of the just. Or rather the pissed, as I said. So yes, probably neither of us would have been aware of the other going out. But for the record, I'm quite sure that neither of us did that. The first thing I was conscious of was screaming from Ally Durkin at whatever time it was the next morning. I wondered what on earth all the noise was about. And I had to waken Jason, even then. He was out to the world.'

'How long had you known Mr Durkin?'

He had a habit of putting his questions very abruptly, as if by surprising her he might catch her out in some deception. Lisa wondered if it was part of his normal technique, or something which denoted a special animosity to her. Probably the former. She was pleased that she sounded so calm and matter-of-fact as she said, 'Four or five weeks, I suppose. We all moved into the close at about the same time.'

'You didn't know him before you became his neighbour?'

'No. I knew his garage. I drive past it quite often. I've seen it grow and become more prosperous over the last few years. But I didn't know Robin until we found ourselves neighbours in the new houses.'

'Do you know of anyone who had reason to dislike him?'

'No. He's been helpful to most of us since we moved in. He had contacts and he seemed to enjoy using them. He saved us quite a bit by getting the booze for the party at a good discount. I suppose he has business enemies – I'm sure most people who've become successful quickly make enemies – but I don't know anything about that.'

Lambert noticed again the inclination to push this crime outside the close, to suggest that their killer was some anonymous figure from the larger and more violent world outside. But that was natural enough: even people who are totally innocent do not like to take on the idea of an immediate neighbour as a murderer.

They left her with the usual injunction to get in touch if any useful thoughts occurred to her. Lisa Holt decided that it had been straightforward enough, and less fraught than she had feared. Nevertheless, she was glad that it was over. She spent the rest of the afternoon working on the conveyancing of a three-hundred-year-old rectory in a Gloucestershire village. It was detailed, straightforward, even slightly boring, work, which demanded the whole of her attention. She was glad of that.

At the end of the day, she went home and chatted to her son about his day at school whilst she made a meal. At the first opportunity, she went up to the bedroom where she had slept with Jason Ritchie on Saturday night. That was less than two days ago, but it seemed much longer.

She stood for a long minute looking out of the bedroom window into the back garden of her neighbours, gazing at the innocent-looking patch of grass on which a man had died.

Nine

'The bank manager will see us this morning. I spoke to him as he was leaving last night.' DI Rushton greeted his chief with the news as he came into the CID section at Oldford nick on Tuesday morning. It was still only ten to nine; he wanted Lambert to realize he had been at work at his computer for almost an hour already.

'You go, Chris. Bert Hook's delayed at home, but he'll be in shortly. I want to talk to the Chief Constable about the crime figures, and clear the overtime budget for this Durkin murder enquiry. Go and get the details of Robin Durkin's finances for us. I'll hold the fort here for the time being. You need to get out more.'

Rushton looked at him suspiciously for a moment. He decided this was probably a light-hearted remark rather than a real criticism, but he wasn't sure. He was never quite sure whether the long-established partnership of Lambert and Hook was pulling his leg. He was surprised how reluctant he felt to get up from his familiar chair and leave the winking screen of his computer: perhaps the chief was right when he said he should get out more.

The bank manager put up the token show of resistance to revealing the details of the dead man's finances. It was very British, Chris thought: you could fairly easily discover all sorts of intimate details about a man's sex life; from an examination of the records, you could discover in a few minutes any crimes he had committed and where he had done time. But money was sacred, and unless there was a very serious crime involved, the details of a man's financial situation were jealously guarded by all concerned.

Today there was a serious crime, the most serious one of all. Murder sounded a note of grisly glamour, even for a bank manager who was twenty years older than DI Chris Rushton. Charles Ferguson, manager at Barclays, made both the Durkins' private accounts and the account for the business the dead man had run from the garage available within minutes to the young inspector, once he had played the murder card.

The joint private account told the story Rushton would have expected for a prosperous businessman. Never in the red, with plenty of small and medium cheques passed by Alison Durkin over the last few months as she planned the furnishing of the comfortable nest of her new house. It was an expensive business, moving house, but there was no sign of any financial straitjacket for the Durkins.

It was when he turned to the business account that Chris Rushton found the entries more interesting. He studied them for a moment, then pushed them across the desk to the silver-haired manager. 'Is this the sort of financial profile you'd expect for a prosperous small garage?'

Ferguson was immediately defensive. 'I'm really no expert on these things. We don't interfere with our customers' transactions:

we're here to provide them with a service, which includes confidentiality. We don't pry into what they are doing, that's not our function. We provide advice when clients want it, but don't interfere.'

'Unless they get into financial difficulties. When you can be most unhelpful.' Chris Rushton had been through a divorce, and had certain residual resentments about banks.

Charles Ferguson said stiffly, 'There are certain financial constraints. We have to protect people from themselves, sometimes. Prevent them from getting themselves into deeper financial trouble. And people don't realize that individual managers have less room for manoeuvre than they once had. Policy decisions are taken at a much higher level than was once the case. We are not allowed to go against the guidelines.' He had dropped into his defensive mode automatically, trundling out the tired phrases which had become a large part of his life over the last ten years. For the third time in a week which had only reached Tuesday morning, Ferguson thought that he wouldn't be sorry to retire in a few years.

Rushton was wondering how to arrest the flow of clichés. Because there was something interesting here. He said bluntly, 'Look at the deposits into that account, please. Tell me if they seem to you typical for a business like that of Robin Durkin. If you don't feel able to comment, no doubt you can refer me to someone with the appropriate expertise.'

He had hit upon the right approach, almost by accident. The manager was stung by the suggestion that he might not be up to this. He studied the figures carefully for the first time. It was a full minute before he spoke, and when he did his voice was animated, even startled. 'You're right! This isn't typical at all. The sums are much too large, even for a prosperous small business like Durkin Autos.'

'There seem to be very large sums moving in and out.'

'Yes. And it's not just that.' Ferguson could not keep the excitement out of his voice; detection was a totally new and unexpected pleasure for him. He came round the desk and pulled up a chair to sit down beside his unexpected visitor. He pointed at certain entries with a well-groomed finger. 'The dates are wrong. There should be a lot of money passing through at the time of the new car registration numbers. There's always a flurry of new sales then, for any dealer with an agency. There should be a lot of financial activity in the account at those times, as they pay out money on cars taken in part ex-change and bank the larger sums taken from the sales of new cars. Those trends are there all right: you can see them in April, for instance, after the spring change in registration letters. But there are very large sums coming in at other times, when I would expect a garage account to be very quiet.'

'Coming in and going out.'

'Yes. These large sums don't seem to stay there very long.'

Their roles were almost reversed now. It was the manager who was animated, Chris Rushton who was attempting to sound calm as he said, 'It's a pattern which would be typical of someone engaged in money laundering, wouldn't you say?'

It was a suggestion which this sober man would normally have automatically resisted. But it was the first time he had been asked to confirm anything like this, and he could not resist it. 'Yes. I must say it has all the hallmarks of money laundering. Which is embarrassing for us: we're supposed to be vigilant about these things nowadays. It might take a lot of proving. But we have fiscal experts who would take on any further investigation. They would work with you, of course: serious crime is much more your field than mine, Detective Inspector.'

'It's something we'll need to follow up. It will be interesting to see where this money has been transferred to. And in due course, to find where it came from.'

'Yes. Yes, it will. I hardly knew Robin Durkin myself, unfortunately.' He said it with genuine regret. And then, in a belated fit of caution, he said, 'There may be a perfectly innocent explanation, of course.'

There was not. The money had been transferred to an account in the Halifax Building Society in Cardiff, opened three years previously in the name of someone calling himself Mark Durkin. There had been no withdrawals from it. The balance now stood at eight hundred thousand pounds.

'Do come in and sit down! You'll have to take us as you find us, I'm afraid. We're still settling in. Everything takes longer to do than you expect, as you get older!'

Ronald Lennox gestured vaguely towards the sofa in their bright new room, which already looked like a well-established living area, despite his introduction to it. There was a vase of roses in the hearth, a smaller bowl of roses on the north-facing window sill, pictures of English landscapes on the walls, a photograph of a handsome youth who was obviously their son in pride of place on the sideboard.

Lennox was patently nervous. John Lambert watched him with interest. He did not speak, did not oil the wheels of social exchange as the man expected him to do. It was an unfortunate effect of CID experience that you enjoyed nervousness in people you were interviewing. Anxiety made your opponents more vulnerable in the bizarre games you had to play. Bizarre because ninety per cent of the time people were innocent, but had to be treated with suspicion until this innocence was proved.

Rosemary Lennox saw what was happening. She said coolly, 'We want to offer you all the help we can, Superintendent. That goes without saying. But I can't think we can add anything to what you already know.' She was wearing a dark-blue cotton dress with a pattern of small white flowers. The flowers in her dress and her white sandals picked up the silvery threads in her grey hair, which was surprisingly becoming above her neat, intelligent face. It was cut short and tidy, but with a wave over her forehead which took away any severity. She looked very comfortable on this very warm day, in contrast to her husband. Ronald Lennox sat sweltering in the suit and tie he had donned when he heard that the superintendent in charge of the case was coming to see him.

Lambert said, 'I'm sure you want this business cleared up as quickly as we do. Normally, I would have Detective Sergeant Hook with me to take notes, but he can't be here today. This morning's meeting may prove to be no more than a formality, but I must ask you to give it full concentration. Small things sometimes emerge which turn out to be highly significant at a later stage.'

'What sort of things?' Ronald Lennox was in almost before his visitor had completed his sentence.

'Little discrepancies in the way people remember things. You'd be amazed how much people's recollections differ, even when they're recounting events which occurred very recently. Even the recall of totally innocent people is sometimes quite varied.' Lambert gave Lennox a smile which did nothing to allay his nervousness.

Rosemary took over in her efficient, matter-of-fact way and gave him their story of Saturday night's events. Lambert listened without interruption to her lucid, economical account, watching her husband's reactions to what she told him. Then he said, 'And whose idea was this gathering? A street party, I think you called it.'

Rosemary smiled. 'It was mine. And it wasn't really a street party. I called it that when I suggested a gathering because I remembered sitting at a table in the street at the end of the war in 1945, when I was only three. We had sandwiches and home-made cakes and lemonade. It must have made quite an impression on me, because I can still recall it quite vividly.'

'So you suggested a street party for the new residents of Gurney Close.'

'Yes. I think because we were a group of disparate people drawn together by the accident of residence. All we really had in common was that we'd become occupants of these new houses at more or less the same time.'

'Or in our case, a bungalow. The only one in the close,' said Ronald Lennox pedantically.

'But the party was your idea, Mrs Lennox?'

'Yes. I dare say someone else would have suggested a get-together of some kind, even if I hadn't.'

Ronald Lennox bristled, suddenly and unexpectedly. 'They certainly would have done just that. Are you trying to suggest that Rosemary set this thing up deliberately, just so that someone could have the opportunity of killing Robin Durkin? That's ridiculous!'

Lambert smiled, not at all displeased to find the man losing his sense of proportion. 'I'm suggesting nothing, Mr Lennox. One of the things we have to establish in a case like this is who set up the situation. It is simply a fact to be determined, like any other fact. When we have all the facts, some will emerge as highly significant. Neither I nor anyone else is yet in a position to say which ones those will be.'

'Of course you aren't! And I can see that there is nothing sinister in your enquiry.' Rosemary Lennox tried to be as calm and equable in her answers as this polite but determined superintendent was in his questions. But she noticed that he hadn't refuted her husband's suggestion about the meeting being set up as a possible prologue to murder.

'There is one other thing I wanted to clarify about the evening and your impressions of it. Both of you can help here. You have confirmed what other people have told us, that a fair amount of drink was consumed. I know it's difficult to be accurate about these things, but how drunk would you say people were, at the end of the evening?'

Ronald Lennox responded promptly to the invitation, as Lambert had somehow known that he would. 'Oh, we'd all had quite a lot over five hours or so. And none of us had to worry about driving home. I remember us congratulating ourselves on that, at the time.'

'Repeatedly,' said his wife, with a touch of acid.

'I'd say that no one was blind drunk and reeling about, but we were all pleasantly pissed, if you'll pardon the modernism,' said Ron.

'Yes. That tallies with what Mrs Durkin and Mrs Holt have told us,' said Lambert thoughtfully. 'And how drunk would you say Mr Durkin was? In the same state as everyone else?'

Ronald Lewis's thin face cracked into an indulgent smile. 'Oh, Robin was pretty far gone. We'd been drinking for hours, remember, and you usually drink rather more than you think you're taking, in circumstances like that, don't you? I know I realized that the next morning, when I had the biggest hangover I've had in years. Wasn't fit for anything on Sunday, was I, Rosemary?'

'You certainly weren't. And of course, we had to contend with the news of Robin's death, before we were far into the day.'

Lennox grinned ruefully. 'I must have drunk a lot more than usual on Saturday night, because Rosemary had some difficulty waking me to give me the sad news. But to answer your question, I'm sure Robin was as merry as anyone at the end of the evening. I remember him going round with the brandy bottle, giving everyone a nightcap. And I'm sure he didn't miss himself out.'

'That's interesting,' said Lambert tersely.

'May we ask why?' said Rosemary Lennox quietly.

There was no reason why they should not know. 'The post-mortem report shows that Robin Durkin had drunk only a moderate amount last Saturday night.'

They both looked surprised. Ron Lennox said, 'He didn't give either of us that impression. Perhaps habitually he didn't drink as much as we would have thought he did. Or perhaps he was one of those men who get drunk quite easily, so that you assume they've drunk more than they have.'

'That is a possibility, of course.'

Rosemary looked at him sharply. 'But you obviously don't consider that the likely explanation.'

'From what you and other people have told us, it doesn't seem likely, no. His wife, for instance, thinks he usually let himself go on occasions like Saturday night. She says that he was no drunkard, but she thought like you that he had drunk quite a lot during Saturday evening.'

'But why would it be important?'

Lambert thought from Mrs Lennox's shrewdly intelligent features that she had already guessed why. 'We don't know for certain that it has anything to do with this crime. But one explanation could be that Robin Durkin knew that he had an assignation coming up when your party was over. A meeting with someone, for which he wanted to keep his brain sharp, and unfuddled by too much alcohol.'

Ron Lennox frowned. 'I can see what you mean. But surely this chap who came into his garden and killed him took him completely by surprise? I can't think that Robin was anticipating a meeting. Not by the way he behaved with us in that last hour.'

Lambert shrugged. 'I offered that as a

possible explanation. It's not the only one. I'm confident that we shall know a lot more about this by the end of the week.' It was always as well to give the public the impression that you were in confident control and that things were moving steadily forward. Especially when there was a possibility, however remote, that the killer of Robin Durkin might be one of the two people confronting him so earnestly in this comfortable room.

He said, 'Thank you for your time. We may need to see you separately at a later stage of the enquiry. Am I right to presume that neither of you knew Mr Durkin before you moved into Gurney Close?'

Rosemary Lennox smiled. 'That is correct. One of the interesting things is how a disparate group of people can be brought together by the common problems of moving into a new neighbourhood. Hence my suggestion for the street party. I remember thinking on Saturday night how good it was that such different people should be enjoying themselves together. And then this happened.' She looked past Lambert and out of the big window of her sitting room at the dangerous world outside, and shook her head sadly.

It was her husband who broke the silence which followed. He said quietly, 'I knew Robin before we moved in here.'

They both turned to look at him, more

113

because of his tone than because what he said was particularly startling. He forced a smile to disperse their solemnity. 'There's nothing sinister about it. I know him for the same reason that I know hundreds of other people in the local community, Superintendent. I taught him, years ago.'

'How many years ago, Mr Lennox?'

'Sixteen, seventeen years ago. Something like that. We could check the dates in the school records, if it's important.'

'And is it, Mr Lennox?'

He smiled, as if he were pleased to have thrown his little surprise into the exchanges. 'Of no importance at all, in my opinion. A matter of supreme irrelevance, as one of my colleagues used to say.'

Lambert answered his smile. 'What kind of a pupil was he?'

Ron Lennox grinned at the recollection, and his lined face looked suddenly more attractive with mirth. 'Bit of a nuisance, if you want to know. In fact, I'm aware of the convention that one shouldn't speak ill of the dead, but Rob Durkin was a right little bugger when he was at school!'

'In what way?'

'Oh, nothing vicious, you know. High-spirited adolescence, you'd call it. But high-spirited adolescence can be a pain in the arse when you have to deal with it. Especially without the sanctions you used to have when

I started teaching forty years ago!'

Rosemary was surprised to hear her normally fastidious husband describe the vanished schoolboy as both 'a little bugger' and 'a pain in the arse'. She sensed that a familiar diatribe about modern discipline was in the offing. She said hastily, 'You never said you'd taught Robin, Ron. Not even on Saturday night, when everyone was being relaxed and indiscreet.'

'Professional discretion, Rosemary. Robin never acknowledged that I'd taught him, so I thought he might not wish to have those days recalled. Perhaps he wasn't proud of the way he behaved at school: I think some of the other teachers had more trouble with him than I had. I'd have been perfectly prepared to have a laugh with him about the peccadillos of his youth, but I didn't think it was up to me to raise the matter.'

'And his school career was the only contact you had with him until the last few weeks of his life?' asked Lambert.

'Indeed it was. And I wouldn't like you to go away with the idea that the young Rob Durkin was anything more than a high-spirited boy. There was nothing vicious at all about him. He was the same as hundreds of other boys with a lot of energy and a little mischief in them.'

'Nevertheless, thank you for recalling those days.'

'Not at all. I only mentioned them because I felt I must be strictly accurate in answering your questions. We don't want to be hauled into the police station and given the third degree because of some small omission at this stage, do we, Rosemary?' Ron laughed at his little witticism, a high, startling sound in the quiet room.

Lambert took an amicable leave of them then. And Mrs Lennox was left wondering why her husband had never mentioned this previous acquaintance with Robin Lennox, even to her.

The man was surly, tight-lipped, cautious. Police officers are used to dealing with such attitudes, but DS Liz Brown had problems of her own to contend with.

As a newly promoted CID sergeant, she was anxious not to make mistakes. She had been thrilled to be assigned to the team of Chief Superintendent John Lambert, who had acquired almost mythical powers in local police folklore, through a combination of longevity and sustained success as a villain-taker. But now that she was actually working as part of his murder team, excitement had turned to trepidation. The old dinosaur would surely eat her for breakfast if she made mistakes.

And here was this surly man putting up the barriers against her and making her life

difficult. She glanced at the gawky uniformed constable who was standing expectantly
beside her in the airless office which had
been assigned to them for this interview. No
help there. He looked scarcely more than a
boy to Liz, and he was watching her expectantly, as if he expected to learn things.

They were in the rambling buildings of the
Ford main dealers in Gloucester, where
Mark Gregory was a sales manager. He
looked at his watch and said, 'I hope this
won't take much longer. I've a busy schedule
to cope with.'

'It will take as long as it needs, Mr Gregory. This is a murder investigation.' Liz
spoke with a firmness she did not feel, and
got a tiny crumb of comfort from the sight of
her acned colleague nodding his support.

'And I've already told you I know nothing
about this crime. I've even offered to prove
to you that I was out of the area at the time.'

'No one has suggested that you killed Mr
Durkin.' At this moment, I'd like to suggest
it, you sullen sod, but I can't. 'We need to
find out all we can about the murder victim.
And we expect the public to cooperate with
us.'

'Which I'm doing.' Mark Gregory became
suddenly all sweetness and reason. No point
in alienating the forces of the law, especially
when they came to you in this unthreatening
guise. And he didn't want them prying too

closely into the past.

'You were a partner of Mr Durkin.'

'Not for the last three years, I wasn't.'

'A former partner. We need to know about those years when you worked together.'

He resisted the impulse to tell her to go to hell. That would only prolong this. 'There isn't much to tell. We established a successful small garage. Built up quite a good reputation. He was in charge of the workshops and servicing, I handled the showroom and car sales. I thought the partnership was working well. But that wasn't enough for Robin bloody Durkin. He had to control the whole thing. He had to get rid of me.'

There was already enough of CID in Liz Brown to make her pulses quicken. Usually people were polite, even unctuous, in the face of death. Normally any hostility was veiled, and defences had to be stripped away to reveal the enmities beneath. This man was making no secret of his resentment: that had to be interesting. With luck, she would only need to lead him on. She said rather lamely, 'You didn't part on friendly terms?'

He smiled grimly. 'As friendly as they could be, when you'd stopped speaking to each other. He bought me out.'

'So it was a straightforward business transaction.'

Again that bitter twisting of the lips, as if he wanted to say much more than he was

118

going to allow himself. 'In so far as anything was straightforward with Rob Durkin, yes. He said the business needed capital to expand, that I must provide as much as he was prepared to put in or get out. I got out. Not because I wanted to, but because I had no alternative.'

'But he paid you a proper price.'

Gregory's mobile face turned to stone. 'That's between us. He had me over a barrel, because he knew I was strapped for cash at the time. He drove the kind of bargain you'd expect from a bastard like him. But I was a good salesman. I got a job here and I'm doing pretty well. I preferred being my own boss, but at least this way I'm away from the tricks of Rob Durkin.'

Liz wondered whether to press him about the terms of the partnership buyout. But she sensed that Gregory would resist, and she hadn't any weapons to use against him. He was simply a member of the public helping police with their enquiries, as a good citizen should. And John Lambert would have other methods of getting the information, if he thought it relevant. She said, 'You make it sound as if Mr Durkin must have had a lot of enemies.'

'I'm sure he did, DS Brown. And in case you still have any doubts, I shan't be mourning his death. As far as I'm concerned, it's good riddance to him.'

'Do you want another coffee?' he said.

'No. I've had far more than I want already.'

The hospital, or rather this particular section of it, was very quiet. Abnormally quiet, surely. And the time passed more slowly here than anywhere else in the world, when you were waiting for news.

Eleanor Hook looked up at the round white face of the clock on the magnolia wall, watched the red second hand ticking silently round it. She wondered why she and Bert were suddenly so stiff and wordless with each other, why two people who normally communicated so effortlessly and easily could become awkward and tongue-tied, sitting here like strangers on these uncomfortable plastic chairs.

'How long is it since the specialist went in?' Bert Hook knew perfectly well how long it was. He was talking for the sake of talking, because speech seemed less threatening than silence.

'Twenty minutes. It seems longer, but I don't think it is.'

'That's long enough to decide what's wrong with him, surely. He should be out here talking to us by now.'

'He'll be putting the right treatment into operation. Getting the nurses organized. Making sure that he's regularly checked, monitoring his progress towards recovery.'

Eleanor was surprised how positive and cheerful she made it sound as she tried to convince Bert. How could you manage to do that, when you were sick with the worry of it?

'He's always been a strong lad, Luke. Much stronger than he looks.' It was the first time either of them had mentioned his name in hours. Bert felt as though he was tempting fate as he voiced it.

'He didn't look strong when they brought him in here. His temperature was sky high. And his head was hurting, despite the pills. Poor little scrap!'

And suddenly she was in tears, and Bert was holding her clumsily against him, muttering over and over again, 'He'll be OK, Elly. He's strong, is young Luke. He'll be OK!'

They were still like that when the registrar came out, looking to Bert absurdly young in his white coat, with his wrists sticking out too far at the cuffs. He said, 'He's in the best place now, Mrs Hook. The very best! We'll pull him through for you, I'm sure.'

'What is it?' Bert's voice was rough and challenging, dispensing with the normal courtesies.

The registrar had wanted to take them off the corridor and into the office, to talk quietly and reassuringly to them, infusing them with a confidence he could not feel himself.

But he was caught up now in Bert's urgency, in his brutal and primal helplessness in the face of catastrophe. 'It's what we feared, I'm afraid. Meningitis.'

Eleanor felt the colour draining from her face as she prised herself away from her husband. 'How bad?'

'Pretty bad. His temperature's very high and he's lost consciousness. The crisis will be in the next thirty-six hours.' The registrar felt absurdly relieved that he'd got all his bad news out at once, like a child blurting out a confession.

He said again, as firmly as he could, 'But we'll pull him through, I'm sure.'

Ten

'First question: was this extra money coming from the garage business?' said Lambert.

Rushton was staring at the page he had put on to his computer, giving the startling details of the dead man's finances. 'No. Quite certainly not. The agency for new cars was for the Seat range of models. There's nothing wrong with them, but it's not the most lucrative dealership to have. When you look at Durkin's new and used car sales, he wasn't doing much more than making a living. Perhaps a comfortable living, depending on how tightly he controlled his overheads, but nothing more than that.'

'Second question: why was he hiding it away so carefully? Was he merely dodging the taxman, or was the money itself illegal?'

Rushton had no hesitation about that. 'That money's dodgy. It's got to be. No small businessman makes sums of that size without them being dodgy.'

Lambert grinned. 'How sad that one so young should yet be so cynical. But I agree. Unless you inherit it, which we know he didn't, or have large sums of capital to invest, it's virtually impossible to acquire getting on for a million pounds by legitimate methods. And if that money had been accumulated legally, he wouldn't have been taking such steps to hide it. So now question three: how did Robin Durkin contrive to get his hands on an extra eight hundred thousand pounds?'

Rushton grimaced, knowing that he was being asked to voice the obvious. 'Drugs? Fraud?' The two great modern sources of illegal gains. The two means by which the fly boys of the criminal industry build up capital and finance even bigger coups. The two crimes which policemen suspect automatically when unexplained sums of this magnitude turn up.

'Not fraud. There's nothing in Durkin's background or the world in which he operated to suggest that. I don't think the opportunities were there. Drugs are certainly a possibility. I'll get in touch with the Drugs Squad to see what they think.'

The Drugs Squad enjoys a great degree of autonomy within the police service, as befits a unit operating in the most dangerous and most lucrative of all crime divisions. The personnel of the Squad guard jealously the information they take such risks to acquire, even from fellow police officers. Secrecy is vital, both to the safety of the many officers operating under cover and to the success of their operations. But murder overrides normal practice, and Lambert knew the man he would contact.

He said thoughtfully, 'There's a fourth question to add to the other three, you know. And that is, how many other people knew that Durkin was making money of this sort? Did anyone who was at that party on Saturday night know anything about it? Did even his wife know?'

'You sure you want to do this, Bert?'

Lambert had never seen the normally rubicund Hook looking so pallid. The detective sergeant nodded more firmly than he felt. 'I'm better working, John. There's nothing I can do, is there? You just sit around feeling helpless.'

'All right. I won't raise it again. You must let me know if you want out. And if there's anything Christine or I can do, you know that—'

'There isn't!' There was an awkward pause, which seemed to stretch whilst Lambert took the car round a long bend under the trees, then Hook said, 'There's nothing any-one can do, except the medics. But thanks for asking.'

The caravan was old, but its exterior was surprisingly spruce. Its paintwork gleamed softly, even though, at this time of day, it was in the shade of the great oak which stood twenty yards from it. It would probably never be towed on the road again, but its tyres were fully inflated and it stood exactly level on its concrete footing. The metal step beneath its door had neither leaf nor dirt upon it; it looked as if some diligent house-wife had recently brushed it thoroughly.

The man looked a formidable figure as he opened the door and stood looking down at them. His frame filled the whole aperture of the doorway, shutting out any light behind him.

Jason Ritchie didn't even try to manufac-ture a smile for them. He saw no need to pretend that they were welcome: the fuzz had never given him anything but grief in his life. He said, 'You'd better come in, I suppose.'

They climbed the single step and sat where he indicated, on the bench seat with its thin covering of foam cushioning. Everything in the place was cramped, so that when the occupant sat down opposite them, he was abnormally, unnaturally close. No more than two feet away, thought Bert Hook; this was a closer and even more claustrophobic environment than the inhibiting box of a police interview room at the station.

The difference here was that the man was on his own ground, showing no signs of the inhibitions which the interview room at the nick often brought to people questioned there. Ritchie said, with a belated, clumsy attempt at welcome, 'You want a mug of tea? I was making a brew anyway.' He spoke as if he felt a need to apologize for the gesture, as if he was already regretting something which ran so counter to his principles.

To Hook's surprise, Lambert accepted the offer, and they watched Lisa Holt's gardener moving with brisk efficiency around the tiny area which was so familiar to him. The caravan was even more clean and tidy inside than outside. The stainless steel sink gleamed softly, the blankets on the bed were tucked in as tightly and neatly as those on the hospital beds still fresh in Hook's memory. The windows were bright and clean, and even the small chintz curtains on them looked as if they had enjoyed a recent wash.

They didn't compliment him on this, nor offer any other casual words. These particular policemen felt no need to fill conversational voids with small talk. They chose to let a silence build, heavy with implication, hoping it was increasing tension in the man at the centre of it. In this confined space, Jason Ritchie's movements sounded unnaturally loud as he took milk from the tiny fridge and put it into the three large china beakers he had set on the side of the sink.

Perhaps he felt some of the unease they wanted to see in him, for it was he who eventually broke the conversational hiatus, as he said roughly, 'You're wasting your time here, you know! There's nothing I can tell you that you don't already know.'

Lambert smiled at him, picking up the first trick in the game. 'Neither you nor I know whether that is true or not, at this stage, Mr Ritchie.'

'Let's get it clear then. I know bugger all about this killing. I hardly knew Robin Durkin before Saturday night, and I don't know anything about the way he died. Full stop.'

But his aggression was already a weakness: that thought struck Jason himself now, even as it became apparent to his visitors. Lambert said calmly, 'We have to be interested in anyone who was close to a murder victim in the hours before he died. I expect you know enough of our procedures to appreciate that.'

Ritchie glanced up at him sharply above his beaker, then nodded a sullen acquiescence. They took him through his account of the now familiar Saturday night party by a series of questions, since he seemed reluctant to give them a continuous statement of his own. Then Lambert said, 'When was the last time you saw Robin Durkin?'

'You know that.' The brown eyes stared hard into Lambert's grey ones. The thick, strong fingers moved over the tattoo of barbed wire on the upper arm, tracing its line upwards and under the cotton. It was a habitual gesture, as if it was a tangible thing he could feel under his fingers, rather than a tracing beneath the skin. 'I said goodbye and thank you to him at the end of the party on Saturday night, and I left with the others. If you're implying anything else, I want a brief.'

'You're entitled to retain your own legal advice at any time. You're not entitled to free legal representation unless you've been arrested and are being questioned in connection with an offence.' Lambert's eyes, looking into his from no more than two feet, seemed to Jason to see everything and never to need to blink. 'Did you see Mr Durkin again after you left his house at just before one a.m. on Sunday morning?'

'What the hell are you implying?' He watched Hook make a formal note of his reply, resting his notebook on the spotless melamine surface between them. 'I've no idea what you're on about.'

But they all knew what was behind the question. Jason felt himself having to work up his anger, when he knew that he should have been more naturally and spontaneously outraged by the suggestion.

Lambert ignored his reaction and said, 'You don't seem to have spoken much directly to Mr Durkin during the evening. Perhaps not at all. Was there a reason for that?' No one had reported that directly to him: it was something he had deduced from the various accounts, including the one Ritchie himself had just given to them.

Jason did not refute the idea. He said gruffly, 'I was there on sufferance, the only one who wasn't a resident of Gurney Close. I was watching myself a bit, making sure I didn't step out of line. All the men were older than I am. I hadn't a lot in common with them.' It sounded a little desperate; he hadn't expected to be pressed on this.

'Robin Durkin was the nearest in age to you among the men. One might expect that you would have found it easier to talk to him than to the others.'

'I didn't. I don't know why.'

'Even when drink had relaxed you and

everyone else? I would have thought that might have loosened your tongue.' Lambert had no idea where this was going, but he had located a weakness, almost by chance, and his instinct was to go for it.

'We were all quite relaxed by the end of the evening. I kept close to Lisa, because I was only there because of her. But the others were friendly enough, once we'd had a few drinks.'

'But not so friendly in Robin Durkin's case that you felt able to talk to him. Did you see him again after you had left his house with Mrs Holt at the end of the party?'

'No. I've already told you that I didn't.'

'You hadn't, actually. Never mind, you've answered the question for us now. So tell us what happened after the party broke up.'

'I spent the night with Lisa.' Jason wondered whether to enlarge upon the delights of this, but decided against it.

Lambert looked at him keenly. 'Did you know Mr Durkin before you met him in Gurney Close during those last weeks of his life?'

How abrupt the man was. How quickly he switched from one area to another, just when you felt you were getting to grips with him. 'No. I'd passed his garage, like other people. I didn't recognize that this man was the Durkin who owned the garage until I met him when we were doing the gardens.'

130

'So you hadn't had a relationship of any kind with him before that.'

'No. I've told you I didn't. Why should it be of any interest to you if I had?' He wished as soon as he'd said it that he hadn't asked that question, that he'd left them merely with a blank negative.

Lambert smiled, as if he too recognized the error. 'We've got to be interested in any previous dealings people had with someone who is now a murder victim. Particularly when one of them has a previous history of violence.'

So they had come to it, as he told himself now that he had known they would. He forced himself to appear calm, to take a long breath before he responded to them. He tried to speak evenly, but found his voice rising as he said, 'This is always the way with pigs, isn't it? Once a villain, always a villain. You don't look any further than someone with a record, when you want to pin a crime on someone. I told Lisa you'd be after me. I knew it would be like this.'

Lambert waited for the torrent of protest to dissipate itself. 'We bear in mind what has happened before. That is no more than common sense.'

'Then bear in mind that I've never killed anyone. Take your blinkers off and look at the facts.'

'One of which is that you have a conviction

for Grievous Bodily Harm. Another of which is that you could easily have been facing a murder charge on that occasion, if the cards had fallen slightly differently for you. Facts we need to bear in mind, as you indicate, when we are looking for the perpetrator of another violent crime.'

'Not my style, Lambert. This man was garrotted with a piece of cable. I've never attacked anyone like that in my life.'

'But you attacked someone with a knife. Stabbed him three times. Nearly killed him.'

'Self-defence.'

'The man attacked you with his fists. You took a knife to him. Very nearly killed him.'

'He was a violent man. Attacking me outside a back street pub, with other violent men. They were wearing boots, and they'd have used them, if they'd got me down. Very likely kicked me to death.'

'Not what the coppers who arrested you thought.'

Jason allowed himself a small smile. 'It's what the court thought though, isn't it? What my brief told them and what they accepted. British justice triumphant against lying PC Plods. And thank the Lord for it.'

Lambert permitted himself a mirthless answering smile. He wasn't going to get involved in mudslinging over a battle which had been lost long ago. 'I hope you did thank the Lord. Or at least thanked a persuasive brief. A suspended sentence for taking a knife to someone must have sent you away laughing at the law.'

'Learned my lesson, though, didn't I? That po-faced woman judge told me to go away and keep my nose clean, and I've done just that. For five years, now. A triumph for British justice and the liberal ideal, that's Jason Ritchie.' He found to his amazement that he was enjoying this, that winning the argument with this senior policeman was giving him a kick. 'So don't think you can breeze into my home and arrest me for something I didn't do. British justice won't allow it, see? Police harassment, they'd call it, in my view. I'd go for the brief I had last time.' He nodded a couple of times, trying to control his excitement as the adrenaline pumped in his veins.

Bert Hook looked up from his notebook, avuncular and concerned. 'So you're thinking in terms of briefs already, Jason? Not a good move, that. Might have suspicious coppers believing you had something to hide. Might make them think they were on to something, wouldn't you say?'

Jason Ritchie was thrown by this sudden intervention, when all his hostility had been concentrated on the gaunt superintendent. 'I'm not hiding anything. I know the way cops try to trip you up, that's all.'

Hook nodded. 'Very wise, that. Not hiding

133

anything, I mean. I've seen a lot of people get into trouble, over the years, when they've tried to hide things. You're sure that you hadn't met Mr Durkin before you encountered him in Gurney Close, are you?'

It was slipped in almost casually, as if Hook were acting in the interests of the excited young man who sat on the other side of the table in the cramped little caravan. Almost as if he were a brief for the defence, thought Jason. 'No. I've already said I didn't know him.'

Hook nodded. He looked as if he were about to make another note, but then thought better of it. He said almost casually, 'So who do you think killed Robin Durkin, Jason?'

The query which set the pulses racing in Jason's temple had been uttered so quietly that it seemed paradoxically to be more significant, more menacing. He found himself wishing that it was still Lambert who was putting things like this to him: it seemed easier to fight a man who was more openly aggressive. 'I don't know. Someone who came in from outside, I should think, after we'd all gone.'

'And why do you think that, Jason?'

The quiet repetition of his forename was ringing like a taunt in his ears, an intimacy he didn't want to hear but could not avoid. 'I – I can't think that anyone who was drinking and eating with him on Saturday night would have killed him. We were all getting on so well together!'

It sounded lame, even to him. Hook nodded quietly a couple of times, as if weighing that idea. Then he said, almost reluctantly, as if it pained him to recall it, 'Except for you, Jason. Who didn't speak directly to Mr Durkin at all during the five hours of eating and drinking and laughter, on your own admission.'

He wondered how they had prised out this, who among those there on Saturday night had been observant enough to watch how he was behaving towards their host. He was not experienced enough to realize that these two were experts in making bricks with very little straw, in picking up some small admission he had made and exploiting it as a weakness. He said rather desperately, 'You asked me what I thought, and I'm telling you, aren't I? I think someone came in from the path by the bank of the river, after we'd all gone. Perhaps he'd been waiting there for hours, watching for his opportunity.'

'It's a possibility. But you'd all been out there, through the gate at the back of the Durkins' garden, wandering down to the banks of the Wye, we're told. Surely you'd have seen anyone lurking there with malicious intent, wouldn't you? Still, we're considering every possibility, however unlikely.'

They left him then, with the injunction that he must not move out of the district without giving them a new address. This familiar environment of his, what he thought of as his little private castle in the woods, seemed sullied by their visit. Jason sat for twenty minutes, motionless in the neat and spotless interior of the old caravan, recovering his composure, telling himself that, however he had felt, they hadn't prised anything out of him that he hadn't been expecting to give them.

Lambert drove slowly back towards Oldford, through a Forest of Dean which was heavy with fresh new leaf, as if the pace of his driving could be an encouragement to measured thought. It was several miles before he said, 'It was good having you with me in there. But you don't have to do this, you know.'

'I told you, I'm better working. It occupies the mind. Some of the time, anyway. And I thought you weren't going to raise it again.' Hook stared out of the window at the forest sheep, scampering away beneath the trees, as if they were of surpassing interest to him.

Two more miles passed before he said, 'I wonder what exactly it was that Jason Ritchie was concealing from us.'

Bert Hook felt as if he was watching a scene in someone else's life, not his, as he paused for a moment at the door of the hospital room.

The woman sitting by the bed, looking down at the too-tiny conformation beneath the sheets, was surely some other woman, not his wife. That grave and grey-faced female was ten years too old to be his smiling Eleanor, who played like a fellow-child with her boys, who united with them in their teasing of their staid and anxious father.

And that slight, amorphous shape beneath the sheets could surely not be his ebullient, noisy Luke, the exhausting embodiment of perpetual mobility that he had so often called upon to be still. This must surely be some other, private drama, in someone else's life. Not his.

Bert had visited hospitals often enough, in his younger days, following up road accidents and serious incidents of assault, waiting for statements from victims, statements which sometimes never came. He had witnessed far too often the moment when life was pronounced extinct, when the relatives were escorted from the scene and the curtains were drawn around the bed by the professionals.

People had told him then that you never believed that it was happening to you.

He shook his head and went forward, divesting himself of the conceit that this was tragedy being played out in some other family. Eleanor looked up at him, and he saw the blankness in her eyes which told him that she was so involved with the closed world within three feet of her that he, too, was an interloper.

She spoke reluctantly and very slowly, as if she were loth to admit anyone else into her private drama. She said dully, 'He's holding his own, they say. It's still on a knife-edge.'

In the leafy suburb of Birmingham, the man was perfectly relaxed.

It was part of the training: when you were not on a job, you relaxed. Not that there was any training available for the work he did; he was thinking merely of the training he had devised for himself and steadily imposed upon himself as he became a specialist. You could scarcely think of it as a calling, and he did not do so. But he knew he was working in one of the most exclusive of occupations.

Even in a more violent age than the country had ever known, there were still very few contract killers.

His commissions were sporadic, though they had increased steadily over the five years in which he had operated. But he was never impatient. He knew now that other jobs would come along before too long: his efficiency and his anonymity had ensured that for him. And he had no problems with money: liquidation was expensive. His remuneration was such that he could afford to be patient between jobs.

The people who used him knew his rates and his terms of business; the word got around quickly along the dubious grapevines of the underworld. A third up front when he was commissioned, two-thirds when the death was achieved, safely and anonymously. Watson knew that some of his rivals operated on a half-and-half basis, but he thought it showed his confidence in his abilities that he only asked for a third in advance.

And one of the benefits of working in a dangerous field was that the people who used your services were always reliable. You didn't have to worry about credit ratings with people like this: Watson's thin lips widened into one of his rare smiles on that thought. He never pressed for payment, because he knew that it would come.

The e-mail had been in his in-box for several hours before he read it. It said simply, 'The River Wye has reached the sea.' He looked at it for a few seconds, then deleted the simple seven words of code.

The money was now in his account. It had never come to him more easily.

Eleven

Lambert was glad to have Bert Hook back at his side as they visited Gurney Close in the early evening.

Pressing a bereaved widow for information is never easy. It is vital to establish facts as early as possible in an investigation, but families often feel that police officers are being crass and insensitive during what, for them, is an agonizing period.

At least there were no children involved here. And Alison Durkin appeared to be perfectly composed as they made their apologies for intruding at such a time. 'You have your job to do. I understand that. I hope to get back to my own job later this week. They told me to take the week off, but I think the best remedy for brooding is to get back to work. And I've no funeral to organize. Not for the moment: not until you are able to release the body.'

It sounded almost heartless, but they had seen grief in too many forms to draw any conclusions from her demeanour; brave faces were sometimes put upon the most painful private sufferings. Lambert said,

'One or two things have emerged about your husband's business dealings which we cannot explain. We hope that you might be able to help us.'

The smooth face beneath the dark hair clouded, then turned blank. She was very pale, but appeared perfectly composed. Alison Durkin wore elegant black trousers and sandals with a crisp, white, sleeved blouse. She said, 'I know very little about how Robin conducted his business. The money came in, and I was happy about that. And he was the kind of man who didn't take kindly to questions.'

'Even from his wife?' said Hook gently.

'Even from his wife,' she said firmly, almost as if she were resisting interrogation. She looked at the brown-eyed, observant Hook and found that he was waiting for her to enlarge upon her denial. Hook was good at waiting, and surprisingly often people responded to his quiet, unthreatening expectancy. Alison Durkin said, 'He provided me with anything I needed. I'm afraid I didn't ask him too many questions about how things were going at the garage. He was really very generous.'

But her tone made what should have been a routine wifely compliment to the dead man sound almost like a complaint. Hook said, 'We have been investigating his finances. It's standard practice with a murder victim. It sometimes throws up interesting statistics.'

'Shows up people who might have had a good reason to kill him, I suppose.' She nodded thoughtfully, when they would have expected her to bridle at this intrusion into her husband's private affairs. For a woman who had been widowed less than three days earlier, Alison Durkin was remarkably controlled. 'Have you found anyone like that?'

'Not yet. But we have found some interesting information. Some unusual and very obscure sources of income. And some expenditure that needs explanation.'

'I won't be able to help you there.' It was a very prompt assertion, as if she wished to sever all connection with the enquiries into her husband's finances. Then, almost unwillingly, she said, 'Tell me about these payments Robin made.'

Did she suspect that the dead man had been spending on things she knew nothing about and of which she would not have approved? On other women, perhaps? Lambert, who had been watching her keenly during her exchanges with Hook, said, 'At present, we're more interested in where some large sums came from. We're already certain they weren't from the garage business. Can you help us with this?'

'No.' Again the negative was blunt and very prompt. As if she wished to mitigate the severity of it, she added, 'I deliberately kept out of his affairs. I'm sorry if that means that I can't help you now, but he preferred it that way, and it suited me as well.'

Hook said quietly, 'Was that because you preferred not to know, Mrs Durkin? Was it because you suspected that not everything was above board in his activities?'

She looked from his unthreatening, weather-beaten face to Lambert's thinner and more intense one, wondering how much she should say, how secretive she could be without them deciding she was uncooperative and therefore becoming more hostile to her. 'I sometimes thought that I wouldn't approve of some of the things he was doing, if I knew the full story. Perhaps that was one reason why I was quite content that I didn't know.'

Lambert studied her alert face, trying to let the tension build in her, marvelling silently at her composure. Eventually he said, 'Would it surprise you to know that we have unearthed a sum of over eight hundred thousand pounds, in another bank account entirely from the one he used for the garage business and your domestic accounts?'

She gasped. 'Eight hundred thousand?'

She sounded appropriately incredulous. But the size of the sum might have ensured that, even if she had suspected her husband had some more shady source of income.

Lambert watched her closely, keeping his own face carefully impassive. 'This didn't come from buying and selling cars. We're sure of that. Have you any idea what other activities your husband was engaged in?'

She looked as if she was still astounded by the size of the sum. She sounded quite dazed as she said slowly, 'You should call me Ally. Other people do: short for Alison, you see.' She paused, looking past them and out of the window at the innocent world outside, where the sun shone and small birds fluttered among the trees at the end of the garden. She took a deep breath, gathering her resources for what lay ahead. 'It wasn't legal, this other activity you're thinking of, was it?'

Lambert gave her a small smile of encouragement. 'You think like a cynical policeman, Mrs Durkin. And we agree with you: it's difficult to see how a sum like that could have been acquired legally.'

She said slowly, 'I don't know how Robin got that money. Really I don't. And I want you to believe me.'

Hook leaned forward. 'But you must have some ideas. Some thoughts on the matter, at least. You lived with him as his wife, for eight years. You're in a better position to speculate about this than anyone in the CID team.'

It looked for a moment as if she would descend into anger. But all she said was, 'I don't know. He didn't talk to me about it.'

'And you want us to find out who killed Robin, don't you?' Hook went on as if he had not heard her denial. 'There's a strong possibility that the people who are connected with this money are also connected with Robin's death. You must see that.'

She nodded. 'I do. And I want you to arrest them. But I feel helpless, because I know so little.' She looked down at her hands, clasped still and unmoving in her lap. 'He knew things, Robin. Took a delight in knowing things.'

'What kind of things, Ally?'

'Things about people. He made a point of finding out things that people didn't want him to know.'

It wasn't what they had been expecting. Their thought was that Durkin had probably been involved in the supply of illegal drugs, that she might have been prepared to tell them whatever she knew about that. But Hook knew better than to appear surprised by what she was now suggesting. It was much better to imply that this is what they had been expecting, that what she said was no more than a confirmation of what police enquiries had already thrown up.

Bert gave her an encouraging, complicitous smile. 'You think he used this information, don't you, Ally? You think he used it to blackmail people.'

He had voiced the word she hadn't wanted

to use herself. Somehow, that made it easier for her to go on. 'I think he might have done, yes. If he was getting money of that sort, he must have been doing something illegal, mustn't he?'

Indeed he must. But he would have needed to be a blackmailer on a massive scale to amass eight hundred thousand pounds. Nevertheless, the information was useful, perhaps even crucial. Blackmail is one of the most despicable of crimes, and also one of the crimes which most often lead to violence. Blackmailers almost always come back for more, despite repeated assurances to their victims that this is their final demand. Those victims become desperate, and desperation triggers wild reactions, including murder.

Hook said gravely, 'I know this isn't easy for you, Ally, but we need to know facts. We need you to tell us the sort of information Robin had and the people against whom he was using it.'

'I don't know that. I'd tell you if I did. But I didn't want to know about what he was doing. I was a coward, if you like, turning a blind eye to it. Content to live off the proceeds, I suppose, without asking too many questions. It doesn't reflect very well on me, does it? But I loved him, you know. A lot of the time I wished I didn't, but I loved him.'

There was something desperate about her

avowal, something febrile in her manner, as if she was nearer to breaking point than she had revealed in the earlier part of the interview, when she had appeared unnaturally composed. It seemed that this declaration of her feelings for the dead man had brought back the reality of his death.

Lambert took up the questioning, but they could get nothing more useful out of her, beyond what they already knew: that Durkin and his former partner in the garage, Mark Gregory, had parted on bad terms. It seemed probable that she had told them all she knew, that Robin Durkin, like most blackmailers, had hugged his dangerous knowledge to himself and kept his own counsel about his activities.

She promised to get in touch immediately if the names of any possible victims occurred to her, and they went quietly out to the car and reversed it out of the drive. They were conscious as they drove away of other eyes in Gurney Close watching their actions, wondering what progress they were making in finding the killer of their neighbour, a man who was proving a more sinister figure than most of them had ever imagined him to be. Except one of them, perhaps.

They had driven over a mile before Hook said, 'You didn't raise her criminal record.'

'It didn't seem the right time. It's still only two days since she found her husband's body. I wanted to talk about Durkin and his activities, to find out how much she knew about what our victim had been up to. If she murdered him, she's not going on to more killing. No one else will be in danger.' Then, lest Bert thought he was becoming softer with the passing years, he added, 'We shall be seeing her again, in the next few days. She's still holding things back from us.'

In the bedroom of her new home, Alison Durkin stood and looked at herself in the full-length mirror of the new wardrobe. She didn't think her visitors would have found it strange that she was wearing a sleeved blouse, even on such a stifling day: the white cotton still looked crisp and cool, even after the ordeal of the interview. Men wouldn't have thought it strange that she had full-length sleeves, as a woman who knew her might have. Men were like that: they would think it no more than the present fashion.

She took off the blouse, wincing a little as she slid it from her shoulders, noting with approval how her new bra made the most of her small bust without any vulgar redistribution. She moved a little closer to the mirror, looking at the discoloration at the top of her left arm. The bruising was turning from black to green and yellow now. In a few days, it might be gone.

Lisa Holt was finding, like millions of others

before her, that divorce is a strange thing to have in your life. It was an experience which no one could anticipate, she decided: you would never have taken on marriage if you had envisaged even the possibility of divorce. Divorce was a horrible, messy business. And even when it was over and you were picking up the pieces, it was a thing which stirred you with unexpected emotions; they hit you when you least expected them and least wanted them.

As her ex-husband stooped under the low doorway of the room at the back of the pub in Gloucester, she found herself experiencing an unexpected spurt of affection for him. He looked so vulnerable, so beaten down by life. And she was a part of the life which had beaten him down.

He wore the brown sweater with the fawn diamonds, which she knew he had bought at least six years ago. That was the kind of stupid, unwelcome knowledge which would only be available to an ex-wife. Martin glanced at her drink, asked her if she wanted another.

She refused. She didn't want to prolong this any more than was necessary. And Martin wouldn't have much money, after the divorce settlement. She didn't want to thrust him back into the things which had driven her away from him: that would be the worst of all legacies from a failed marriage. Of course, if he'd been more considerate, he wouldn't have left her sitting here on her own in the pub for ten minutes before he arrived, a target for any man looking for an easy pull. He knew that she hated being first into a pub on her own, but he had never taken any account of it in his actions.

Martin Pearce came and sat down with her at the small round table, awkward as a stranger. But that was what he was going to become, she told herself: that was why she had gone back to her maiden name and changed the name of their child. Nevertheless, she was pleased to see that he had bought himself only half a pint of bitter, that he was clean-shaven, that his shirt was clean. It was a curious and unnatural business, sharing your bed and the most intimate moments of your life with someone for years, and then not seeing them at all. She didn't want to think of Martin going downhill, even though she wouldn't be seeing him from now on.

She said, 'The lawyers seemed to have agreed on the details of your access to George. Are they all right for you, the arrangements they've suggested?'

'Yes, I suppose so. They're more or less the standard thing, my man says. I'll have to think what to do with him on those weekends, won't I?'

'You'll have to make sure you don't spoil

him. Access and how to cope with it are problems lots of fathers have, and lots of kids have to cope with. It shouldn't be too difficult.' She sounded cold, deliberately so. She didn't want Martin back in her life, didn't want him bringing his problems to her, as he always had. She ran a well-manicured nail around the edge of her glass. 'What was it you wanted to see me about?'

'You can guess that, can't you? Robin bloody Durkin!'

'And what can I do about Robin? He's been murdered, for God's sake. A little charity wouldn't come amiss, surely?'

He looked at her closely, a small smile touching the corners of his mouth. 'You didn't kill him, did you?'

She thought that he couldn't be serious. But then she saw how he was looking at her, with real curiosity, sizing up her reactions to his question. Probably he had always planned that question. Probably he had planned how he would come out with it abruptly, as soon as he had arrived, to see how she reacted to it. Lisa found herself hoping that the police didn't get to Martin, an eventuality she had never considered before.

She said firmly, 'Of course I didn't kill him!'

'You'd have had ample motive.'

'And so would you!'

He smiled, then took a pull at his bitter

and wiped his mouth with the back of his hand, that old mannerism she had always found annoying. 'But I was at a dinner party in Bristol on Saturday night. Getting myself together after our divorce, the way you told me to do.' Martin delivered the last phrase with relish, enjoying the waspishness of the reminder. 'So, unlike you, I've got seven people who can swear to the police that I was nowhere near the scene of the crime.'

'Clever old Martin.' She was realizing anew why the marriage would never have worked, why it was such a relief to be rid of him. 'Well, I'm glad, in view of your previous associations with Durkin, that you can prove you're in the clear.' She paused, making herself take a sip of her gin and tonic, trying to avoid wrinkling her lips at the sourness of it in her mouth. 'You could have employed a contract killer, I suppose.'

'With what you've left me after the divorce? You must be joking!'

She felt the bitterness coming at her across the small round table. In this ridiculous setting, in this small room at the back of the pub in the early evening, they would soon be hurling insults at each other, the way they had in that tiny, claustrophobic kitchen at midnight and beyond. She wondered how the concern which she had felt a few minutes ago for this man who had shared her life could have dissipated so quickly and completely. She tried to keep the irritation out of her voice as she repeated her question. 'Why did you want to see me?'

'I wanted to know what was happening. Whether they'd arrested anyone yet for killing the bastard. How my child came to be involved in such a traumatic situation.'

'George wasn't there. He was away for the weekend with his grandparents, as you should know.' She made herself speak evenly: he wasn't going to have the satisfaction of seeing her losing control. 'And as far as I know, the police haven't made an arrest yet.'

'Pity, that. From your point of view, I mean. You must be one of their suspects. Being on the spot, with your toy boy.'

She didn't know that he'd found out about Jason. She should have expected it, she realized. Martin had always had a capacity for intrigue, for finding out the things you didn't want him to know. She said, 'That's ridiculous! I lived near Durkin, that's all. The police have no reason to treat me as a suspect.'

'Told them that you'd known him for years, have you?'

'What I've told them is no longer your concern, I'm happy to say.'

'Not quite true, that. Not when my only child is in your tender care. I've a right to be concerned, as long as there's still the chance that you're a murderess.' This time he took a longer pull at his beer, emptying the glass and setting it down with a little sigh of satisfaction. 'Keep me posted on what happens, won't you? I don't think I'd like to be in your shoes, when they find out the full facts about you and Robin Durkin.'

He departed as abruptly as he had arrived, leaving her sitting alone in the pub again.

Twelve

At nine o'clock on the morning of Wednesday the thirteenth of July, Superintendent Lambert had an unexpected visitor.

Like many people who have never been in trouble with the law, Carol Smart was diffident, even apprehensive, about entering a police station. The Oldford one was a busy place at this time of the morning, with the latest duty rosters being implemented and John Lambert concluding his briefing to his murder team on the latest developments in the Robin Durkin case. But as soon as she told the station sergeant why she had come, Mrs Smart was shown straight through into the office of the superintendent.

'How can I help you?' Lambert was all smiling urbanity; it wasn't often that suspects in a murder case came voluntarily into the lion's den.

'I felt that there was something you ought to know. Something I'd kept from you previously. Something you were probably going to find out for yourselves, which might look bad for me.' The ideas came tumbling out in a rush, and she could feel that she was speaking too quickly. Now that she had finally come here, she felt foolish, as if she had been caught out in some naïve over-reaction to events.

'Always a good policy, to be frank with the police, when you're an innocent party.' Superintendent Lambert was civilized, reassuring, relaxed, not at all the intense figure she remembered from that earlier meeting they had had, when her husband had prattled so idiotically at her side and she had taken the wrong decision about concealing things.

For his part, Lambert saw an attractive woman in her early forties, probably a little plumper than modern fashions would approve. Comely, or buxom, the Elizabethans would have called her. Bedworthy, when he was an impressionable young constable thirty years ago. Shaggable, they'd say now. Language, like standards, seemed to deteriorate with the years. God, he *was* getting old!

155

He'd been shocked when he heard a young woman PC using that word 'shaggable' about a new male recruit in the canteen the other day. It really was time to think about retirement.

Carol wondered where that stolid detective sergeant who had sat beside his chief had gone. She had somehow thought of making her confession to him, had assumed that he would always be sitting at his senior's side, ready to be understanding and forgiving of human weakness. She found herself saying absurdly, 'Is your sergeant not here today? The one with the notebook, I mean. A local man, I think.' What an absurd thing to say! As if an intelligent woman like her would find it easier to talk to a man with a Herefordshire accent! It just showed how nervous she was.

Lambert said, 'DS Hook isn't here at the moment. I'm afraid one of his sons is very ill. Suspected meningitis. Hopefully the hospital is pulling him through.' He smiled and picked up the pen on his desk. 'I'm not as reliable as Bert Hook, but I can make the odd note when I have to. What is it you wanted to tell me, Mrs Smart?'

Now that the moment had come, she wished that she was anywhere but here, sitting like a guilty teenager in front of the man's big desk. She had to force herself to speak, when she wanted to get up and run. 'I said I didn't know Robin Durkin before we moved into Gurney Close. That wasn't true. I'm sorry I concealed the fact.'

Lambert nodded understandingly. 'Not a good idea, concealing things. But just as well that you've now decided to put things right. Do I gather that this is easier without your husband at your side?'

'Yes. I don't want Phil to know anything about this.'

'There can be no guarantees, if it proves to be information relevant to a murder enquiry. But we respect confidences, whenever that is possible. Which is more often than not.'

She nodded, scarcely hearing him, preparing herself for what she must say now, trying to recall the words which had seemed so apposite when she had rehearsed them at home. 'I did know Robin in the past. Ten years ago, I had an affair with him.'

After all the careful, mitigating phrases she had prepared, she had blurted it out, just like that guilty teenager she had felt herself to be, in this quiet room, with this attentive, school-masterly man. He didn't even raise an eyebrow. He sounded sympathetic, almost conspiratorial, as he said, 'I can see why you didn't feel that you could tell me this in front of your husband. We'll need a few more details, I'm afraid.'

'There isn't much to tell. I blame myself for any pain that it caused me. I should have known better. I'm ten years older than Robin, and I think I represented the novelty of the experienced older woman for him when he was twenty-three. He certainly wasn't struggling for partners, but I think I was the first older woman he'd got involved with. Possibly at that time the first middle-class housewife, as well: he always said that he was my bit of rough on the side.' Her contempt for herself grew with each phrase of her account.

Lambert was used to the familiar feeling of being an intruder into another person's life, of hearing intimacies he would never have heard without the committing of a murder. He could no longer see the carefully made-up eyes which had looked so directly at him when she had come into the room. He studied the well-groomed fair hair on the head which had dropped forward in front of him and said gently, 'All this will only be of interest to us if it has a connection with a murder. How many other people know about it?'

'As far as I am aware, no one.'

'You think that not even Mrs Durkin knows about it?'

Carol considered the question she had often asked herself. It was tempting to suggest that Ally Durkin had probably known about this: it would make her a suspect, as a betrayed wife, and divert attention from herself. Instead, Carol said, 'I don't think so. He was a secretive man, Robin; he enjoyed having information, but not sharing it. I don't see him telling Ally things like that, even during marital pillow talk.'

'But you aren't sure of that?'

She took her time, trying to show him that she was quite objective, was taking this in her stride, was not at all the sort of woman who would commit murder because of some old, half-forgotten wound. 'These things took place a long time ago now and I don't think they meant very much to Robin. From what I've seen of him in the last few weeks, I'm sure they didn't. I've noticed nothing in Ally's behaviour to suggest that she knows. I'm not suggesting I'm very experienced in these things, but I feel that I would know if she was aware that I'd been to bed with her husband.'

Lambert was studying her, quite unembarrassed that she should be aware of his close observation. She wondered if he was going to draw attention to the fact that this made her more of a suspect in this case. Instead, he said quietly, 'Are you sure that your husband knows nothing about this liaison?'

'I am. Phil isn't the most perceptive of individuals.' For a moment she sounded almost affectionate; perhaps she was merely grateful for his blindness in these things.

'But he's been a good father to our two daughters: surprisingly good, some people might say. He's eight years older than I am: I think he couldn't believe his luck when I said I'd marry him. But I doubt whether he's capable of monogamy. He thinks I don't know about his affairs, whereas I'm usually well aware of what he is about. But despite his philanderings, Phil can be positively naïve about those closest to him: it doesn't even seem to occur to him that I might occasionally fancy a fling myself.'

'Do you know of any other relationships which Robin Durkin had? More recent ones, possibly?'

'No. I wasn't in touch with him. It gave me quite a shock when I found out that the Durkins were to be our new neighbours.'

'It has emerged since his death that Mr Durkin seems to have had some eccentric sources of income. Do you know anything about where his money came from?'

She smiled, apparently perfectly at ease now that her confession was over. 'Eccentric! I like that word. Police euphemism for crooked, is it? No, I don't know how he came by his money, just that he always seemed to have plenty of it. And it doesn't surprise me to hear that he was using shady means to acquire it. But I'm afraid I can't help you with any detail.'

She felt quite buoyant as she left the police

station which she had been so hesitant to enter. This must be how Catholics felt after listing their sins for the priest, she thought. She had never before been able to understand why they felt that confession was such a relief.

And the great boon for her was that she had told the superintendent in charge of the case only as much as she wanted to tell him.

Chris Rushton came in as soon as Mrs Smart left Lambert. He tried not to look too pleased with himself as he said, 'Some information has just come in. I thought you'd want to hear it right away.'

'Let's have it.' Lambert in his turn tried not to be irritated by his younger colleague's smugness.

'We haven't had a lot of success yet in checking where Robin Durkin's extra money came from. But we've been checking his outgoings, to see where he was spending. And we've come up with an interesting payment to the Westview Private Hospital.'

An abortion clinic. Familiar territory to the police, and others like them, who deal with the various forms of human distress. 'For some young woman he got pregnant, no doubt. The convenient way out.'

This time Rushton could not conceal his pleasure. 'Not quite. This payment was for a termination, all right. Just over three years ago. But the patient was one Alison Durkin.'

'Jack's here for his lunch,' said Christine Lambert to her husband as he came into the house. With a wife's sensitivity to these things, she picked up his look of incomprehension and elucidated. 'Jack Hook. Bert's boy. I told Eleanor to drop him off here, while they're at the hospital. He's out in the garden, I think. He doesn't know what to do with himself.'

Lambert went into the long garden at the rear of the house and saw the boy at the end of it, smelling roses, a thing he had possibly never done before in his life. John Lambert said, 'There's not much grass here for games, is there, Jack? My children have grown up and left home, now, so we don't need the lawn for games much any more. They were girls, anyway, so they wouldn't have made good use of grass, like us.'

He tried to make it sound as if they were partners in the great male conspiracy against the fripperies of female relaxation. 'Test match starts tomorrow,' he said cheerfully. 'Your Dad tells me your cricket's coming on well, now.'

'I'll never be as good as he was, Mr Lambert,' said Jack dolefully. He would not normally have confessed to anything so humiliating: Lambert supposed it must show how this totally unexpected business of his brother's illness was affecting him.

'Nonsense!' said Lambert breezily. 'He was a good bowler, your dad, one of the best. But there's no reason why you shouldn't be as good as him and better, if you put your back into it and keep practising.' Already I'm sounding like the dusty schoolmaster, he thought, with exhortations to duty and the rewards of the manly virtues. I'll be telling the lad to take cold showers and runs before breakfast next.

His own children had both been girls: he found that he didn't quite know how you talked to thirteen-year-old boys. They were always gauche and ill at ease, and Jack was as good an example of that as anyone. The boy said awkwardly, 'It's very good of you to have me here. I know you're very busy with this murder in Gurney Close.' He'd read eagerly every fact the local papers printed about the killing, as he did always when his father was involved in a case.

'Not as busy as you'd think. I let my team get on with the real donkey work. I expect your dad's told you what an old fraud I am!'

'He says you're the best there is. That the Home Office must recognize that, or they wouldn't have given you an extension of service. Not that I'm saying you're old.' The boy was suddenly blushing furiously at his imagined gaffe, the blood rising red and full in his long, pubescent neck.

163

Lambert grinned at him. 'I'm old all right, Jack. Ancient, in your terms. Have to make my brain work to save my legs, now.'

There was an awkward silence, which the boy felt more keenly than the tall man beside him. He stooped to a deep crimson rose, sniffed deeply at its heady bouquet, recoiled in surprise at the strength of it. Then he said suddenly, 'Will Luke be all right, do you think?'

Lambert said woodenly, 'I'm sure he will.' He wanted to put an arm round the slim young shoulders; he would have done so instinctively with his daughters, but he didn't know whether a thirteen-year-old boy, poised so agonizingly between childhood and adolescence, would resent the gesture.

'But you don't know, do you?'

'No, I don't know, Jack. But I know that he's in the best place. That people who know far more than either of us are fighting with all their skills and all their energies to make sure that he'll recover.'

The boy nodded slowly, weighing the logic of this and apparently finding it convincing. 'People fob you off with things all the time when you're young. When you're a child, it's all right, because you believe them. But when you're as old as I am now, you don't know what to believe and what to reject.'

Lambert felt a tug at his tough old heart-strings from this confused, ungainly, honest boy. He put his arm round him this time, and felt the boy hugging him back, like the child he still wanted to be at this moment. 'I won't fob you off, Jack. Luke's very seriously ill, or your mum and dad wouldn't be at the hospital like this. But it's my honest belief that he'll be back home with you by this time next week, and well on his way to being a thorn in your side again.'

There was a tiny shudder from the face against his chest, which might have been an involuntary giggle or a sob of pain. Then a muffled voice said, 'I should have been kinder to him.'

Lambert turned the small, narrow face away from his chest and back towards the world. 'I'm sure you've treated him just as well as a younger brother deserves to be treated. They're irritating creatures, aren't they, when you're trying to get on with more important things?'

'It's his first year at the comp, you know. I should have made things easier for him.'

'I expect you did what you could. And we all have to learn to stand on our own feet, don't we?'

Jack began to shake his head unhappily, but fortunately at that moment Christine called down from the house to say that lunch was ready. 'It's just sandwiches and fruit and a bit of cake, I'm afraid. We have our main meal at night, as you do, Jack,' she said.

The insistent appetite of a thirteen-year-old took over, and the clearly distressed Jack demolished a substantial allocation of sandwiches, seemingly without registering the fact of their disappearance. Christine, who was much in demand as a part-time teacher herself, chatted knowledgeably to him about his progress and his problems at school.

John Lambert found it a relief to listen to the two of them, to have the responsibility for this awkward, touching, alien presence in his household taken away from him. It allowed his thoughts to stray back inevitably to the killing in Gurney Close.

In retrospect, Lambert thought that it was during that strange hour of lunch with a suffering schoolboy that the first glimmerings of a solution came to him.

Thirteen

Ronald Lennox watched the police car parking in his drive with what seemed to him agonizing precision. He wanted them in the house, questioning him, getting this over and going on their way.

'I thought we'd talk in the conservatory.

We've been rearranging things in the rest of the house – you can never fit everything in, can you, when you get rid of a bigger house? We're still unpacking boxes and moving pictures about. The sun's moved round. The conservatory won't be too hot at this time in the afternoon.'

Ron was aware that he was talking inconsequentially, unnecessarily, as he took them through a sitting room which had lost its flowers and its photographs on the mantelpiece, and now seemed like any other new lounge in the close. He led them into the light, pleasant conservatory and invited them to sit in the wickerwork chairs. 'We won't be disturbed. Rosemary is at the Red Cross centre. She does voluntary work there on a Wednesday.' He knew he was sounding nervous, knew that these experienced men would have picked that up, wondered what they were making of it.

'We wanted a few more words with you about Robin Durkin,' said Lambert, his economy with words underlining Lennox's unnecessary loquacity.

'At your service,' said Ron expansively as he sat down. 'Though I'm sure I can't tell you any more about him than you already know.'

'Let's see, shall we?' Lambert's manner was not unpleasant, but his words sounded to Ron like a threat. 'We now know quite a bit more about the murder victim than when we last spoke with you, so whatever we learn from you today will be fitted into a fuller context.'

Was that a warning to him not to lie? Ron said apprehensively, 'One doesn't like to speak ill of the dead, but...' He had lifted his hands as he began the statement, but they dropped limply back on to the arms of his chair as the words ran out for him. They were bony hands, sticking out a little too far from the cuffs of the cardigan he had selected to emphasize how relaxed and unthreatened he would feel.

Hook flicked open a new page on his notebook and looked at his man earnestly. 'Tell it how it was. That's much the best policy, Mr Lennox. Especially when it's a murder that we're investigating. Any attempt at concealment only leads to complications.'

Ron looked gratefully at the weather-beaten, honest face. 'All right. Robin Durkin wasn't a very nice man. Rosemary and I like what we've seen of his wife, Alison, and when we spoke to you yesterday we didn't want to say too much about him because of her. And of course we didn't want any trouble with our new neighbours. But I happen to know that Rob Durkin was a nasty piece of work. Rosemary and I didn't plan to have any more to do with him than was strictly necessary.'

'But you were quite willing to go to a party at his house last Saturday night.'

Ron smiled. He was ready for this. 'As was everyone else in the close. It was my wife who had suggested the street party; when it turned out that the venue was to be at the Durkins' house, we could hardly make a sudden withdrawal. I think you'll find if you question them closely that others as well as me had reservations about the man. But perhaps you already have.'

Lennox was speaking in a curious, rather pedantic manner, as if he were outlining the obvious for someone rather dense. Perhaps it was a habit acquired in his schoolteaching days. Or perhaps he had prepared these words carefully before their arrival. Lambert said with a twinge of irritation, 'You'd better tell us exactly what you knew about Robin Durkin.'

'It's nothing tangible. Nothing I'd care to swear to on oath in a court of law. But then I won't have to do that, will I?' A little nervous laugh escaped him before he could suppress it.

'Anything is possible, in a murder case. That's why we need the full story from you now.' Lambert was getting impatient. 'If it will help to loosen your tongue and remove your inhibitions, Mr Lennox, I can tell you that we have already discovered quite a lot of things about Mr Durkin.'

'Hah!' Ron heard the breathy monosyllable exploding into the bright room an instant before he realized that it had come from himself. 'That I can well believe! If your investigative techniques are as efficient as I am sure they are, Superintendent, you will have discovered by now what an unsavoury character Rob Durkin was.'

'We are in the process of getting a fuller picture. And you are in the process of help-ing us,' said Lambert tersely.

'Yes. Right. Well, Durkin was a black-mailer, you know, among other things.'

'What other things?'

Ron was sure the blood was rushing to his face. It was an unfamiliar and disconcert-ing feeling. He had expected to talk about blackmail, to deliver the sentences he had prepared on that, not to have the ground switched so abruptly to this. He looked down at his brilliantly polished brown toe-caps and decided that city shoes were in-appropriate footwear to go with the informal dress he had donned for these exchanges. 'Well, I'm sure he had some pretty un-savoury business dealings. Cut plenty of corners in his working methods, from what I heard. Have you talked to his partner in the garage?'

'We have, yes. What he said rather confirms what you are telling us now.'

'Well, there you are, then. An unsavoury

man, and it's not just I who think so!'

That seemed to give Lennox great satisfaction; Lambert noted with interest how important it seemed to him. 'Mr Durkin had accrued a very large sum of money, seemingly not by legitimate means. Have you any views on how he might have come by such a fortune?'

Ron pretended for a moment to be struggling with his scruples. Then he said, 'In my view he was involved in supplying illegal drugs. That's a lucrative business, they tell me. The kind of thing where you can quickly accumulate money, if you're the kind of man he was.'

'Indeed it is. And what kind of man was he?'

'I've already told you that. The worst kind. A man who did not operate by the moral canons which the rest of us use to regulate our lives.'

There was a curious combination of passion and fastidiousness in this man, as if he sought to control his emotions by the precision of his words, to disguise a real hatred for the dead man by meticulous vocabulary. Lambert strove for a wavelength which would encourage him to cooperate. 'It's true that if we left now we should be in no doubt about how you felt about our murder victim. But as an intelligent man, you will appreciate that we need rather more chapter and verse about this. We can't simply take your strong feelings as establishing the worthlessness of the man.'

Lennox pursed his lips, thought for a moment, nodded slowly. 'I see that. You mean that, in a court of law, some clever defence counsel would say I was just voicing an opinion.'

Lambert smiled. 'We're not talking about courts of law. We're a long way from that yet. I'm asking you to support what you're telling me with something more tangible than your own dislike for Robin Durkin.'

'Well, I wouldn't normally go around exchanging gossip.' The eagerness in his face made Lambert doubt that. 'But one picks up quite a lot, around a secondary school, you know, if one keeps one's ears open. People think we educationists exist in ivory towers, but we certainly don't. Not these days. I used to listen to the sixth formers talking and pick up quite a lot about what young people were up to.'

Lambert leaned forward conspiratorially and said, 'And you asked a few pertinent questions, too, I'm sure.'

'On occasions I did, yes.' Ron rocked back and forward a little on his chair, folding his arms and hugging his thin chest. This was better: they were treating him now as a valuable source of information. This was a chance to put the boot in on that awful man who had died on Saturday night. 'Within two years of leaving school, Rob Durkin was dealing in drugs in quite a big way. I'm certain of that. We had one or two cases of drug abuse in the school – all schools do, nowadays, they tell me. And of course they had to be followed up. Where possible, we kept the police out of it. But Rob Durkin's name came up every time. He was an ex-pupil who was exploiting his contacts with the school. Anything but an alumnus, you'd have to say!'

His little cackle of laughter at his bon mot flew oddly round the glass walls of the conservatory. Lambert said, 'We have been made aware of these activities over the last two days. But Durkin was a clever man. He seems at that time to have established a network of dealers, without direct involvement in selling drugs himself. He was never charged with offences because the CPS didn't think there was enough evidence.'

'That's him exactly! That's just what he'd do. Let others take the risks, and keep his own back well covered.' The vehemence of Lennox's feelings overcame his air of objectivity. 'I don't know any more about it than that, as far as hard evidence is concerned. If I had known, I'd have reported it to you at the time, as a responsible citizen who wanted to see the law upheld. But I'm sure he went on to bigger things, that he wasn't involved just in dealings at the school gates any more.'

'We think you're right, Mr Lennox.' Lambert smiled encouragingly. He didn't often flatter people, but he would use whatever was necessary to hurry on his investigation. 'So let's agree off the record that Mr Durkin was a thoroughly unsavoury character. What else can you tell us about the way he made his money?'

Ron nodded sagely. He liked this. They were fellow-professionals now, in the pursuit of a villain. A dead villain, but then villains were better dead. 'I'm pretty sure he was a blackmailer. The worst sort of crime, wouldn't you say, blackmail?'

'Apart from murder, of course!' Lambert and Lennox had a little dual smile about that. 'Most policemen find blackmailers pretty despicable, yes. And when they turn into murder victims, they are often the worst sort of victims, too, for us. They usually prove to have a lot of enemies, you see.'

'Among the people they've tormented, you mean? Well yes, I can quite see that. Must make things difficult for you. In that it gives you a wide field of suspects, I mean.'

'That's one of the reasons why we hate it when a blackmailer is murdered, yes.'

Ron Lennox nodded several times, enjoying the logic of the discussion, appreciating having his ideas treated seriously by these professionals. 'You can't have much sympathy, though, for a man who's been battening on to people like that. I think I'd feel that he'd driven his killer to such extremes, if it was someone who hadn't been violent before.'

'The law has to be observed, nevertheless. I'm sure a man like you wouldn't condone murder.'

Ron smiled at him, continuing to relish the exchange, experiencing an excitement he had never felt before, that of being close to the heart of a very serious crime. 'No, of course I wouldn't. I'm just saying that one must feel a certain sympathy with a killer, in these particular circumstances.'

Bert Hook nodded encouragingly. 'So who was Robin Durkin blackmailing, Mr Lennox?'

The question shook Ron out of his complacent enjoyment of the situation. He hadn't expected anything so direct, and certainly not from this lumpish sergeant who hadn't spoken now for several minutes. 'I wouldn't know that, would I? He wouldn't be a very good blackmailer, if an innocent schoolmaster like me knew about his victims, would he?'

His involuntary cackle of laughter at the silliness of that idea rang round the huge panes of conservatory glass. Hook didn't respond with a smile. He said, 'But you keep your ear to the ground Mr Lennox, as you told us a few minutes ago. It was by doing so in the school that you came to suspect that the man was dealing in drugs: a suspicion which our present enquiries have proved to be well-grounded. And no doubt you have continued your habit of acquiring useful knowledge.'

Of sticking my nose into other people's business, he means, thought Ron. He's not as harmless or as blockish as he looks, this man. But nor am I the sucker for flattery that he thinks I am. He said primly, 'I take an interest in the people who were once my pupils. It's one of the satisfactions a man gets, in a poorly paid and increasingly demanding profession. It gives one pleasure to see boys and girls becoming adults and going on to do great things in life. One feels one has made some small contribution to their success, and to society as a whole, when one sees such things.'

'And naturally you take an interest in following the after-school lives of the less savoury characters as well. People like Robin Durkin.'

Ron rocked back and forth a little on his chair, clasping his arms across his thin chest in an involuntary gesture of satisfaction. 'I can't deny that there is a certain ghoulish interest in failure as well as success. Though of course one is delighted when boys and girls who have been nuisances at school shake off their adolescent peccadilloes and become responsible citizens.' His expression rather belied this pious sentiment.

This time Bert Hook did smile. 'And no doubt there is also a certain macabre pleasure when those that you have predicted will become villains justify your judgement.'

'Oh, I wouldn't say that.' But Lennox's wicked grin showed his pleasure in the proposition. 'One is not pleased to see people turning out badly, but I won't deny that it gives one a certain confidence in one's estimation of people when one sees one's judgements vindicated.'

'And in the case of Robin Durkin, you saw what you had predicted becoming fact.'

'Yes, indeed I did. He was a thorough nuisance at school: a lot of boys are just high-spirited and mischievous, but I found Robin Durkin to be underhand and malevolent. It looked to me then as if he was going to be a bad lot, and so it proved.'

'So who was he blackmailing, Mr Lennox?'

Hook's brown eyes looked hard into his face now. Ron felt he had been led round in a circle to where they had begun, and been shown in the process that there was nothing for it but to voice his suspicions in full. He found that he was not averse to doing so. 'I don't know. Not for certain. I just felt from his manner, from his smugness, that he was still up to his old tricks. I'd known Durkin a long time, don't forget. I remember that even when he was at school he liked to have a hold over people, liked to exploit his knowledge of any breakage of the school rules, for instance. And what was more, he took a delight in showing people that he had a hold over them.'

'And you'd seen signs of that in him again, all these years later.'

'I had indeed.' Lennox could not conceal his own satisfaction in this.

This was a petty man, perhaps, but maybe also an important one, in the context of a murder investigation. Hook said patiently, 'You must see that any knowledge, even any conjectures you have about this, are of interest to us. So who do you think Durkin was blackmailing at the time of his death?'

Lennox nodded contentedly. '"Conjectures", you said. That's the right word, you know. I haven't any certain knowledge, and I'm not pretending to any.'

Lambert said curtly, 'We understand that. Are you going to give us any names?'

Ron looked from one to the other of the contrasting faces, and was satisfied to see that he had their complete attention. 'I think it possible – no more than possible, mind – that he had some sort of hold over Mrs Smart.'

He looked to see surprise and satisfaction in their faces, but they were disappointingly noncommittal as Hook wrote the name in his notebook. Perhaps this was a professional inscrutability, Ron thought. Or perhaps their enquiries had already thrown up something in that area. He said, 'I think it possible that Durkin had something on Jason Ritchie, as well. There was some sort of tension between them on Saturday night, I think.'

Lambert gave him a small, acerbic smile of encouragement. 'You seem to be very observant, Mr Lennox.'

'One picked up the habit, I suppose, over forty years in the classroom. Children always have their secrets, and it's as well to try to pick up the undercurrents of what is going on amongst them. I suppose one transfers these skills into the adult world, without realizing it.' He looked immensely pleased with himself.

Lambert said without any change in his quiet tone, 'Was he blackmailing you, Mr Lennox?'

For a moment, Ron could scarcely believe his ears, so unexpectedly had the question come to him. He was striving for control as he said, 'No, of course he wasn't! Whatever made you think that he was?'

'It's just that you seem to be very aware of his methods. Acutely conscious of both his practices and his mannerisms, in fact, for one who claims not to have been in touch with him for many years.'

'But what possible hold could Rob Durkin have had over me?'

Lambert smiled, seemingly becoming more at ease as his man's discomfort grew. 'I wouldn't know that, would I, Mr Lennox? That's the nature of the crime of blackmail, isn't it? If I knew what it was that you needed to conceal, a blackmailer wouldn't be able to extract money from you, would he?'

'Well, let me formally assure you then, that Rob Durkin was not and never had been blackmailing me. There is no possible way in which he could have secured a hold over me. My background is blameless, if rather dull. Sorry to disappoint you.'

'No disappointment, Mr Lennox. Simply another fact that can now be recorded. Who do you think killed Mr Durkin?'

Again the abruptness of the question caught Ron off his guard. He made himself take long seconds before he replied. 'I've no idea. I don't envy you your task, Superintendent, because I'm sure there are lots of candidates. People in the lucrative but violent world of illegal drugs, I have no doubt. And also people who were or had been the blackmail victims of this unsavoury man. I'm privately sure that you'll eventually arrest someone that I've never even heard of.'

After they had gone, Ron Lennox stood looking out of the window, across his back garden towards the spot where Rob Durkin had died, still feeling a residual buzz of excitement.

He could not for the life of him decide whether the meeting had gone well or badly.

Fourteen

Philip Smart thought sometimes that his wife knew. When he said on Wednesday night that he was going out to the club, she accepted it not only without any objection but without any question.

Sometimes he wondered whether he would have liked a little more wifely opposition, a little more curiosity about his activities. But another part of his complicated psyche told him that he should be grateful that he did not have a jealous harridan of a wife, screaming at him and making his little escapades impossible.

Little escapades. They weren't anything more glamorous or exciting than that, if he was honest with himself. He had assured himself for years that monogamy wasn't a natural state, that free spirits like his would always need to break the monotony of it. But he couldn't deceive himself any more that there was anything glamorous in his pursuit of women, or in the beds he nowadays dwelt in so briefly.

He had left it late to go out, and he thought that that in itself might have excited Carol's interest. But she did no more than nod at him and go back to her book, nettling him illogically by her indifference to his activities. He needed to leave it late at this time of the year, because he had a prejudice about going to these liaisons in broad daylight. They should be secret, even furtive. It was that clandestine element which contributed to the excitement which he found it increasingly difficult to conjure up.

The woman gave him a drink, then draped herself languorously over the sofa, which was new since his last visit. He knew that he would be expected to comment on this addition to the room's furnishings and he duly did so. But it was but another feature of a conversation that felt to him increasingly stilted and artificial, even though the woman seemed to find the exchanges natural enough, as she sipped her gin and watched the level in his own glass going steadily down. Her neckline was a little low for her declining bust, but he knew that it was adopted for him, so such thoughts were churlish.

She seemed to be listening to the meaningless things he said, putting in her own conventional and rather vapid responses at the appropriate moments. At least he wasn't being hurried, he told himself; at least she was maintaining the semblance of affection, of a relationship which went beyond the sheets. He wondered as they spoke how often she had said these or similar words before, how many other men had sat upon this new couch and said similarly meaningless things as their preludes to sex.

She topped up his glass, measuring the gin carefully before she poured in the tonic. She shouldn't be wearing that sleeveless dress: her upper arms were running a little to flab. Phil noticed that she gave herself only tonic, caught her glancing at the clock on the mantelpiece. His observation seemed to be at its most acute when he required it to be least so.

And the coupling when it came was curiously unsatisfying, though Phil could not have said why. Her expensive perfume was heavy upon the pillows, but he found himself wondering whether it was there to disguise the scent of other males who had been there before him. When she opened her legs and received him, he thrust away like a younger man, trying to put out of his mind the comparisons with those other men she must have rolled with here, the men who might have had more urgent and thus more satisfactory comings than his. She seemed willing, even grateful, in her responses to him, but perhaps that was merely an aspect of her professionalism.

She shouted the rough words that she knew excited men, arched her back and groaned and moaned as his own cries became more urgent, told him when it was over and they lay together on their backs that he had the energy of a much younger man. But how much was genuine; how much was part of the flattery which was one of the tools of her calling?

Because that was what this was, for sure. She wasn't a common prostitute, trawling the streets of a city in search of trade. This was a pleasant, discreet suburb of Cheltenham, where the innocent would never suspect that such things went on, that such transactions took place. But Philip Smart could not delude himself that this was anything other than that: a sexual transaction. A discreetly managed and scarcely acknowledged transaction, but a piece of well-paid business, nonetheless, as far as the female partner was concerned.

He put the bank notes on the mantelpiece beside the clock as usual, saying nothing, checking from her quick smile that the price was correct, that nothing had changed since his last visit six weeks ago. He stood for a second looking at the money, feeling the surge of revulsion pulsing through him like a physical thing. It was coming to something, when you had to pay for it! All the things he had said in his youth about the sad old men who bought their women, all the cruel jibes about the pathetic randiness of men who had to pay for sex, came surging back into his head when he least wanted to hear them.

He left as quickly as he could, conscious that the woman too wanted him out of her house quickly, now that she had endured his clumsy tumbling and had secured his money. She came with him to the door, and he noticed lines in her face that he had not seen before, a tiredness, perhaps even a desperation about her eyes, as she told him to come again whenever he fancied a visit.

He felt a sudden, belated pity for her as well as himself, for her desperate attempt to retain her fading looks, for the uncertainty which she must feel about the future. His feet dragged a little as he walked back towards the car, which he had left a discreet two hundred yards away in a pub car park. It was difficult to walk brisk and erect when you had lost all pride in yourself. His mind fled back to childhood, to his long-dead father's warning that his soul would be damaged if he did things with women which would make him ashamed. That old-fashioned man had always refused to answer his questions about the detail of these things, but he knew for certain now that this was one of them.

He drove around for a little while, trying unsuccessfully to dispel the feeling of misery which had dropped so heavily upon his shoulders as he walked back to the car. At this moment, it did not seem long since those days when the father he had almost forgotten had warned him so vaguely about the dangers of sex. Where had all those years fled to so quickly, and why had he descended into such a useless life?

It was ten to twelve when Philip Smart eased the car into the new garage at Gurney Close. He was surprised that the light was still on in the sitting room: he had hoped that Carol would have gone to bed. He sat for a moment in the driving seat after he had turned off the ignition, trying to muster the bright, false, cheerful face which he felt his re-entry into the house now demanded.

'Sorry I'm late, dear,' he said. 'I got dragged into a last frame of snooker with the lads, and it went on a bit.'

Carol Smart was in her dressing gown, clutching an empty beaker. She was without make-up after her bath, and she looked to her husband curiously young and vulnerable. She glanced at him for a moment. He thought he caught contempt in her face, but it might have been no more than the reflection of his own guilt and self-loathing.

Then she said acidly, 'That Superintendent Lambert wants to see you in the morning. On your own, his sergeant said. I hope you've nothing you want to hide!'

Philip Smart endured a very disturbed night. As he lay on his back and stared at the ceiling in the first light of the early summer dawn, he told himself that he had nothing to fear from the police, that they could not possibly know what had passed between him and Robin Durkin. Once he heard his wife snoring softly in the adjoining room, and was filled with envy. Carol seemed to him to be sleeping the undisturbed sleep of the innocent.

But when Lambert's big old Vauxhall turned slowly into Gurney Close the next morning, it eased itself into the drive of the house next door to the Smarts. Lambert climbed out stiffly, glanced for a moment at the azure of the sky, then looked unhurriedly at the four newly-erected residences in the tiny close. The superintendent said a few words to the burly man at his side before he went into the house of Lisa Holt.

Lisa glanced briefly along the close towards the window where Philip Smart stood before she shut the front door, almost as if she expected the older man to be watching her. He drew back instinctively a little further into the room, even though he knew that she could not see him.

The two big men sat down in the seats she had intended for them in her sitting room, leaving her with her back to the light, as she had envisaged it. That at any rate had gone according to plan. Lisa said, 'Thank you for coming to see me here. I thought people might begin to gossip if we talked again at work. It can't be good publicity for a solicitors' office, if the police make a habit of interviewing murder suspects there!'

She followed her little joke with a nervous laugh, which elicited no more than a quiet smile from Lambert. He looked at her for a couple of seconds before he said, 'Is that what you feel you are? A murder suspect?'

She had expected him to deny the idea, to tell her it was ridiculous but normal, to reassure her that everyone who was questioned felt like that. She drummed her fingers on the arm of her chair. 'I suppose everyone feels threatened. I'm not paranoid enough to think it's just me. I've noticed the tension, even in a quiet place like this. Even in the close, I mean. We all seem to be looking at each other with a new sort of reserve. It's as if we think it preposterous that anyone here could have done anything like that, and yet we still have the thought at the back of our minds that there might just have been someone among us who committed a murder.'

She felt she was saying too much, that he

should have defused the tension with some relaxing dismissal of the notion before now, but he said nothing. Indeed, he listened as if her thoughts were of surpassing interest to him, and she was left to try to dismiss the idea for herself. 'But I expect that's how most people feel when they're involved in something like this.'

'When a murder occurs in a closed community, it's not unusual for people to look at each other with suspicion, yes.'

He was much less sympathetic than she had anticipated. He had not said that the notion was ridiculous, as she'd expected him to. Lisa said rather desperately, 'But we're not a convent or a hospital. We don't work together. It's just an accident of life that we happen to live our separate lives in this little cul-de-sac. And you're talking as though the murderer lives in one of these houses.'

'You don't think he does? Or she does?' There was a ghost of a smile about Lambert's lips as he added the gender qualification.

'No, I don't. I find it a ridiculous idea, if you want the truth!'

'Oh, we want that, Mrs Holt. There have been far too many attempts to conceal the truth.'

She ignored the challenge in his words. 'And you think that it might have been someone in the close who killed Robin

Durkin? Even though it would have been perfectly possible for someone to get into his garden from the path by the River Wye behind it?'

'We are keeping an open mind. It has not been possible to rule out many possibilities when we have been told so many lies. They tend to induce suspicion, do lies.'

It was the second time he had thrown the gauntlet at her. This time she felt she had to pick it up. But she felt she was making but a feeble response as she said, 'I hope you're not suggesting that I concealed things from you when we spoke in the office on Monday.'

Lambert said evenly, 'I'm suggesting rather more than that, Mrs Holt. I'm asserting that you did not merely attempt to conceal things from us but told us outright lies. That you attempted to deceive the police in the course of a murder investigation.'

She felt her mind reeling; told herself that she should have been ready for this; that she should not have been taken by surprise by it. She said stupidly, 'If anything I said gave you a wrong impression, I can assure you that there was certainly no deliberate attempt to—'

'You implied that you had no acquaintance with Robin Durkin before you moved into Gurney Close. That you had known him for no more than four or five weeks. That he was a name on a garage to you and nothing more than that. This was not a simple misunderstanding. You were attempting to deceive us.'

'All right. You make it sound more sinister than it was.'

'What we now have to ask ourselves is why you did this.' Lambert went on as if she had never spoken. 'I'm not sure how serious you were when you said that you felt you were now a suspect in a murder investigation. I have to tell you that it is you who have placed yourself in that position. And that as the person directing this investigation I regard it very seriously indeed.' He spoke as though it was a situation which gave him considerable satisfaction.

Lisa was beginning to hate this quiet, implacable man, with the lined face and the intense concentration upon a single issue. She wondered if the fear she felt showed in her face. She said lamely, 'If I lied to you, it wasn't in an attempt to conceal a murder.'

'You will need to convince us of that, Mrs Holt. I'm sure you can see that for yourself.'

'I don't know where to start.' It was true: she felt more helpless than she had done for years. She did not know how much they knew, how much she could still hope to conceal.

Just when she had focussed all her resources upon Lambert, on the contest she felt herself fighting against him, it was the less threatening presence beside him who

191

now said, 'Perhaps you should tell us all about your previous acquaintance with the murder victim. And then tell us why it was that you chose to attempt to conceal it from us.' Bert Hook's tone was quiet, even friendly, and accompanied by an encouraging smile. But there was no evading the directness of his suggestions.

'I'd known Robin for years.' The flat, defeated voice seemed to come from someone else.

'Yes. Since when?' Hook's quiet acceptance implied that she was merely about to confirm for them what they already knew, that she had better now be completely frank, if she wished to restore even a measure of credibility to her battered reputation for honesty.

'Seven years. Just over seven years.' She was suddenly very precise, as if she hoped that this might compensate for her earlier deceptions.

'And what is your opinion of him? The truth now, please. You should know that we already know a lot more about Robin Durkin and what went on in his life than we did when we spoke with you on Monday.'

Lisa took a long breath, forced herself to take her time. She was thinking on her feet now, discarding the evasions she had planned, determining how much she needed to reveal of herself and her dealings with the dead man. 'Rob was into drugs, I think. Dealing, I mean, not using. In a big way, by the time he died.' She forced the staccato phrases out, waiting for them to intervene, to help her with their confirmation, to signify that what she was saying was accepted now as the truth. Neither of the men opposite her said anything; they continued to watch her with that unwavering, unnerving intensity. She said unwillingly, 'And he made it his business to know about people. To know – well, things that they didn't want him to know.'

They were as inscrutable as medieval torturers. She could not tell whether or not she had surprised them. Then Bert Hook said quietly, 'And he knew things about you, didn't he? Knew things which he could use for his own purposes. To blackmail you.'

The word was out, the word she had feared to use. She said in a hurry, 'Not me. My husband. The man I have now divorced.' She wanted to pour out her hatred of the man who had ruined her marriage, had ruined the proud, optimistic man who had taken her to the altar and fathered her child.

It was another scorching day, and she had put on shorts and a sleeveless blouse for this meeting, had come to it barefoot and with minimal make-up; she had wanted to show these CID men how unconcerned she was. Now she regretted her boldness: she gazed down at her bare feet and felt naked, stripped of the disguises and the defences which more formal clothing might have given to her.

A voice within Lisa said that showing her hatred was not a good idea, that revealing the full extent of her detestation of Robin Durkin would not be a sensible tactic when she was speaking to the men charged with the investigation of his death. That voice lost out. She could not keep the repugnance out of her tone as she said, 'Durkin supplied Martin with what he wanted. At a price. Then he used his knowledge to drive him into a breakdown.'

She was almost in tears at the recollection. The composure which normally came naturally to her, which she had thought it would be so easy to maintain with these strangers, was in tatters now. She had seemed younger than her thirty-nine years when they had spoken to her on Monday. Now she seemed older and more careworn. It was Lambert who said softly, 'Officers in our team spoke with your husband on Monday, Mrs Holt. We already know something of his dealings with Robin Durkin.'

It was at once reassuring and disturbing, a confirmation that she was not on her own in this, but a reminder of the resources they were applying to discovering things about the people involved in the case. She tried to be as dispassionate as if she were speaking about some stranger as she said carefully, 'He supplied Martin with what he wanted. Drugs: just pot at first, then coke. I'm not sure what else. And women: there was always a ready supply of nubile girls ready to meet a young man's needs.'

Lambert nodded, then said dryly, 'Your husband was an adult and a married man. He must have been a willing partner in this.'

She gave him a bitter smile. 'That is why he is my ex-husband, Superintendent. He may have been easily led, but he was a man in his thirties: he has to take responsibility for his own actions. This is a conversation Martin and I had many times over the years. But unless you were involved, it would be difficult for you to appreciate the part played by Rob Durkin in the process of his disintegration. Oh, Rob pretended it was just lads in the pub together at first. That he was merely indulging the high spirits which were natural in Martin, that what my husband wanted was not vicious or illegal, but perfectly natural in an intelligent man who liked to "experiment" and "live life to the full". He used phrases like that a lot, did Rob Durkin. My mother used to talk about people having dark angels in their lives. I thought it was all romantic nonsense, until Martin met his.'

'Are you sure that Mr Durkin was any more than an undesirable companion for your husband?'

'I'm very sure indeed. He knew exactly what he was doing. He took a delight in seeing my husband going downhill. And when Martin had reached a certain stage, when his destiny was moving out of his own control, Rob didn't just turn his back on him: nothing as simply despicable as that. Oh no! That would have been far too simple for Rob. He used what he knew to blackmail Martin, did the admirable Mr Durkin!'

She had a sense of losing control, of displaying things in herself that she had planned to conceal, but she could no longer help herself. Lambert wondered a little at the depth of the emotion she could still display over this man whom she claimed so insistently was her ex-husband. He let her listen to her own breathing for a moment, allowed her to regain a measure of control, before he said, 'We need to know the details, Mrs Holt.'

She gave him again that acrid smile which seemed to go with the recollection of her pain. 'At first, he just threatened to tell *me*. The women had all been provided secretly, you see, as if the two of them were no more than naughty schoolboys enjoying breaking the rules. But Rob Durkin had kept a record of every occasion and every woman and every squalid hotel room involved, and he waved it in front of Martin and said he was going to post it to me. Unless Martin did what he wanted him to, of course.'

'Which was?'

'He made him a dealer. Small-time. I don't think he'd have trusted Martin with anything important, any real knowledge of what was going on: Martin wouldn't have been reliable enough for that, by then. I'm talking about four years ago: Durkin was well-established in the drugs business at that stage, but I knew nothing about it, and Martin had no idea of the scale of his operations. I don't think Rob particularly needed Martin. I think it just amused him to get him further involved, to give himself an even stronger hold upon him.'

'That's interesting. Because you're right that Durkin was making big money from drugs by then. One of the questions we have to ask ourselves is what was in this for him, why he should bother with small-time blackmail against someone like your husband.'

She nodded. It was a logical enough question, if you didn't hate Robin Durkin with the unswerving hatred which she had felt – still felt, even with the man dead and out of her life. 'You wouldn't need to ask that if you had been anywhere close to Rob Durkin whilst he was alive. He enjoyed making other people vulnerable, enjoyed watching their pain and distress. And to ensure that he could watch it, he had to have a hold over them. I'm sure you're right that Martin should have been far too petty a being to exercise Durkin's mind, with the bigger concerns he had. But he loved being able to control people, and he loved exercising that control to make them suffer.'

'You feel that it was the power he was exercising rather than any actual money he was making which was his motivation in this case?'

'I know it was. I've met other control freaks, but never one quite like Durkin. He delighted in seeing people go off the rails and in making sure they remained there. I spoke of a dark angel, and that's what Rob was for Martin. He was an evil man, Superintendent Lambert. He was the only man I've ever met who carried an aura of evil about him.'

Lambert nodded slowly, frowned a little, said, 'And yet you elected to go to a social gathering at his house last Saturday night. That was surely a strange decision, wasn't it?'

She wasn't as thrown as she would have expected to be by the question. 'I've been asking myself just that. Part of me said I couldn't refuse to go without the other people in the close asking why. Part of me said that I found that I liked Ally Durkin, whom I'd never met before I moved in here, and didn't want to insult her. And part of me, if I'm honest, was determined not to let that man Durkin determine where I should go and where I shouldn't! And I think I was anxious to see how he behaved, in the context of being a neighbour. I hadn't spoken to him for two years, at least, before I found that he was moving in alongside me here.'

Lisa saw Lambert weighing her explanation: she found it a curious and wholly novel feeling to have a man coolly and undisguisedly estimating what you said and deciding whether it was rational and whether you were honest. Then he said, 'And how did the evening go?'

'From my point of view, better than I had expected. Rob Durkin behaved himself impeccably, as if he was anxious to go on playing the role of the good neighbour, which he had been doing in the weeks building up to the street party. Perhaps that's the persona he intended to adopt in Gurney Close. I was guarded with him, of course, watching that I didn't give away too much of myself and what had passed between us in the past, though I think I managed to be relaxed with the others. But I had a feeling that other people as well as me were being careful with Durkin on Saturday night.'

'Which people?'

She was ready for him this time. 'I couldn't really tell you that. There was nothing I could put my finger on at the time, and nothing I can recall now and pinpoint as being odd. I just felt that other people as well as me had reservations about our host. But maybe I was projecting things into the atmosphere which weren't really there.'

Lambert gave her a small, encouraging smile. 'I doubt that. Who else as well as you seemed to have other concerns?'

'I really couldn't say. I was much too anxious about my own odd position to take much account of the detail of what was going on. When I think back on it, Ally Durkin herself seemed a little over-excited, a little brittle, considering that she was in her own garden and her own house. But of course I don't know that her nervousness had anything to do with her husband, do I? That's if it even existed: maybe it was no more than a figment of my over-active imagination.'

Lambert thought it was probably more than that. There were too many people who had reasons to fear or resent the host for it to have been anything other than a rather odd party. Everyone maintained that they had drunk quite a lot, which would have been a natural release in such circumstances. Yet the one man they had been able to test, the dead Robin Durkin, proved to have drunk relatively little. That would tally with this woman's description of him as a control freak, who liked to observe and manipulate those around him. But it would also have been logical if he had been anticipating a meeting with someone after the night's jollities were over.

Lambert said with his usual abruptness, 'Mrs Holt, who do you think killed Mr Durkin?'

'I don't know. Not Martin, though he would have had ample reason to do so.'

'You might like to know that your ex-husband has a perfect alibi. He was in the company of other people throughout the evening, some thirty miles from the scene of the crime.'

'Yes, I know. And for your records, I didn't kill Durkin, either.'

'So who did?'

'Someone who came in from outside, I should think. He had plenty of enemies. And he was swimming in some pretty dark pools; I imagine there were some pretty nasty fish around him.'

It was true enough. Lambert noted again the suggestion, the wish, that it should be some anonymous villain from outside the world of Gurney Close who had killed this resident. Natural enough, perhaps, but also putting Lisa Holt herself outside the frame for the crime, if they accepted the idea. He said, 'Jason Ritchie confirms that you were with him throughout the night.'

'So neither of us could have slipped out

and killed Durkin. Or both of us could have been partners in a murder.'

He did not respond to the smile with which she suggested that this was an absurd idea. 'Had Mr Ritchie any reason to wish him dead?'

'I shouldn't think so. You'll need to ask him that yourself, though. I haven't known Jason very long.'

Lisa Holt was certainly cool enough to commit murder, as Bert Hook pointed out to Lambert as the superintendent drove back towards Oldford. And she had not tried to disguise the fact that she was delighted that Robin Durkin was dead.

Fifteen

It was like a painting, thought Bert Hook. Standing at the door of the room in the Intensive Care ward, he suddenly did not want to disturb the scene. Some superstition, deep-rooted in the human psyche, told him that if he disturbed this quiet tableau, there would be ill consequences for the figures in it. For Eleanor perhaps, sitting still and upright as a statue with her eyes closed and her right hand on the sheet at the head of the bed. Or perhaps, worse still, for the pathetically small shape which lay so susceptible beneath that sheet.

The only patch of skin he could see in the patient was a few inches of unnaturally white wrist, where a drip was feeding fluids into the small, ominously quiet body.

Bert went forward and stood beside his wife, looking down at the boy, saying nothing by way of greeting because there was nothing to be said. He moved into the tableau as a third presence, standing as still and as silent as the two figures beneath him who had composed the original scene.

Eleanor was as silent as he was, weary with her vigil, fearful that any optimism might break the spell and cast the fragile subject of all this care back into the chaos between life and death. A full minute passed before she said, 'It's well over the twenty-four hours now. Well on the way to the thirty-six hours they said would be crucial.'

'And he's come through it. That's got to be a good thing.' Bert Hook looked down at the slim shape beneath the sheet, willing it to survive, watching the slight rise and fall of the cotton which proved there was life underneath it, helpless because he could not volunteer some of his own strength to drive on those small, faltering lungs.

Eleanor fought back her absurd fear that it was tempting fate to voice even the smallest hope. 'He's still in the crisis. But his temperature's down a little, the nurse says. And his pulse is slowing.' Illness in your children did odd things to you. She was resentful of her husband for extracting this information from her, as if he were stealing something which was hers and hers alone.

Bert felt a sharp pang of love for her. Eleanor looked ten years older than when she had begun this vigil at their son's bedside. There was a button on her blue shirt undone, a drop of dried, unheeded coffee on her jeans. He noticed that she had forgotten to comb her normally very tidy hair; you'd think one of the hospital people would have reminded her about that. But no doubt they had other and more pressing concerns.

He put his hand on his wife's shoulder, feeling the bones of it, thin and delicate under his broad fingers. He felt very helpless: nothing he said could distract either of them from the momentous event which was working itself out in the bed beside them. He said, 'You should get some rest, love. You've been here a long time.'

For a moment, she felt only more resentment at his intrusion, at the intrusion of anyone into the cocoon of suffering she was enduring. Didn't he see that if he broke the concentration of her love, Luke would suffer for it, might even slip away, whilst her attention was diverted? She said dully, 'I'm all right. Don't you worry about me!' and refused to look up at him.

Bert reached out a hand carefully to touch his son's forehead, as tentatively as if he were establishing contact with a tiny, injured bird, feeling that any sudden movement might damage the unconscious flesh. It felt very dry, very warm. He said, 'Perhaps he's turned the corner now.'

Eleanor felt the irritation again. What right had this man to come in here from the world outside and offer his notions, when she had been here all night and had watched every nuance of her boy's progress? What right had he to wander in off the streets and offer his banal opinions? She was the one who knew. She had been here all the time. She had sought every informed opinion, had watched the mystical electronic pulses recording the variations of heart rate and temperature. She resented his arrival from that wider world outside where he worked, which seemed to her at this moment quite remote from her. Even to think about that world, to hear the tolling of the town's clocks in the silence of the night, the distant sounds of the traffic, now seemed to her a sort of treachery.

Eleanor was silent for so long that Bert thought she was not going to speak. Then she said reluctantly, 'I think he has turned the corner, yes. I just didn't dare to say it, you see. The nurses think so: I don't think they're just saying things for me. They say there's a bed for me in the family unit when I want it. I might use it tonight, Bert.'

With the use of his name, the bond between them was re-established. She reached out a hand in slow motion and gently removed his larger one from the boy's brow. Then she intertwined her slim fingers with his thicker ones and made herself give him a squeeze.

Philip Smart couldn't stand the waiting. Once Carol had told him at midnight on Wednesday that the police wanted to speak to him, he was unable to think of anything else. When they had come to the close and gone in to see not him but Lisa Holt, it only made the tension worse. By half past eleven on Thursday morning, he could stand it no longer.

He picked up the phone and made arrangements to go into the CID section at Oldford.

He was quite relieved to be ushered in to see Detective Inspector Rushton. A younger man had to be easier than that battle-hardened and all-seeing superintendent. Phil went forward and held out his hand. 'The better half said the CID wanted to see me. Thought I'd bring the mountain in to Mahomet. One volunteer is worth a dozen pressed men, eh?'

Chris Rushton's file on Smart told him that the man was fifty-one; Chris didn't think he'd met anyone under seventy who spoke like this. It wasn't just what he said, but his manner of speaking: the man was almost a caricature of the English bounder he thought had disappeared with Ealing films. Rushton, who was used to dealing with much nastier villains, found the noisy appearance of this man in his office almost refreshing.

Smart looked at the computer winking in front of the inspector and said, 'Nice to have a fresh view on the case. I was rather expecting to see your Superintendent Lambert and the PC Plod who takes notes for him.'

Chris Rushton said stiffly, 'Detective Sergeant Hook has family troubles at the moment. His son is seriously ill in hospital.'

'Sorry to hear that. But I expect you're able to spare him from the team more easily than the brainboxes of the enterprise.'

'Detective Sergeant Hook is about to complete an Open University degree. With a very high honours classification, if his results in previous years are anything to go by.' It was the first time that Chris could remember springing to the defence of Bert Hook, whose lofty refusal of promotion to inspector had always seemed to Chris an unspoken comment on his own ambition.

'Oh! Well I didn't mean to cast any nasturtiums, you know! Still waters run deep, and all that.'

Chris was well used to clichés from a nervous public, but he found himself noticing them and being irritated by them in this man. He picked up the internal phone. 'Mr Smart is here, sir. Interview room two is free. I thought we might see him together, if you have the time.'

This wasn't going as planned at all. Phil Smart found himself ushered into an intimidating square box of a room, with no windows and a single high-wattage light in the centre of the ceiling above him. He was left on his own in there for a couple of minutes, staring at the plastic chairs and the square, scratched table with its cassette recorder, which were the only furnishings in the room.

When he came in, John Lambert said, 'I think we'll just record this, if you've no objection.' He leaned forward, pressed a button, set the cassette turning silently and went on, 'There's nothing official about this, of course: you haven't been cautioned or anything like that. It's just that it's useful for us to have a record of what you say. You would be surprised how often people recall things differently at a later time.'

He sounded as if he expected Philip Smart to change his story, to be trying to wriggle off the hook in a few days' time. That, at any rate, was how it sounded to Phil, who said weakly, 'This is a bit over the top, you know. I can't see that anything I have to say will be worth hearing, never mind recording.'

'Really? Well, I think you'll find you're underestimating yourself there. What you have to say will form part of a much larger picture. We shall see whether it fits into the pattern of what we are hearing elsewhere. We try to put whatever everyone tells us together, then see if there are discrepancies in the pattern, and in people's impressions of what happened. Then we follow up these discrepancies. It's surprising how often the discrepancies lead us to the solution in a criminal investigation.' Lambert found that he enjoyed watching the tension mount in the face opposite him as he voiced the familiar ideas.

'I've already told you what happened on Saturday night.'

'Yes, you have. And we've compared it with what other people remember of the occasion.'

'And found none of your "discrepancies", I'm sure.' Phil gave a nervous laugh, which brought no response from the two grave faces opposite him.

Chris Rushton said stiffly, 'I have already recorded on our computer files what you told our officers about the events of Saturday night. Do you wish to change anything?'

Phil had already revised his opinion and decided that he preferred the rubicund Bert Hook to this unsmiling young automaton. He said, 'There is nothing I wish to change. Nor have I recalled anything further to add to what I told the detective constable who took my statement on Monday.' He switched his attention to John Lambert and said abruptly, 'I understand my wife was in here yesterday. What was it she told you?'

Now Lambert did smile at him. This was never an easy situation. 'I'm afraid that remains confidential, Mr Smart. We never divulge what anyone tells us: it only becomes public if it becomes evidence in a murder trial.'

'But we're husband and wife.'

'That is a line of argument you must take up with Mrs Smart, not with us.' Lambert smiled again, trying to relax the tension, to suggest that nothing of great moment was involved here. 'Similarly, whatever you have to tell us this morning will not be revealed to your wife, unless you choose to relay it to her yourself. You must surely see that this is the only way for us to proceed. People will only reveal what is potentially embarrassing to them if they know that we will respect their confidences.'

Phil eased his position on the hard seat, raised his hand unconsciously to make sure that his plentiful, greying hair was still in position, then made himself fold his arms and look straight at Lambert. What the man said made sense: he certainly wouldn't want Carol to hear some of the things he might have to say here. But he didn't want to concede anything, at this stage; he might get out of this without revealing anything more, if he was lucky. 'I understand that. I just don't see what I can have to tell you.'

'We'd like to hear what you thought of the dead man, without any of the tact you might think appropriate. We've heard from a lot of people about him now. We'd like to know how you saw him and compare that with what other people remember of him.'

'I hardly knew him. We'd only been living in the close for two or three weeks when he died.' Phil found that his resolution to look his questioner fully and frankly in the eye hadn't lasted very long. He wished now that he hadn't dressed so formally. His tie felt tight on his neck, and before he knew it he was running his forefinger round the inside of his collar, feeling the dampness of his neck in this airless place.

'You're telling us that you didn't know Robin Durkin before you met him as a neighbour.'

Phil found himself trying to work out what they knew. He couldn't afford to be caught out in a direct lie at the beginning of this, but

Lambert's tone was even and unrevealing. Phil was sure now that he was sweating, that there was a sheen of damp about his temples which he could not wipe away. Some other unfortunate who had sat on this seat had tried to scratch his initials into the shiny top of the table; Phil found himself trying to decipher them as he said, 'I did know Durkin. From years back. And I didn't like him.'

It sounded like a confession – was a confession, of sorts, an acknowledgement that he had just tried to deceive them. Phil wanted to shout that it wasn't a confession to murder. Lambert said quietly, 'Don't you think that it's time that we had the full details of that? I shouldn't need to remind you once again that this is a murder enquiry, but I'm now doing so.'

'He was a nasty piece of work, Durkin.' The latest of his clichés, and one they had heard before about the dead man. 'He made plenty of money, and not much of it from that garage of his, if you ask me.'

'Which is what we are doing, Mr Smart. Asking you for everything you can tell us about the man and your dealings with him.'

'He was into drugs. Selling them, I mean. But not dealing himself, not him. He wouldn't be on the streets taking the risks, would he, Robin Durkin?'

'I don't know, Mr Smart. I'm looking for you to tell us.'

'I can't give you any details. You asked me for my impressions of the man, and I'm giving them to you.'

'Were you one of his dealers?'

'No! I've never been involved in the drugs business.'

'So if we get a search warrant and go through your house, we won't find any illegal substances?'

Phil tried not to show the panic in his face. Part of his salesman's training was to keep a smiling, untroubled face when things were going wrong, but this was different. This was for real. He fancied he could feel a vein throbbing in his temple; wondered if it was apparent to these men who watched him so carefully. 'Of course you wouldn't find anything.' But his mind was opening and shutting drawers, racing through the house as if he were in some manic farce. 'What is it you want to know?'

Lambert smiled now, acknowledging that the man had been softened up, was ready to make concessions, was going to cooperate with them. And letting his opponent know that he expected all of this. 'We need everything you know about Robin Durkin, Mr Smart. It's as simple and as comprehensive as that.'

And as hazardous and complex as that for me, who is determined that you shall not know everything, thought Phil. He returned his own, more sickly, smile. 'It won't take long to tell you that.'

'Take as long as it needs, Mr Smart. You weren't completely frank with our officers on Monday; it's important that you hold nothing back today.'

'I've already told you that Durkin was into drugs. That he was making big money from coke and horse and LSD and E.' Phil had a desperate and ridiculous hope that by listing all these drugs he could convince them that he was being frank and honest. 'I should think he was into the rape drug, as well. Rohypnol, isn't it?'

'Do you know that he was supplying that?'

'No, of course I don't. Not for certain. It's just that—'

'Confine yourself to what you know at this moment, please. We are interested in your speculations, as I've said, but we need to be clear about what is fact and what is merely your informed opinion.'

Phil didn't think he liked the use of the word 'informed'. It seemed to make him more of a player in this than he wished to be. 'I don't know any of the details of his dealing. A few years ago, I knew a few users, that's all. I picked up things from them. No more than rumours, but enough to make me think that Durkin was becoming a big player in the drugs game.'

Rushton leaned forward and said, rather

prissily to Phil's mind, 'It isn't a game, Mr Smart. It's an evil and criminal business which makes billions of pounds for a few and leads to death for many thousands. So tell us everything you know. We have been in contact with the Drugs Squad and already know quite a lot about Robin Durkin and his activities.'

It was a warning and he took it as one. 'I don't know very much, actually. I didn't like the man, so I suppose I was prepared to listen to gossip about him, especially gossip which wasn't to his credit.'

Rushton flicked rapid, almost silent fingers over the letters of his keyboard to record this. Philip Smart was looking earnestly at the detective inspector, trying to convince him he had yielded everything about this, when John Lambert said quietly, 'Blackmail was Durkin's other criminal interest. Were you one of his victims?'

It was like a lateral blow, thrown at him from the edge of his peripheral vision. Phil's senses reeled for a moment. He tried desperately to marshal his resources, to decide how much they already knew, whether this devilish superintendent was merely inviting him to compromise himself by lies which would then be truculently exposed. He found himself staring again at those in-effectively scratched initials on the table as he said, 'I was one of the people he had a hold over, yes.'

Lambert was unexpectedly quiet, almost supportive. 'You need to tell us the nature of that hold, I'm afraid. The information won't go any further, unless it proves to have a connection with this death.'

The words were said sympathetically, but they sounded in Philip Smart's ears like a knell of doom. He found that his mouth was very dry as he said, 'He knew things about me. Things which he threatened to reveal to my family and my employers.'

'What kind of things, Mr Smart? Things about the women in your life?'

He looked in alarm from one to the other of the two very different faces on the other side of that silently-turning cassette. Like many serial philanderers, Phil was absurdly optimistic about keeping his bed-hopping secret. It came as a surprise to him that these men seemed to know all about his weakness for the ladies. 'No, not that. Well, not just that.'

'What, then?'

He was ashamed, now it came to it. He had convinced himself that with Durkin's death he would never have to reveal this to anyone. But these people might be playing cat and mouse with him: he couldn't afford to lie about it to them. 'Something at work. I fiddled a few figures, made my sales seem a little higher than they were. It was easy enough. A colleague had left and gone to a new post in Canada. I appropriated a few of his sales to me. It made no difference to company profits, but it made my own performance look pretty good. And I couldn't see it was doing any harm to the man who'd gone. He'd got his big job, moved on to become a bigger fish in a bigger pond.' This time a little of his envy of the younger man's success flashed out on the cliché, as the confident, handsome features of his departed colleague flashed momentarily across his memory.

'But stealing these sales made a difference to you.'

It sounded like a statement to Phil, drawing him on to reveal everything, to confirm what they already knew. 'It gave me a bigger bonus. And the Sales Manager's post was coming up. It helped to get me that.' The admission was drawn from him like a painful tooth.

'And Robin Durkin knew about this. Used this.'

'Yes. I don't know how he got to know; perhaps he knew someone in Accounts. He took the bonus I had obtained from me, down to the last penny. He threatened that he was going to take the rise I got with the promotion from me, but that only happened in the first year.' Confession was almost a relief: he must be careful that he did not tell

217

everything about himself to this persuasive man. 'What I paid Rob must have been peanuts, compared with what he was making from drugs in the last year or two. But he enjoyed having a hold over me, I think. Enjoyed the feeling that he held my destiny in his hands.'

Lambert knew as he heard the words that this was a phrase Durkin had used to this abject man. He said quietly, 'No doubt he kept coming back to remind you of what he knew. To taunt you and tell you that there would be further demands.'

Phil found himself nodding eagerly, seizing on this chance to explain himself and the awfulness of the position in which the dead man had placed him. 'Yes. It wasn't just the threat of further extortion. He kept reminding me that he could have me sacked at any time he chose. That he could cause a major local scandal for me and my family.'

'You must have felt quite desperate.'

Phil found that he couldn't stop nodding, even though he felt he must be looking ridiculous. 'I did.'

'Desperate enough to kill Robin Durkin?'

'No!' He heard himself shout the word, appalled at the unfairness of this. The man who had been talking like a therapist had now turned on him and thrown the logic of his confession back into his face.

'People who are blackmailed do kill people,

Mr Smart. When they get desperate, they do things which are out of character.'

'And blackmailers deserve to die.'

'Did you take the law into your own hands, Mr Smart?'

'No.' He wanted to embroider the simple negative, to say something which would emphasize to this relentless man that the idea was ridiculous. But no words would come into his brain, which seemed to be pre-occupied with the problems of a dry tongue against the roof of a dry mouth. He found that his finger was running round the inside of his collar again.

DI Rushton looked at him steadily for a moment, seeming to Phil to savour his discomfort. Then he said, 'The statement you gave on Monday claims that you left Mr Durkin's house at the same time as everyone else on Saturday night. Is that correct?'

The man was underlining the fact that he'd held things back on Monday, that the whole of his story would now be suspect. Phil knew he was in no position to take offence. 'Yes. We all left at the same time. Around one, I think. Carol could confirm the time for you.'

'And you didn't go out again that night?'

'No.' He tried to take his eyes from the slowly-revolving cassette, which seemed to be atrophying his thought processes.

'Presumably your wife could confirm that also.'

He almost nodded, almost gave them a weary, automatic yes. But Carol had been in here herself yesterday, had talked to Lambert; she had been mysterious, even evasive, with him at home, and he did not know what she had said. He couldn't afford to chance his arm with these two: not again, after they had exposed what he had said on Monday. So he said wearily, 'She couldn't, actually. We sleep in separate rooms at present. I expect she told you that.'

She hadn't, of course, though Lambert was quite content that Smart should think that she had. Lambert wondered how much these two confided in each other, how many secrets they held back. He said, 'This means that neither of you can confirm that the other one did not go out again after apparently retiring for the night.'

'You're not suggesting that Carol could have killed him, surely?'

'A woman could have done this, Mr Smart. The method of killing required no great physical strength.'

'Not Carol. She couldn't have done this.'

'And how do you know that? Because you did it yourself?'

'No.' This time he did not shout. This time it was vital only that he made it clear to them that Carol could not have killed Durkin. 'I simply know that my wife is incapable of murder, that's all. It's important that you

220

should realize that. I don't want you wasting your time on Carol.'

For the first time since they had come into the interview room, Philip Smart had a kind of dignity about him. This florid, dishonest, rather ridiculous figure, who dealt in clichés and conventional reactions, was lit up by the startling intensity of his love for the wife he had wronged so often. It was totally unexpected in this middle-aged Lothario, but more striking as a result.

Lambert and Rushton reminded themselves soberly when he had left the station that he was still a very realistic candidate for the role of murderer of the man who had blackmailed and taunted him.

Sixteen

Bert Hook looked at the anxious faces of his colleagues and didn't wait for them to voice the question he had no wish to hear. 'Luke's holding his own,' he said. 'The hospital people seem to think the worst might be over, but Eleanor's waiting to see the specialist.'

Lambert and Rushton muttered their relief

at this terse summary, and Hook said, 'Now, can you bring me up to date with what's been happening in the Durkin murder case? I'm afraid I can't claim to have been single-minded about my work over the last day or two.'

Neither of them ventured to suggest again that he should take time off because of his son's illness. Indeed, Lambert was secretly delighted that Hook wanted to be here: he had grown so used to Bert's comforting, complementary presence at his side that he now found it difficult to conduct key interviews without him. He said, 'It's time we reviewed the case anyway. It would help to clarify my mind, as well as yours. I can't recall a murder victim being as universally disliked as Robin Durkin.'

Rushton nodded, flicking up the relevant list of files on his computer. 'Blackmailers are a pretty odious crew, as we all know well enough. But even among blackmailers, Durkin seems to have been notably nasty.' Chris smiled at an alliteration he had not intended, then gave a professional grimace. 'That has ensured that the list of suspects is still much longer than any of us would like it to be, five days after the killing.'

Hook thought of his white-faced Eleanor at Luke's bedside as he said heavily, 'Have we eliminated the wife yet?'

Lambert shook his head. 'We need to see

her again, in the light of what we now know about her husband. And because of Chris's discovery that she had an abortion, three years ago.'

Rushton tried to look modest. 'I didn't turn it up myself; I merely recorded it. And it may have no connection with this death.'

'It's certainly not the sort of thing which women go bragging about to strangers,' agreed Lambert. 'But we need to ask her about it, when there's a murderer to find. We need to know why she had the termination, and how it affected her relationship with her husband.'

Hook remembered the dark-haired, distressed widow very clearly, though because of the momentous events in his own life it seemed much more than two days since he had seen her. 'She said when we first saw her that they didn't have secrets from each other. I remember thinking at the time that that was probably very unlikely. This job makes us cynical.'

Lambert could think of few people less naturally cynical than DS Hook, who tended to see the best in most people, despite all the evidence provided by his work. 'And you were right, Bert. She admitted to us when we saw her again on Tuesday that she knew about his blackmailing activities. Now that we know a lot more about Durkin, it seems unlikely that Alison knew much of the detail of what he was up to. Or if we decide that she did, we need to follow up that knowledge. We now know that she was holding things back from us when we spoke to her on Sunday. I felt that we couldn't press her then, only a few hours after she'd found the body of her husband on the back lawn. We got a little more out of her on Tuesday. But the answer to your original query is that Alison Durkin is certainly still in the frame as a suspect for this killing. We know that she has a previous episode of violence towards a partner, albeit a long time ago, and we need to investigate with her what she felt about her abortion. She had the most obvious opportunity of all. And she was very anxious to suggest that some stranger had come into the garden through that back gate to kill Durkin. It's natural enough for those closest to a murder victim to prefer an outsider as the killer, as we all know, but Alison Durkin was very quick to stress the possibility.'

Rushton said, 'She may be justified, though. Something's come in only an hour ago to support her theory. There was a call from Birmingham whilst we were talking to Philip Smart,' he added apologetically to a frowning Lambert, who was wondering why this had been withheld until now. 'It now seems that there was a known contract killer in the area at the time of this death.'

'Which known contract killer?' Lambert

was dangerously terse.

'Watson.' Anthony David Watson, the records said. But you somehow didn't deal in forenames when you spoke of contract killers.

'Don't know him.'

'He hasn't any convictions. Ex-army, like a lot of them. He was a mercenary in Africa for a year or two. Finds he has a lucrative career here, now.'

With the spectacular growth in the British illegal drug trade, there is plenty of work for people who deal in swift, anonymous death. If dealers disobey orders, or get too greedy, or stray into rival territory, or even get to know a little too much, they disappear swiftly and quietly. Liquidation is one of the necessary expenses of billion-dollar crime.

'And you say he was in Herefordshire on the night when Durkin died?'

'He was staying in Cheltenham. But the Serious Crime Squad have a reliable sighting of him in Ross-on-Wye on that Saturday night. About three hours before Durkin was killed.'

'What's his usual MO?'

'Rifle, with silencer when appropriate. Or pistol at close quarters. He's a marksman. Won a prize at Bisley, sixteen years ago. But he's a killer first and foremost: if he saw a silent and reliable method of dispatching his man, he'd take it in preference to a bullet.

Garotting is one of the swiftest and surest methods of killing, if you can take people by surprise. And it doesn't leave slugs behind for forensic to identify.'

The three of them were silent, imagining the horror of sudden, silent violence in the small hours, in that quiet spot beside the River Wye. Then Lambert said, 'What chance is there of pinning this on him, if he did it?'

The professionals were always the most difficult to arrest. They moved in and out quickly, killed swiftly and unemotionally, and left few traces of themselves behind. Received police wisdom argues that there is always an 'exchange' at the scene of a killing, that the criminal always leaves behind something of himself, which forensic science can use to put him behind bars. But professional assassins are as aware of this as their police opponents. They leave minimal evidence of their crime; often, indeed, it is not even possible to be sure of where it took place. Bodies are dumped in rivers, or on building sites, or even entombed beneath the concrete of bridges or motorways. CID may suspect the contract killer, may even be privately certain that he is guilty, but without convincing evidence the Crown Prosecution Service will not even consider bringing a case to court.

Rushton shrugged. 'There's going to be very little chance of making out a case against Watson, I'd say, unless we can come up with more than a sighting in the area. I'm trying to secure copies of his bank accounts, but I'm not hopeful.'

Lambert sighed. 'We'll need to see him, in due course, unless we can be sure that he wasn't involved in this. I might want you to come with me for that, Chris.'

Both of them half-expected Hook to express his dismay at being deprived of such a meeting. Instead, he looked at his notes and said, 'What about the older couple? Ronald and Rosemary Lennox. They always seemed unlikely candidates for this. Have you been able to eliminate them?'

Lambert shook his head. 'Not yet. I agree that when you compare them with a contract killer they seem outside possibilities, but they both have motives, of a sort. And opportunity, especially if you envisage them being involved in it together. That, I'm afraid, is a possibility we have to bear in mind for all three of the couples involved.'

Rushton said, 'Rosemary Lennox set up the evening where the victim died. A street party, I think she called it.'

Lambert grinned a little at his puzzlement. 'Yes. She remembers the street parties at the end of the war, when she was only three. I saw the Lennoxes together on my own, on Tuesday. Ron actually taught Robin Durkin at school, about sixteen years ago. He said he was a high-spirited, rather mischievous boy, but nothing worse than that, at the time.'

'But Lennox rather changed his tune when I saw him with you on Wednesday,' said Hook. 'He admitted then that Durkin had been more vicious than that in his final years at school, and also that he knew Durkin was dealing in drugs within a year or two of leaving school.'

'He also pointed the finger at Durkin as a blackmailer. He suggested that he was blackmailing Carol Smart and Jason Ritchie, though he claimed he had no clear evidence on that. Ron Lennox also said that Durkin was certainly not blackmailing him, that the idea of his having anything in his blameless past which could lead to blackmail was ridiculous.'

'Which on the face of it seems likely to be true,' said Rushton, scanning his file on the recently retired schoolteacher. 'He looks far too boring to be a murderer.'

Lambert gave them a wry smile. 'I seem to recall something similar being said by policemen in Cheshire about a certain Doctor Harold Shipman, until the full extent of his killings became clear. Although I agree that Ronald Lennox looks more of a pedant than a killer, we'd better leave him in the frame for the moment. And I think we should see Rosemary Lennox on her own. She may be an unlikely murder candidate, but she hasn't been eliminated yet. And she does a lot of voluntary work in the community: she may know important things, even if she's not directly involved in this herself.'

'Both the Smarts are still candidates for murder, in that they both admit being blackmailed by Durkin,' said Rushton.

Lambert shook his head. 'Not quite, in Carol Smart's case. She admits to having an affair with Durkin in the past, but not to being blackmailed about it. But the effect is almost the same: Durkin had a hold over her and she was frightened that he was going to reveal things to her husband or her daughters.'

'What about the only one who was there on Saturday night who doesn't live in Gurney Close? This Jason Ritchie has a history of violence. Stabbed a man three times. Only got off so lightly because of a good brief and police evidence which wasn't convincingly presented.'

Chris Rushton worked on the well-established police precept, 'Once a villain, always a villain'. It is a deplorable assumption, of course, but statistics support police cynicism; most criminals are recidivists, and the number who start badly and end as model citizens is depressingly small.

Bert Hook said, 'The GBH was five years and more ago. Ritchie's kept his nose clean since then.'

'Or he hasn't been caught.' Rushton voiced the experienced copper's normal reservation.

Lambert said, 'He's another man we need to see again, now that we know more about the murder victim. I'm sure he was holding something back from Bert and me when we saw him on Tuesday. He claims he hadn't had previous dealings with Robin Durkin, but it seems odd that he hardly spoke to him throughout that last Saturday evening. Ron Lennox says that he thought Durkin was blackmailing Ritchie, that he had a hold of some sort over him.'

'Could that be anything to do with his relationship with Lisa Holt? She seems to fancy him as her toy boy.' Rushton, as a divorced man himself, was always sensitive to such issues.

Lambert tried not to smile. 'I doubt it. The pair of them seem to have been quite open about their association, even to the extent of Lisa taking him along to the street party on Saturday night. She's divorced now from her husband, and it's difficult to see what anyone could make out of her pairing up with someone else, whether permanently or temporarily. Even a pillar of rectitude like you can't make much out of it nowadays, Chris.'

Rushton said stiffly, 'I wasn't taking a moral stand. I was simply searching for anything which would make either of the pair vulnerable to a man like Robin Durkin. And thus candidates for his murder.'

'Fair enough. Lisa Holt's already admitted that Durkin ruined her marriage and almost killed her ex-husband. She makes no bones about the fact that she hated him. And if Jason Ritchie was as drunk as they both say he was after the street party, she could have sneaked out of her house to meet Durkin without lover boy being aware that she was gone.'

'And vice versa,' said Rushton, stubbornly reluctant to let his chief suspect get away with anything.

Bert Hook grinned. 'So it seems that you haven't managed to eliminate anyone whilst I've been preoccupied with Luke. Any one of the six residents of Gurney Close – or seven if we include Jason Ritchie in that number – could have killed Robin Durkin. His wife, the Lennoxes, the Smarts, Ms Holt and her lover, could all have done this.'

Lambert nodded ruefully. 'I'd say there are varying degrees of probability among that lot, but I can't claim that we've ruled out any one of them whilst you've been preoccupied with more important things at the hospital, Bert.'

Rushton added gloomily, 'And there's still the strong possibility that Durkin was eliminated by an outside agency. By a contract killer, retained by one of his rivals or former partners in the drugs trade.'

Bert Hook sighed theatrically. 'It seems that it's just as well that I'm now back to throw my mighty intellect on to the side of justice.'

Seventeen

Alison Durkin seemed perfectly calm. She didn't ask about the progress of the investigation. When a rather weary-looking John Lambert apologized for arriving at six thirty in the evening, at a time when she might have been planning to eat, she said, 'It doesn't matter. I don't eat early. I don't have young children to consider, like some other people.'

It was a lead-in to the most important question he needed to ask of her, but it seemed too abrupt to pitch it at her now, almost before they were in her house. Lambert let her take them into the sitting room which looked on to the lawn where the body of her husband had been found, then seat them in the chairs she had planned for them, as if they were more conventional visitors. She said, 'I've made a pot of tea. I thought you might be ready for a cup. I could certainly use one.'

Then she poured tea into three cups very deliberately, as if demonstrating the steadiness of her hand and the extent of her recovery. Her rather white, almost translucent skin looked less drawn than when they had seen her in this room on Tuesday, and her whole bearing was quite different from when they had seen her in shock on Sunday. Her dark, straight hair seemed more lustrous and healthy than it had been in the aftermath of this sudden death. Her every move proclaimed that, a mere five days after the violent event which might have shattered her life, she was coming to terms with life as a young widow.

As if she read this thought in them, Mrs Durkin said, 'It's a good thing there are no children who have lost a father in this house. That's the kind of thing people say after a divorce, isn't it? Well, I feel this is like a divorce, in some respects.'

Hook nodded, took a sip of his tea, tried to dismiss the thought of his own son fighting for his life. He said quietly, 'But you still have to come to terms with it, Ally. And you don't have to put on a show of bravery, as you would have to do if you had children to consider.'

He had remembered that she had asked him on Tuesday to call her Ally. She found that she was absurdly pleased about that. She took a deep breath and said, 'You said when we last spoke that you were finding things out about Rob. Things which would not please me. No doubt you have gone on digging, and continued to unearth unpleasant facts.'

She had clearly planned this recognition of realities, this acknowledgement that her husband had been a villain and that she was prepared to hear about it. Lambert wondered whether it could possibly be also an assertion that what she had done to him on Saturday night was justified. He said gravely, 'I'm afraid that we have to go on digging, as you put it. It is our duty to find who killed Robin. To discover that we need to know all about the life he lived. You helped us yourself, when you told us on Tuesday that you thought he had been blackmailing people.'

'Yes. You've no doubt unearthed some of his victims.'

'We have, yes. We are continuing to discover things about his activities in that field.'

'He liked to have a hold over people, you know. He didn't open up very often, even to me, but once or twice I heard him positively gloating about something he knew. Usually it was when he thought it would give him an opportunity to pay off old scores.' She offered first sugar and then a plate of ginger biscuits, for all the world as if she were discussing the weather and this were a normal social occasion.

'Have you thought of any people who might be victims? As you imply, blackmail victims often become desperate.'

'And turn into murderers, you mean. I see that, but I'm afraid I can't offer you any names. I kept out of that area of his life. Or he kept me out of it. Either way, you could say I was prepared to enjoy the affluence which came from his behaviour, without wishing to dirty my hands with the knowledge of it.' For an instant, the hint of a private trauma of self-loathing threatened her control.

Lambert said, 'I don't think he raised substantial sums from blackmail; you're probably right that he enjoyed having a hold over people and the feeling of power which that gave him. We think the majority of his money came from trafficking in illegal drugs.'

'I suspected as much. I suppose I didn't want to know for certain.' She fingered the top of her arm, winced a little, said bitterly, 'I'm now having to confront the things which I wouldn't acknowledge to myself when Rob was alive.'

'Yes. I'm sorry about that. But I'm sure you want us to find out who murdered him.'

'Are you? I'm not certain I want to know who killed Rob. Not certain that I want you to know.' She voiced the daring, outrageous thought and hid the lower half of her face behind her cup as she drained it, then set the cup back on its saucer and said, 'More tea, Superintendent Lambert?'

For the first time, there seemed something brittle about her control. But she had almost invited him to take up the issue of her own life, and Lambert said quietly, 'In the course of routine enquiries, we have turned up things about you, Mrs Durkin. Things which we have to raise now.'

'Then go ahead.' She tried to think what these things might be, but her mind was blank when she most wanted it to be active.

'Our records show that you attacked a previous partner. That you have a conviction for occasioning Actual Bodily Harm.'

'It's irrelevant.'

'You should have told us about it.'

Alison Durkin felt curiously calm. She had expected this. 'Of course I should. You only had to check your records to find it. But it's something I've long ago put behind me. The habit of concealment dies hard, I suppose.'

'You took an offensive weapon to a man you were living with.'

'That sounds very dramatic. You make it sound premeditated, which it wasn't. I picked up the nearest weapon to defend myself, from the table behind me, when I was being attacked myself. My hand fell on a pair of kitchen scissors. I did the man no lasting damage.'

'But you pleaded guilty to a serious charge.'

'The legal advice was that it would be technically difficult to do otherwise. And it could have been more serious, couldn't it? It could have been GBH. But I was given only a conditional sentence, which I understand is a rarity with an assault charge.'

'It is. Did your husband know about the case?'

She smiled a bitter smile. 'Of course he did. He taunted me with it whenever it suited him. But I never took scissors or anything else to him, even though there were times when it would have been very satisfying.'

Lambert found her confidence about this violence she had concealed unusual and a little disturbing. He said, 'We have found out something else about you in the course of our enquiries, Mrs Durkin.'

'And what might that be?' Alison found that her confidence over the way she had handled the assault issue made her truculent now.

'We discovered that you were a patient in Westview Private Hospital just over three years ago.'

Her confidence drained away as the shock hit her like a physical blow. She had not expected this, had made no plans to deal with it. Her face froze into a mask. 'In April 2002, yes. In the abortion unit. I had a termination, yes.'

'Forgive me, Mrs Durkin. But in a murder investigation, we have no alternative but to pry. We need to know how this event affected your relationship with your husband.'

She wanted to tell this quiet, insistent man, who was almost old enough to be her father, to go and hang himself from the nearest tree. Instead, she heard herself saying, 'Yes. Because it could turn me into a murder suspect, this, couldn't it? Or enhance my status in that respect: I suppose I was already a suspect.'

Hook said, 'This isn't easy, Ally, for any of us. Did you have the termination on medical advice?'

'No! On Rob Durkin's bloody advice, that's all! He said we didn't want children, not at that moment. In a year or two, he said, but not then. He even said that we needed my income! I must have been even more stupid then than I am now!'

Hook said, 'It's probably as well that you haven't got a toddler who had to be told about a father's death this week. You said that yourself, a few minutes ago.'

She looked at him as if he had thrown a new and revolutionary idea at her, rather than merely recalled her own platitude. It was suddenly important to her to make the degree of her suffering clearer to this kindly, avuncular figure. 'I wanted that child. But I persuaded myself that I had come to terms with the abortion, for the sake of my marriage. Then I found a year later that Rob had a child by another woman. A child that he was supporting.'

Hook nodded, as quietly as if he was about to record a car registration number. 'We'll need the details of this woman, if you have them.'

'She's dead. I think she was on drugs. One of Rob's pushers. She became an addict; the child was taken away from her. I suspect she committed suicide. I only found out about the child because I ferreted out a paternity order in Rob's bureau. He wasn't pleased about that.' It might have been the first time he had hit her, but she was no longer sure about things like that. She found herself fingering the cotton which covered the bruising at the top of her arm again, as she recollected that moment when she had discovered that another child had been born, almost on the day of her termination. It seemed now to belong to another and darker life.

Hook waited a moment, thinking of the child he had left in the hospital, before he said, 'Were you planning to have children at some future time?'

She left it so long before she answered that they thought she was going to ignore the question. Then she said very quietly, 'I think that it was that abortion which marked the real end of our marriage. I didn't see it at the time, but when I look at things now, I'm sure that I should have known then that it was time to get out.'

Hook knew that his role now was not to question but merely to prompt, to keep this revelation going. He said, 'But you didn't leave him. You bought a new house together.'

Ally Durkin smiled the disillusioned smile which should have come from a much older woman. 'I'd loved Rob Durkin since I was fifteen, when he was a high-spirited boy. You don't give up when you love someone, even when you should. You don't see things clearly. You turn a blind eye to things you should see as significant. Above all, you hope. Hope that you can change things. Hope that people will change, that they will see things as wrong which you see as wrong.'

It was a bleak summary of dreams turning to ashes, of scales dropping away too late from innocent eyes, of aspiration turning to despair. She shook herself a little, as though she felt a cool draught on this sweltering evening. 'I'm sorry. You're meant to be detectives, not therapists.'

Hook gave her a smile, acknowledging that she was re-establishing contact with them after the revelation of her private nightmare. 'It's not our job to sort out the messes people make of each others' lives, Ally. But I now need to ask you formally whether you killed your husband.'

Ally nodded slowly. This hadn't gone at all the way she had expected it to, but she was prepared for the question. She found herself in fact much calmer than she had expected to be. She would deny murder, of course. But she had a need to convince them that Rob had deserved to die.

Instead of answering immediately, she slowly rolled up the sleeve of her blouse, revealing the yellow and green of the healing bruise below her shoulder. 'That's my last souvenir of the man I loved. I didn't kill him. But someone did me a favour on Saturday night.'

It was after eight o'clock when Bert Hook finally contrived his return to the hospital.

Visiting ended at eight, and he moved against an ebb-tide of departing vehicles as he manoeuvred the silver Focus into the car park. The staff on this ward were familiar with him now. No one tried to prevent him from entering the Intensive Care Unit.

He was into the single room which had grown so familiar before he realized that something was wrong. The bed was empty. It was neatly, even severely, tidy, with crisp new sheets turned sharply back and the single pillow exactly in place at its head. The chair where Eleanor had sat for days like a watchful statue was gone. The multitude of tubes and machines which had been connected to the tiny, inert shape of his son stood quietly in the corner, yards from the bed where they had functioned.

Bert's heart seemed to stop beating for a moment. His head swam, his brain reeled, and he found himself reaching out for the jamb of the door, to keep not so much his physical but his mental balance. They had been told that the worst was over. Surely it couldn't all have gone wrong at this stage! That would be too cruel to bear.

Then a familiar voice said, 'They've moved him. He doesn't need twenty-four hour care any more.' Eleanor Hook was looking puzzled, not relieved, when her husband turned to her. She felt she should have been able to infuse the simple words with a portentous weight which was quite beyond her.

She led him into a different room, quiet, peaceful, invested with hope after the feverish agonies of anxiety which had filled the air in that other place, where their son had seemed a tiny, scarcely human focus of too much technology. There were no tubes, no monitors, no quietly winking screens around the bed here. And what lay beneath the neatly arranged white sheets was small, but now demonstrably human.

Eleanor said, 'He was conscious earlier. He spoke to me. What he said didn't make much sense, but he spoke.' She sounded as if she was announcing miracles and did not expect to be believed. But she did not care about that; she scarcely knew indeed what she was saying.

Bert didn't want to say anything. He was overcome by an overwhelming relief, which made him realize in a few seconds how near to exhaustion he felt. He reached out his hand and put it on top of his wife's hand, which felt warm and dry and very small beneath his. 'You'll be able to sleep tonight,' he said, with heavy, welcome anticlimax.

Bert Hook could think of nothing else to say, nothing which would reflect what either of them was feeling. After a few long seconds he managed only, 'Better get to bed soon. I expect you'll be woken up at six. Things start early, in hospitals.'

Eleanor looked at him for a moment as if she did not understand him. Then she managed her first smile. 'I'm coming home with you, tonight, Bert. He's out of danger, they say.'

Bert knew that, in the obscure code which had been dictated to them by this crisis, this was a speech of love. He tightened his grip on the hand within his and said nothing. After a moment, he gently freed his fingers and reached them almost fearfully towards the occupant of the bed. He brushed the back of his fingers lightly against the small forehead, touched the fine hair above it, confirmed to himself that his son Luke had come back to replace that small, frail shape which had lain between life and death.

In the twilight of this corner of the teeming world, the eyelids beneath his thumb fluttered briefly open, and dark pupils looked at him, first in puzzlement, then in recognition.

'Hello, Dad,' said Luke.

In his cosy retreat in Birmingham, Anthony David Watson watched the television news and waited for the Central (South) local items. There was a mention of the murder in Gurney Close, but only to say that there had been no arrest as yet. There was a shot of the tiny, quiet close of new houses, then a sequence of that photogenic reach of the River Wye behind them, which must have been taken from a helicopter. The victim was described as a prominent local businessman with no obvious enemies. Watson smiled at those phrases: he knew a lot more than that about the late Robin Durkin. The police also would know much more about him and the things he had been involved in by now, obviously, but they weren't releasing anything to the media.

Watson liked what he heard and saw. It probably meant that the CID hadn't made much progress with their enquiries, as yet. He switched the television off and went back to his book.

When the phone rang ten minutes later, he did not answer it. He pressed the button and listened to the coded sentence being recorded on his answerphone. He let five minutes elapse before he rang back; do nothing in a hurry was one of his maxims. You made mistakes when you hurried; you were most efficient when you operated at the tempo which suited you.

The commission was from one of the city's biggest men. He operated gambling clubs and betting shops alongside his illegal drugs racket: they were convenient tools for the money-laundering which was necessary when you made the sums he did from criminal activities.

The man didn't speak himself, of course; it was one of his minions who provided Watson with the facts he needed to know. The hitman thought he recognized the voice, but that did not concern him. So long as you were sure of being paid, it mattered not whether you could put a face to your employer in this trade. For most of the time, it was better for you if you couldn't identify him. When death was your business, anonymity suited everyone; too much knowledge could be highly dangerous.

Watson acquired the knowledge he needed by a series of rapid questions. The target suspected nothing, he was told. Well, he'd heard that before, and he would make his own judgements about it and move in with caution. But he was given a detailed account of the target's movements on the following day, which was much more to his taste. Times as well as the places his man would visit were listed, and his informant seemed confident that the target would stick to the timetable he outlined.

Watson made rapid notes on the pad in front of him, giving no more than the occasional affirmative grunt as the information came down the line to him. The man at the other end of the line finally let out a little of his nervousness. 'Is it too early for you? Do you need more notice than this?'

Watson said, 'No. If it's as you say, if he goes to these places alone, I can take him out tomorrow. But you must let me be the judge of the time and the place. If it's not appropriate, I'll come back to you and get details of his movements on other days.'

'Tomorrow is the ideal day to get him.'

Watson frowned a little at the phone: you didn't pressurize contract killers. Deciding on the right time and place was part of his expertise. 'If he suspects as little as you say, there'll be other opportunities.'

'We'd like him out of the way quickly.'

'If it's safe to do it, it will be done tomorrow. You must let me be the judge of the moment to kill.'

It was the first time that word had entered into the exchanges. Watson put down the phone and went back to his book. He was totally unconscious of the small, mirthless smile which played about the corners of his lips.

Eighteen

Lisa Holt did not want to confront the implications of the ideas which had occurred to her during the night. Still less did she want those experienced, persistent detectives discussing those implications with her, when she was not even clear in her own mind about what she thought.

In the bright light of another blazing day, her fears seemed groundless, even silly. She told herself that three o'clock in the morning was always the worst time for anyone, the time when spectres loomed large and bizarre ideas took hold of the imagination. It reminded her of what St John of the Cross called the dark night of the soul. She'd read a lot of that Spanish mystic, when she was about sixteen and thinking of becoming a nun. When she was a mere girl, in another, more innocent life, which had gone now forever.

She tried to keep up with her son's wide-ranging, innocent conversation in the car. His childish treble seemed louder than usual this morning with his excitement. There was an innocence about nine-year-olds which was taxing as well as refreshing: it made you seem tawdry and jaded, and it emphasized the deceptions which seemed to characterize your more complicated adult life. George ranged over the details of his school life, passing in quick succession from the paintings on the classroom wall to his chances of making the football team when the winter came, then on to the girl who sat behind him in class, whose grandfather had died earlier in the week.

Lisa kept up her end of the conversation as well as she could. Not much was required from her in terms of words, but she had learned long ago that monosyllabic agreements were not enough for George, that her reactions would be measured in terms of the intelligence of the questions she could mount, as her responses to this swiftly-moving panorama of her son's life.

Lisa felt quite exhausted when she had dropped him off at the school gates. She watched him trotting eagerly up to his friends and managed a smile at his pleasure in seeing them, at his immediate dismissal of his mother. Then she sat still and reflective for a moment, until the horn of a four-by-four blasted impatiently behind her.

Instead of going straight to work, Lisa Holt turned the Corsa in the other direction, towards Oldford Police Station.

Watson decided that he would kill during the afternoon. That was unusual for him. He preferred the hours of darkness, when there was natural cover and fewer people were about. Fewer innocent people, that was the important thing. The innocent were un-knowing, and ignorance was hazardous in his world. The ignorant could get themselves involved in things which had nothing to do with them, and that was dangerous.

It wasn't that he was worried about spilling innocent blood: he had long since ceased to operate by the moral conventions which in-formed the lives of ordinary people. Watson's concern was rather that the ignorant could get in the way, bringing with them unneces-sary and dangerous complications. Tidiness was a tool of success, as far as he was con-cerned. If you killed or injured someone whom it wasn't your brief to harm, you were inefficient, which would affect your future employment.

Innocent blood would also bring extra police resources into the equation, a thing he could do without. He didn't make the mistake he had seen in some of his fellow-killers. They showed an arrogance, a contempt for the forces ranged against them. Watson was determined that he would never do that.

He studied his street map, pinpointing in his mind the exact spot where the job would be completed, checking that he could make a swift and undetected exit from the scene of the crime. Three twenty-five, it should be, if things went according to plan. Well before the rush hour traffic would complicate the getaway route.

He put the street map of the city back on the shelf among his other reference books. He would not need it again. He had a photographic memory for the detail of maps, when it was necessary. He needn't even think about the mission again until lunch. It was a discipline for him not to dwell on things, once he was sure of exactly what he was going to do.

The only problem now was how to fill in his morning.

If the CID men were surprised to see Lisa Holt only twenty-four hours after they had last spoken to her, they gave no sign of it.

An impassive DI Rushton ushered her into Superintendent Lambert's office and DS Hook placed a chair carefully in front of the great man's desk for her, as meticulously as if the exact position was somehow important.

These preliminaries only made her more nervous. She was impatient to get on with what she had to say. Indeed, she felt the certainty with which she had made her determined entry into the station draining away with each passing second. She had put on the maroon trousers and dark-red shirt which she knew flattered her slim figure; she had felt a need to dress as differently as possible from the shorts and the bare feet they had seen yesterday.

Now Lisa had an absurd wish to look into a mirror, to check that her appearance was right for this exchange, that her carefully applied make-up had not been affected by the exigencies of the school run with George. She said, 'You'll probably tell me I'm being stupid. But you said you wanted to hear any ideas we had, to collect any information we could give to you.'

Lambert said, 'If I had a pound for everyone who's apologized to me for wasting my time over the years, I'd be living in an affluent retirement by now. But I'd also have solved a lot fewer crimes. We rely on the public for information, a lot more than we like to admit when we're claiming how clever we are.'

'It's just something which occurred to me during the night. It's probably nothing to do

251

with this crime.'

'In which case it will go no further than this room.' Lambert, anxious for her to get on with this, was yet aware that you could not always rush people without them closing up, that it had probably taken this anxious-looking woman in her late thirties quite an effort of will to come here at all. He was quite content in any case merely to observe, aware as always that this innocent-looking exterior could conceal a murderer, who had come here to dissemble and throw them off the scent.

Lisa Holt said, 'It's Jason.'

'Mr Ritchie,' Lambert nodded. 'I thought it might be.' No harm in letting them think that you were splendidly omniscient.

'He knew Robin Durkin before I moved into Gurney Close. Before we met him on that Saturday night.'

'Yes.'

'You knew that?'

'A lot of work has been going on during the last six days. The public does not see much of it, but like the industrious duck, we are paddling hard beneath the surface.' The simile wasn't flattering, but it would divert her attention from wondering how much they really knew.

'I just thought I should tell you about Jason.'

'In case it turns out that you've been

sharing your bed with a murderer, you mean.'

'No!' It was exactly her fear, the thought which had set her flesh creeping in the small hours of the night, but she hadn't expected to hear it put into words by this calm, observant, undramatic man. 'I don't for a moment think that Jason killed Robin Durkin, but you said that we ought to lay every bit of information we possessed before you. That's the only reason I'm here.'

'And very commendable it is that you should be here, Mrs Holt. It would have been even more useful if you'd told us this when we first spoke to you, on Monday. Or even yesterday.'

'I'm sorry. I was coming to terms with this death then. I was too concerned with my own dealings with that awful man to think about Jason's connections with him.'

'I see. Well, you'd better let us have the full details of Mr Ritchie's association with the murder victim now.' Lambert was irritated with this rather attractive woman, who seemed to think they should be grateful to her for coming forward now, when she had impeded the progress of their work by concealing things about her lover.

'I don't know much, really. It's just that Jason has let slip one or two things which made me feel that he knew Robin Durkin almost as well as I did. Jason said yesterday

253

that he was as glad to see the man dead as I was, but he wouldn't tell me why. Just said that Rob Durkin was scum and the world was better off without him.'

'But he wouldn't tell you exactly why he thought that?'

She smiled, trying to lighten the tension she felt building between them. 'He hasn't had much chance. We didn't spend the night together. I haven't seen a lot of Jason since this happened, actually. But there's nothing very unusual about that. My child and my work take over, during the week. And Jason has quite a workload too.'

She wondered if it sounded defensive, if they were really going to believe that she and Jason hadn't talked much about Rob Durkin and the sort of man he had been. She certainly wasn't going to tell them about the way the dead man had come between them over the last few days, abruptly suspending Jason's work on her garden, inhibiting their relationship, making each of them question exactly how much they really knew about the other.

Lambert said, 'We know now that Durkin was a blackmailer. Did he have a hold over Mr Ritchie?'

'No. Well, I don't think he did.' Suddenly, she wanted only to be out of this room and in the open, unoppressive air. 'You'll need to ask Jason about that yourself, won't you?'

Lambert ignored the question. 'Durkin was a drug dealer, employing other people to take risks for him. I expect you know about that. Several other people knew, though they didn't think it necessary initially to inform us about it. Was Jason Ritchie working for him?'

How direct the man was! Almost insolent in his intensity. 'I'm sure Jason was never involved in anything like that.' But Lisa was aware that she didn't sound very sure at all.

Just when she was focussed absolutely upon the superintendent, it was Hook who said quietly, almost persuasively, 'You think Jason Ritchie might have gone back out of your house on Saturday night to meet Robin Durkin, don't you, Lisa?'

It seemed to her more shocking that her worst nightmare should be voiced now by this rubicund, unthreatening figure. 'No. Well, I recognize that it would have been possible. I'd drunk quite a bit and I went out like a light after we'd made love. I told you that. But the fact that it's possible doesn't mean that I think it actually happened.'

But all three of them in the room knew that she wouldn't have been there if she didn't think it was a possibility.

Watson felt very cool, even on a day when there seemed to be not a breath of air in the stifling city. Adrenaline had that effect upon him.

It had always been one of his strengths that he grew calmer as the pressure increased. He had fought as a mercenary in settings as diverse as tropical jungles and the frozen footlands of great mountain ranges. It was in these places that he had discovered that it was when the bullets were flying and danger was at its greatest that his brain functioned with an almost unnatural coolness. Not all men were like that. The discovery of that fact was one of the things which had made him determined to operate alone.

There were twenty minutes yet before he needed to be in position. It was a mark of the amateur to be there too early, attracting attention. Watson turned the car off his route, cruised alongside one of the canals which had been prettified in the last two years. There was a greater mileage of canals in Birmingham than in Venice now, he'd read. Fortunately, you didn't have to make your getaway by water in Birmingham.

He watched scantily-clad girls drinking wine with bare-chested men on barges, opened his car window a fraction to hear the sounds of innocent voices and high-pitched laughter. For a moment, he speculated about those other, innocuous, unremarkable lives, which he would glimpse in passing but never enter. There was a band playing somewhere beyond a high building, a brassy, unthreatening, cheerful sound, which said that some sections at least of the city were at play and beginning the weekend early. Watson drove towards the music but decided not to reach it. He pressed the button and put the windows up, switched on the air conditioning, and isolated himself again within his cocoon of concentration.

It was time to focus again upon the business of the day.

The warehouses were high here, cutting out most of the sky even in this brilliant weather. Many of them had changed their functions with the decline of manufacturing industry. Some of them dealt in less honest trades than in Birmingham's heyday; some of them housed much more dubious goods and much more dubious traders than had been here when these high, blank brick walls had been constructed. It was not a place where you would willingly come alone at night, even if you were as well equipped to protect yourself as Anthony David Watson.

But the place which he had chosen operated within the law. It was a quarter of a mile from the last of the warehouses, on the fringe of the area which was formerly dominated by those small manufacturing businesses which were the foundation of Birmingham's prosperity and reputation. What had once been a toolmaker's busy works had lain derelict for ten years before it had been converted into a gaming club.

Gambling has been one of the growth industries of twenty-first-century Britain. And crime follows economic growth. The men who were already big in the underworld had long seen the possibilities of gaming clubs and betting shops, not just as lucrative enterprises in themselves, but as vehicles for laundering money acquired by other and more devious means. Now the government had seen the revenue possibilities of the nation's taste for gambling and announced the licensing of casinos. The stakes were going up, for the criminal fraternity as well as for the punters in their clubs.

One of the owners was getting far too big for his expensive leather shoes. It wasn't good for you to get ideas above your station in the undefined but clearly understood hierarchy of the underworld. Those people who didn't appreciate that truth had to learn it the hard way. And their fate would be a stern example to a host of other, lesser people, whose ambitions might also be in danger of outstripping their functions.

Watson was here to implement this necessary and educative adjustment.

He eased the Vauxhall out of the side street and into the exact position he needed, twenty yards from the entrance to the club. It would be crowded round here in the evenings, but there was no difficulty with parking in the afternoon, when the roulette wheels were stilled and the cards locked away in the steel cabinets. He had even thought that his presence might be too obvious in the almost-deserted street. But there was a white Transit van, which was obviously the property of some workman operating within the club, a perfect screen for a killer. He pulled in four yards behind it, with his front wheels turned outwards for the getaway.

Seven minutes, if the target came when he should. Watson could feel the tension at last. He forced himself to stare at the bonnet of the car and muse on how perfect the grey Vauxhall was for his needs. Not too new, not too remarkable. Almost anonymous among flashier and more expensive wheels. But absolutely reliable, and deceptively fast when it needed to be.

The target arrived in one of those more luxurious and noticeable cars. Watson's lips twisted into an unconscious smile as he watched the big silver Mercedes turn into the street. He watched it until it disappeared behind the van in front of him. Then he slid silently from the seat of the Vauxhall and pressed himself against the rear doors of the Transit.

He heard the target speaking, caught a few words of his flat Brummagen accent as he gave orders to the men beside him. Watson heard the voices moving away from him before he risked putting an eye round the corner of his white metal cover.

The men with his target were squat and powerful. But they were club bouncers, not a professional bodyguard: Watson would have known them if they had been professionals. These men would be handy enough with their fists, but they probably weren't even tooled up. He wouldn't underestimate them: he never did that. But he could see nothing very threatening here.

As if to confirm his assessment, the men moved into the club ahead of their boss when he told them to. No professional minder would have done that. The target reached into the back of the Mercedes and picked up his briefcase, looked automatically but unseeingly up and down the street, and followed them towards the door of the club.

Watson moved after him on silent, rubber-soled feet. The man in the tailored shirt did not even hear him. His first intimation that he had company was the pressure of the silencer at his temple. It was possible that he did not even have time to anticipate the shot which blew half of his head away.

Watson knew there was no need for a second shot. Not at that range, when you had picked the exact point of entry to the head. He did not even pause to study the effects of his work: that would have been unprofessional.

He was in the driving seat of the car by the time he heard the first shouts of alarm from the doorway of the club. The Vauxhall was at the end of the street before anyone even thought of pursuit. Probably no one would have even noted the number on the false plates – not that anyone in these circles would be invoking the police. His lips curled now into a wider and more deliberate smile at the thought of how ridiculous that would be.

Once he was clear of the immediate area of the club, with no sign of any vehicle behind him, he slowed to thirty. No sense in risking the traffic cops when you had just fried a much bigger fish and got away with it. There was no one around the lock-up garages at this time on a Friday afternoon. Nevertheless, he pulled down the up-and-over door before he moved the old carpet aside and took the cover off the servicing pit beneath the concrete floor. He stowed away the Smith and Wesson .357 Magnum pistol carefully in the secret chamber at the base of the cavity, then set the boards back precisely before dropping the rags and the car tools he never used on top of them.

He enjoyed the walk home in sun and dappled shade along the edge of the park. Schoolchildren, released for the weekend, were playing noisy games away to his left. Mothers with toddlers in pushchairs were conversing near the gates. He wondered why their conversations never seemed to dry up. He was a man who had little time for words himself. The ones he used were mainly functional; he couldn't imagine the kind of desultory exchanges these young women pursued, where the words were an unimportant vehicle for the kind of social exchange he had long since abandoned.

Once he was back within the familiar walls of the flat, he poured himself a stiff whisky, topping it with plenty of water. He scarcely drank at all nowadays, but you had to allow yourself a small celebration of a job well done. It was one of the few conventions he preserved from that earlier life of his, which seemed now to have been lived by a different person.

He rang the number he had been given, waited for the connection, said carefully and clearly, 'The fish has been filleted,' and put the phone down without waiting for any response. These codes always felt ridiculous, but it was what the man had directed him to say. And he who paid the piper so handsomely had the right to call the tune.

He decided he wouldn't eat until much later. He wasn't at all hungry at the moment, and he could easily microwave one of the meals from the freezer whenever it suited him. Life was much easier and more comfortable here than in those places in his past, where he had operated in temperatures of over a hundred or under zero whilst living under canvas. And you didn't need to keep your eyes on the actions of the shady people who served alongside you, in whatever cause was paying the wages this month. Being your own boss had a lot of advantages, whatever trade you were working in.

Watson enjoyed the process of winding down after a job, of gradually relaxing that intense concentration he assumed as naturally as the appropriate clothing for the task. By six o'clock, he was almost asleep in his armchair, with the book closing itself unnoticed on his lap. He never actually went to sleep: the habits he had developed as a younger man did not allow that. At a quarter to eight, he felt perfectly relaxed, as distanced from the events of the afternoon as if they had happened weeks earlier. In a moment, he would go into the kitchen and get himself something to eat.

That was when the knock came at the door of the flat.

He was instantly as alert as a wild animal, his hair prickling as his pulse raced, his fingers coiling around the arms of the chair as he sprang upright. It couldn't be anything to do with what had happened this afternoon, surely? He had reconnoitred the ground as efficiently as ever, and the operation had gone like clockwork.

He put his eye cautiously to the spy-hole in the door and saw two men in jackets standing outside, making no attempt to move to one side and conceal themselves. A tall man in his fifties, with a lined face and grizzled hair, and a man probably at least twenty years younger, with dark hair and a handsome profile.

Rozzers! What the hell did they want? They couldn't be on to him about this afternoon's job, surely? The pigs weren't that good, and certainly not that quick. And he was sure he'd left nothing behind to identify himself. They were flying a kite, whatever this was about. If he gave them nothing, they'd be on their way in ten minutes, and none the wiser. If he kept his nerve, he told himself firmly, there was nothing at all to fear here. And keeping his nerve was what he was good at.

He opened the door carefully, gave them a guarded smile, even managed to look surprised at these strangers on his threshold.

It was the taller, older man who spoke. He said, 'Are you Anthony David Watson?'

He didn't like the use of his full name, and still less that it was the filth pronouncing it. He said 'That is I,' enjoying his correct and sententious use of the pronoun. Such precision would show them from the start that he did not feel threatened.

The man had never taken his eyes from Watson's face. He said calmly, 'I am Detective Chief Superintendent Lambert. This is Detective Inspector Rushton. We'd like a few words with you, Mr Watson.'

Nineteen

The Governors' Meeting of the junior school was conducted with brisk efficiency. That was normal, with Rosemary Lennox in the chair.

The news was generally good, she reported. The intake for the coming September was now finalized, and numbers would be up, for the third year in succession. The number of pupils was important, because there had been a threat to the future of the school a few years ago, when many of the villages of Gloucestershire and Herefordshire had lost the schools at the hearts of their communities as falling rolls in the classrooms took their toll.

This one had acquired a new, enthusiastic head teacher and Rosemary Lennox as chairman of its governing body at the same time, and had never looked back. The reputation of the school was now such that parents from the whole of the surrounding area wanted to send their children here, and the problems were bulging classrooms and crowded play areas rather than threatened closure. But the problems of expansion were always easier than those of decline, as Rosemary and the head constantly reminded staff and parents. The numbers next year would probably justify another extra teacher, with all the advantages that would bring.

The teacher-governors on the committee were glad that the meeting was swift and optimistic, for they had just concluded a busy working week. They appreciated the competence of the woman chairing the meeting and the way she constantly supported their popular head. Once the business of the day was concluded with the agreement of a date for the next meeting in October, the teachers departed swiftly to their weekend concerns, as did most of the other governors.

Rosemary Lennox was left chatting with her new neighbour, Carol Smart, who was also a governor of the school, and who seemed to share most of her own views. 'Thanks for supporting me on the employment of a music teacher,' said Rosemary.

'No problem. I'm glad the success of the school means that we have the resources available. We need things like music to develop the souls of the little hooligans! My own daughters missed out on things like that. I can see the need for minimum standards all over the country, but I sometimes think the National Curriculum seems to squeeze out things like music and drama.'

Carol hoped she didn't sound sycophantic. She was still a little in awe of Rosemary Lennox's grasp of educational issues and clear-sighted pursuit of excellence. But she was getting to know her new neighbour better day by day. She liked what she saw and heard. Rosemary was not stuffy, as she had feared she might be when they moved into Gurney Close; indeed, she had a quite impish sense of humour, on occasions. Carol Smart said, 'I suppose it helps you with this, your husband being a teacher.'

Rosemary grinned. 'Ex-teacher, now. And I'm not sure working in the upper echelons of a comprehensive school, with fifteen-to eighteen-year-olds, has much relevance to the problems of a junior school.' Her punctilious and slightly pompous husband was good with committed sixth-formers; less so, she fancied, with boisterous eight-year-olds. He had even seemed a little diffident and awkward with their own son when Andy had been that age, though there had never been any doubt that Ron loved the boy dearly.

Neither woman voiced the thought which had occurred to both of them during the afternoon. It was surely ridiculous that two such competent but unremarkable women, one a slim, healthy, grey-haired lady in her early sixties and the other a comely and intelligent forty-three year-old, should be involved in the investigation of a violent killing. That two of the governors of this lively and successful primary school should be murder suspects.

Rosemary was gathering her papers from the meeting together and preparing to leave when the head teacher returned to the room, looking surprisingly embarrassed within her own school. 'There's a Chief Superintendent Lambert just arrived. He says he'd like to speak to you, when you've finished here.'

'That's all right,' said Mrs Lennox. 'We've had a murder among our neighbours, you know, Mrs Smart and I. I expect he wants to clear up a few details with us.' She spoke as if murder was just one more thing to be dealt with in a busy working week, no more disturbing than rotas for hospital visiting or rebates on council tax for charity shops.

'There are two of them, actually,' said the head. 'And it's Mrs Smart they say they want to speak to.'

'I'll be on my way, then,' said Rosemary Lennox, sliding her papers into her bulging briefcase. She tried not to show the relief she felt that it should be Carol Smart rather than her that the law wanted to speak with.

Jason Ritchie had never been afraid of hard physical work. Whenever he was confused about other things in his life, he positively exulted in toil that would have put lesser men on their backs for a week. Whilst Anthony Watson was despatching his target into eternity in Birmingham, Ritchie was engaged in more honest and innocent work.

Even a little later, at five o'clock on a roasting Friday afternoon, when most people would have been happy to stop work and declare the weekend had commenced, Jason worked steadily on, feeling the sweat pouring in rivulets down his back and occasionally into his eyes, lifting the mixture of sand and cement and swinging the shovel with steady, rhythmic movements. This shifting of heavy loads with the wheelbarrow was how he had begun the day; this is how he had occupied himself for almost eight hours of it; this is how he would finish his working week. If it took him another hour, even two hours, to complete the job, then so be it.

He was completing the base for a double garage: undemanding work as far as the mental side of it went, but enough to test the strength and the stamina of anyone labouring alone. He was proud of the fact that he was working at the same pace as he had used at nine in the morning, after all these hours when the sun seemed to blaze ever more fiercely. Many men would have been content to stop after the initial preparation, to make two days' work or more out of this. But Jason had worked out his timetable and was sticking to it. It was a hard day, but not an unrealistic one, for a strong man in the prime of life. Jason was delighted to be demonstrating just that, to himself and to anyone else who cared to observe.

He had barrowed and spread the hardcore steadily through the morning, had it laid and roughly levelled within the wooden shuttering by one o'clock, allowing himself the full hour he needed for his sandwiches and his rest, so as to be strong enough to complete the day he had planned. When the ready-mixed cement had been delivered as he had ordered at two o'clock, he had been ready and eager to go.

The woman had looked through the window of the house and marvelled at his strength and his industry as the sweltering afternoon passed without any alteration in his steady, unrelenting application to the task. Her husband had come home half an hour ago, reluctantly offered his assistance, and departed indoors with relief when it had been politely rejected. The task was almost complete now. The last of the mixture had been put into the big rectangle formed by the shuttering and the surface of the concrete had been sprayed and smoothed. The place where the big lorry with the mixer behind it had dumped the two cubic metres of ready-mixed cement hours ago was being hosed down and the surface restored to normal.

A good job done. A week's labour completed. A satisfying as well as a lucrative day. When you worked for yourself, there were financial advantages as well as job satisfaction in working yourself towards exhaustion.

He was so intent on leaving the black tarmac of the driveway as immaculate as it had been when he had begun his operations that he did not hear the police vehicle ease itself softly to a halt in the road beyond the gates. The two occupants of the car stood and watched him silently for several seconds without him sensing their presence. Then a soft Herefordshire voice said, 'Good job, that. Might even employ you myself, when I can afford an extension to the house.'

Jason started in spite of himself. His concentration on the last stages of his task had been so complete that he had no idea that anyone was there until Bert Hook spoke. Now the detective sergeant smiled at him over the gate, ruddy-faced, unthreatening, approving of the thoroughness and quality of the work he was assessing. He said, 'You know me, Mr Ritchie. And this is Detective Sergeant Ruth David.'

A young, dark-haired woman, tall and willowy, observing him steadily through dark-green eyes, taking in the curves of his torso and his biceps, the tattoo of barbed

271

wire winding itself round his upper arm. She nodded at him with a small, quick smile when Hook mentioned her name; she seemed to Jason to be taking in far more about him than he wanted her to know. He tried desperately to refocus, to divert his attention away from his physical tiredness to the mental challenge presented to him by this unexpected arrival.

He said rather stupidly, 'I don't know how you knew I was here. I thought no one knew where I was working.'

'Mrs Holt told us we might find you here,' said Hook, not unpleasantly. 'We tried your mobile number, but it didn't appear to be in operation.'

'I switch it off when I'm working. Don't want calls disturbing me when I'm on a job like this. You have to work the ready-mixed stuff quickly, or it goes hard on you.' He gestured towards the immaculate rectangle of shining wet concrete, wondering why he was telling them this, aware that the phrases were nothing more than an innocent preamble to something much more demanding.

As if he shared that thought, Hook, speaking as affably as if this were a social call, said, 'Things to discuss, Mr Ritchie.'

Jason looked automatically towards the house, towards the people who had paid him to work so hard through this long, hot day. There was no sign there that anyone had realized that he had visitors. He said, 'I've almost finished here. I'll be with you in a minute.' He resumed his hosing of the drive-way, trying unsuccessfully to thrash his brain into furious action.

You didn't know just what they knew and what they didn't know. That was always one of the problems with the fuzz; you wanted to be quick on your feet, but you didn't know at this stage exactly what you were having to defend yourself against. He turned off the hose, dragged the big shovel for one last noisy scrape across the path, and rattled it against the pick and the rake, asserting the virtues of honest labour against whatever accusations they had brought here with them.

He was conscious of the woman sergeant's eyes watching his every move, totally unem-barrassed in her assessment of his move-ments. When he had got his tools together and put on his tee shirt, she spoke for the first time. 'Seems you've been economical with the truth, Mr Ritchie.'

'I don't know what you—'

'Telling us porkies. Never a good policy, that, with the police. I'm surprised you haven't learned that by now.'

A reference to his previous brushes with the law. He didn't like that. 'I don't know why you should think I've—'

'I can understand that you wouldn't want

us to know about some of the things you've been up to. I wouldn't want CID anywhere near them, if I were in your shoes. But you should understand that when you lie in a murder enquiry, you're asking for trouble. Lying invites us to examine your other activities.'

'Which is what some of our officers have been doing, since we spoke to you on Tuesday,' said Bert Hook, as amiably as ever.

'If I gave you a wrong impression, I can only apologize,' said Jason. He was conscious of how foreign this speech pattern was for him, how ponderous and artificial his evasions sounded in these phrases.

'More than a wrong impression, Mr Ritchie. You told Chief Superintendent Lambert a string of lies. Very stupid thing to do, with an eminent man like that.' DS Ruth David seemed to be getting deep satisfaction from telling him about his mistakes.

'Lies. I can't think what you mean.' Jason could envisage exactly what she meant, but he could think of nothing sensible to say. His automatic reaction was to deny the charge of lying, even when he knew that his denial could not possibly be successful.

DS David shook her head impatiently. 'You said you had not known Robin Durkin before the last few weeks, that you had had no dealings with him before the Saturday night on which he died. We now know that you were lying about that, quite deliberately and blatantly. Very interesting to us, that knowledge is, seeing that Mr Durkin is a murder victim.' She allowed herself a smile of satisfaction, whilst Jason strove to dismiss the idea that these assertions were just the preliminaries to putting him behind bars.

This time Jason said nothing, feeling belatedly that silence might be preferable to the useless denial which would constitute a further lie.

Bert Hook smiled at him, as if he was dealing with no more than a village boy who had been caught scrumping apples. 'You also gave us statements about your own conduct and way of life which were completely un-true. Misleading the police in the course of their enquiries, I'd call it.'

'I'm sure I didn't. You can see that I'm running a perfectly legitimate one-man business here. It's hard enough making an honest living these days, without being accused of things you haven't done.'

From the recesses of a pocket in his com-fortable trousers, Hook produced the note-book he had used when he and Lambert had spoken to Ritchie on Tuesday. 'Let me quote your own words to you, Jason, about your previous appearance in court on a GBH charge. "That po-faced woman judge told me to go away and keep my nose clean, and I've done just that. For five years, now." Not true, is it, lad?'

'You buggers never give up, do you? Once a villain always a villain, as far as you're concerned.' But Jason couldn't get any conviction into his voice. He suddenly felt the need to sit down on the low garden wall. He stared dumbly at the brightly coloured marigolds and geraniums and wished he was anywhere but here.

'It's the National Crime Squad who pursue the big boys in drugs, Jason. Along with paedophiles, arms traffickers and major financial criminals. You've been getting yourself into some very bad company, Jason.'

'I can't think what—'

'They employ fourteen hundred police officers and four hundred and fifty civilian personnel. Many of them work under cover, throughout England and Wales. They pick up all kinds of useful information.'

'This has nothing to do with me.' But Jason was aware that he was sounding increasingly desperate.

Ruth David permitted herself a sorrowful smile and a rueful shake of the head at the wrong-headedness of this young man, who was probably no more than six or seven years younger than her. 'We've been talking to the National Crime Squad about you since you spoke to us on Tuesday, Mr Ritchie. Well, not really about you personally: you're not important enough for that.

They're concerned with much bigger fish than you. But occasionally, because they're only interested in catching these bigger fish, a criminal tiddler is allowed to swim into their net and out of it again.' DS David paused, as if to savour her metaphor.

'You've got the wrong man. This has nothing to do with me.' But the denial was wooden, automatic, and all three of the trio in this strange little exchange beside the garden gates knew it.

Bert Hook was avuncular, almost kindly. 'Best admit it, Jason. Let's get on and get out of here, before we bring out everyone in the area.'

Jason had to resist the impulse to blurt out everything to this understanding man. He still didn't know how much they knew. 'What am I being accused of?'

Hook said softly, 'We now know that you have been dealing drugs, Jason. Dealing for Robin Durkin. You'd have been arrested long ago, if the National Crime Squad hadn't been more interested in the men making millions out of the trade.'

Jason lifted his hands, let them fall back helplessly on to his knees. He felt suddenly cold on this broiling day, felt the sweat cooling upon his exhausted body. 'I've been trying to get out.'

DS Ruth David nodded, acknowledging that the man's formal, hopeless resistance was broken. 'You're lucky there haven't already been charges for dealing. The best thing you can do now is to be absolutely frank with us. Then we'll leave it to Chief Superintendent Lambert to consider what to do about your previous lying, about your deliberate obstructing of the police in the course of their duties.'

'I've been trying to get out. I had a scare two years ago. Nearly got caught outside a pub in Gloucester. It's only a matter of time before you get caught, when you're dealing.'

That tallied with the information they had, which said that Ritchie had been much more active in the trade two years ago than now. 'So why didn't you? Why didn't you make the break?'

'Durkin. He said he could drop me right in it, without implicating himself. That a word in the right ear would land me in deep trouble. I wasn't sure whether he meant with the police or the drug barons. They don't believe in half measures, those people. You end up in the river with a bullet in the back of your head.'

It was true enough, though she doubted if Ritchie was important enough to warrant a killing. 'So you're saying that Robin Durkin had a hold over you.'

'He had a hold over lots of people, I think. He enjoyed having that sort of power.'

'You realize that this gives you an excellent

motive for murder,' Ruth David said.

Jason nodded dumbly. He couldn't see any other answer to that. He wanted to deny that he had killed Robin Durkin, but the words wouldn't come.

Bert Hook said almost apologetically, 'In the light of this new knowledge, I have to ask you again the question John Lambert put to you on Tuesday. We know that you left Saturday night's party at about one a.m. That has been confirmed by others. But did you leave Mrs Holt's house and go out again in the small hours of Sunday morning to meet with Robin Durkin?'

He shook his head miserably. 'No. Lisa will confirm that.'

'Mrs Holt admitted to us at Oldford Police Station this morning that she could not be certain of your movements from about one forty onwards. She said that she had had a lot to drink and fell quickly into a heavy sleep.'

It was like a blow in the stomach, a confirmation that his world was falling apart. He felt now that Lisa and he had been moving further away from each other all week, without either of them having the courage to put things into words. No doubt Lisa would have warned him that they were on to him, if he had not had his mobile switched off. He said hopelessly, 'I didn't go out again. I went to sleep beside Lisa.'

DS David said quietly, 'Then no doubt you are not able to tell us whether Mrs Holt left her house again that night.'

'She didn't.'

'Can you be sure of that?'

Jason's mind raced suddenly, when for minutes it had seemed clamped. They'd talked to Lisa, obviously. If what they had just said was true, she'd gone in voluntarily to the station to give them information. What on earth had she been saying to them? 'Of course I can't be sure of Lisa's movements, if I was asleep. When you work like this, you don't wake up easily.' He lifted his arms and gestured vaguely towards the shining rectangle of the garage base, as if the fierceness of his physical labour could somehow demonstrate his integrity. 'All I'm saying is that I'm sure in my own mind that Lisa Holt wouldn't creep out and kill Robin bloody Durkin. Why on earth should she do that?'

Lisa Holt had given them powerful reasons why she might have done it when she told them of how Durkin had wrecked her marriage and ruined her husband, but they weren't going into that with this man. Bert Hook said thoughtfully, 'You must be relieved that you can get on with your life, Jason. Get on with what you called "keeping your nose clean". That's another way of saying that you must be very pleased that Robin Durkin is dead.'

'Yes. I—'

'Did you kill him, Jason?'

'No.' He wanted to enlarge on the mono-syllable, to give them the words which wouldn't come to him to demonstrate his innocence.

'Then who did?'

'I don't know that either. There's no reason why I should, is there? That's your job, not mine.' He was proud of his belated flash of spirit.

DS David smiled at him, her oval face very pretty beneath the dark hair. Somehow that smile dropped Jason's heart towards his cement-streaked boots. 'It is indeed our job, Mr Ritchie. And sadly, we shall have to report back to CID that we have not been able to eliminate Jason Ritchie from our enquiries into the murder of Robin Durkin. Good afternoon to you. Please accept our apologies if we have disrupted your legitimate work.'

She turned back towards the police Mondeo. Bert Hook looked down at the exhaust-ed man sitting on the low garden wall. 'Make sure you don't deal again, Jason. Cut your-self off entirely from that trade, and it's possible that there won't be any charges against you.'

Jason was grateful to the burly DS for his concern, when he considered things later. But it was that other and greater charge of murder which preoccupied his thoughts as he drove wearily back to his caravan.

Carol Smart, well-rounded and attractive, did not look like a killer. But she felt very uncomfortable as the head teacher left her in her office with two senior policemen.

Lambert introduced the tall, dark-haired man she had not seen before as Detective Inspector Rushton. He seemed to be in his early thirties. He was a handsome man when he smiled, Carol decided. He did not smile very much. In fact, after the initial, automatic little response when they were introduced, Carol could not remember him smiling at all.

It was Rushton who now said, 'We need to speak to you rather urgently in connection with new information we now possess.'

'I'm only too willing to help you, of course.' It was bland and meaningless, but Carol could think of nothing better. She bit back the impulse to embroider it, to tell them that there was nothing of interest that an innocent person like herself could possibly have to tell them.

Lambert gave her a small, encouraging smile, but she was already conscious of his unswerving attention. He said, 'We now know a lot more about our murder victim, as you'd expect. Not all of it is very flattering to him.'

'I'd expect that, if you've been talking to lots of people.' Again she had to resist the desire to say much more, to release her tension with a diatribe against Robin Durkin. 'I told you about my affair with him when I came into the station on Wednesday, Superintendent. I don't think that particular liaison was flattering, either to him or to me.'

'It hasn't gone any further than the CID files. And it won't, unless it proves to have a bearing on the case.'

'Then what is it that you want to speak to me about?' An absurd, distracting reservation about ending sentences with prepositions assailed her. Perhaps that was an effect of being interviewed in a school.

'We now know for certain that Mr Durkin was involved in the supply of illegal drugs.'

'That doesn't surprise me.' It didn't surprise her, because she had known it for years. Carol could see no point in admitting that she knew as much as she did about the murdered man.

'He was also a blackmailer, Mrs Smart.'

'I guessed as much.'

'Were you one of his victims?'

'No. I told you when I spoke to you on Wednesday that he was a naturally secretive man, that he liked knowing about people's lapses and having a hold over them. But he never tried to get money from me. Perhaps he knew that I had nothing substantial to give to him.'

'Blackmail has different faces, all of them ugly. Let's accept that Durkin didn't demand money from you. Did he threaten that he would reveal the details of your affair with him to others?'

Carol had planned to deny this. Now she suddenly knew that that would not be a good plan with these perceptive interrogators watching her so closely. Yet she couldn't bring herself to admit directly that Durkin had been threatening her. 'I wasn't happy when I found that Robin Durkin was to be a close neighbour.'

'You felt it was only a matter of time before he told your husband about your affair with him.'

He didn't allow evasions, this Lambert. She suddenly hated his calm and clear-sighted vision, the way he delivered this idea to her as a statement, not a question. 'Rob enjoyed having secrets, enjoyed having people in his power.'

'And someone felt that the only way to escape from this was to get rid of him once and for all. Were you that person, Mrs Smart?'

She denied it, and they let her go. But as they drove away from the school, all three of the people who had been in that room knew that the important question was still to be answered.

Twenty

Bert Hook was ready to leave the station when the desk sergeant buzzed him to say that there was a man who wanted to speak to someone connected with the Robin Durkin murder case.

'I told him that the governor and DI Rushton had buggered off early as it's Friday. That you were the nearest thing to top brass we had available.' The desk sergeant was the public face of Oldford Police Station, wearing uniform and engaging in the long-established ritual of denigrating CID. He had known Bert Hook for nearly twenty years, since they had been coppers together on the beat.

'They've buggered off all right. Beaten it to Birmingham.' Bert enjoyed a bit of alliteration. 'To interview a contract killer. Still be working long after you're at home enjoying your conjugals, Mike.' He sighed. 'Who is this bloke and what does he want?'

'Name of Ronald Lennox. And he won't say what he wants: not to a humble plod like me. Clever-looking sod; also a prat, if you

285

ask me. But I'm biased, of course. I'll bring the bugger through to the purer air of CID and be rid of him.'

Ron Lennox looked round him curiously as he was ushered into the almost deserted CID section, taking in all he could of his surroundings, making sure that this unimaginative detective sergeant knew that being in a police station was a novelty for him. 'I really wanted to speak to Chief Superintendent Lambert,' he said, not attempting to conceal his disappointment.

'Superintendent Lambert is pursuing another strand of the investigation this evening. Whatever you have to tell me will be recorded and relayed to him. Always assuming that it is judged to have relevance to the case.'

Not only have I not got the organ-grinder, but the monkey is attempting to be obstreperous, thought Ron. He said loftily, 'Perhaps I should come back when the man in charge of the case has time to speak to me.'

'I don't think you should do that, sir. There may be an urgent need for us to hear what you have to say. And I shouldn't like a delay to result in charges of withholding information.'

Uppity sod! Ron had expected them to be grateful for his cooperation, not to find himself threatened like this by a man who looked as if he should be chasing kids trespassing. He said loftily, 'You said I should come forward if I had any further thoughts about Robin Durkin. I must tell you that I come to bury him, not to praise him, though.' He glanced at the stolid figure opposite him and decided he had better explain his literary reference. 'Brutus talking about Julius Caesar, Detective Sergeant Hook. Of course, I'm hoping I shan't come to a sticky end, as Brutus did.' Ron's little cackle of laughter rang oddly round the large, low-ceilinged, almost deserted area. His expression said that he doubted whether this pedestrian plod would have any idea what he was talking about.

Hook looked at him steadily for a moment. He did not permit himself a smile as he said, 'Not Brutus but Mark Antony, sir, if you remember. Not the noblest Roman of them all. Antony came to a different but equally sticky end, I think. But he enjoyed himself a little in the intervening years, I believe. Indulged himself in the pleasures of the flesh in Egypt, if I remember things correctly' Bert ignored the pleasing effect created by the dropping jaw in the thin face opposite him and glanced pointedly at his watch. 'What is it that you wish to communicate to us, sir?'

This wasn't going according to plan. Ron said stiffly, 'It was your chief superintendent who instructed me very clearly that I should communicate with you if I could offer any further information on the activities of Robin Durkin. That is why I am here. It wasn't an easy decision for me to take. I don't like implicating other people in the investigation of a serious crime.'

Hook nodded. 'Murder, sir. The most serious crime of all. Murder most foul, as the gloomy Dane's father has it. So you had better abandon your scruples.'

Ron Lennox was seriously ruffled to be out-quoted by this blockish-looking but unexpectedly knowledgeable man. He said sullenly, 'Mr Lambert said that we should go on thinking about the case. I've done so and come up with some new ideas.'

'Admirable, sir. If only every member of the public had such a conscience.'

Ron glared at him suspiciously, but could detect no sign of irony in the stolid features. 'Yes. Well, you may remember that we talked about Durkin's activities in the drug trade.'

'Vividly, sir.'

'I've been thinking about it. I told you that I was pretty sure that he had recruited some of the people from my school to work for him. Illegally, I mean, not in his garage. People who were younger than he was. This was quite a while after he'd left school himself, when he had established himself and was looking for pushers. I believe that is what you call them.'

'What everyone calls them, sir.' Including

you, you supercilious buffer. 'No doubt you now feel able to give me names.'

'One name, Detective Sergeant Hook. Not several. And I should emphasize that I have no definite proof of this theory to offer you. You must understand that—'

'Let's have the name, sir.' Hook had pen poised over the pad in front of him.

'It's young Jason Ritchie. Well, young to me. They always seem young, when you've taught them as boys. The man who has been cohabiting with young Mrs Holt in Gurney Close.'

Lennox's lips had set in a thin line of disapproval. Hook wondered uncharitably how much jealousy there was behind that. He said patiently, 'For what it's worth, sir, it seems that you are right. Mr Ritchie has already admitted to being employed by Durkin as a pusher of illegal drugs. It was some years ago, mind.'

'But it gives him a motive doesn't it? A strong motive.' For a man who had claimed to be diffident about involving others in the case, Lennox was suddenly very anxious to do so. He leaned forward eagerly. 'And Durkin was a blackmailer, remember. We discussed this when we spoke on Wednesday.'

'I do remember, yes, sir.'

'Well, he had a permanent hold over young Ritchie, didn't he? He could have shopped him at any time by revealing the details of his involvement in pushing illegal drugs.'

Bert forbore to point out that Lennox seemed to be doing a pretty good 'shopping' job himself. 'But could he have done that without implicating himself, Mr Lennox? Wouldn't his own much more important role in the trade have been exposed, if he had chosen to expose Jason Ritchie?'

For a moment, Lennox looked cast down. Then the thin, too-mobile features brightened with mischief. 'But this was years ago, as you said yourself. I'm sure that Durkin could have dropped the details about Ritchie's involvement at that time easily enough, without involving himself.'

Bert Hook didn't tell him that less than an hour ago he'd been thinking exactly that himself. He said, 'Your thoughts on this are most welcome, of course, sir. Are there other names you have to offer us? Other people you think might have been involved with Durkin, either as drug pushers or blackmail victims?'

'No. I just thought you'd want to know this.'

'Of course we do, sir.' Hook was at his most blankly polite.

'I'm only doing my duty as a citizen, you know.'

'Of course, sir. Would that everyone took their responsibilities so seriously.'

Lennox withdrew, awkwardly and gracelessly. Bert was left wondering exactly how useful his visit had been.

Half an hour later, Hook was at home and determined to switch off from the case.

The atmosphere in the house was different. Eleanor and he felt almost back to being a normal couple. They looked at the weeds springing up in the small, normally impeccable front garden of their semi-detached house; even had time to stand for a minute and consider how the petunias had burst into full flower since they had last had time to look at them.

They chatted unhurriedly as Bert drove through the rich green countryside of high summer, following the course of the Wye towards the ancient city of Hereford. The conversation flowed easily enough until they reached the outskirts of the town. It was only when they got within a mile of the hospital that Eleanor Hook felt the tension rising again within her, and heard her conversation degenerating into a series of terse, monosyllabic replies to her husband's well-meaning questions.

Bert felt the same disquiet stirring within him. He put his hand on his wife's much smaller one after he had parked the car under the shadow of the high wall of the hospital. 'It'll be all right, you know, Ellie-

Belly.' He couldn't remember when he had last used this childish form of address to her: not since they were newly married, he reckoned. 'They told us yesterday that the worst was over, that he was on the mend. And they're pretty cautious, you know, about things like that, in hospitals.'

'I know,' was all Eleanor said. She thought that her sensible husband was probably right and wanted to tell him that she was grateful for his thoughts, but she didn't feel that she could trust herself with more words. There was a queue for the lift and Bert eventually strode impatiently to the stairs and began to climb the three floors to the children's ward. In that moment, she realized that he was as anxious for reassurance as she was.

There was quite a lot of noise in the ward. That in itself was a shock, after the church-like silence in which she had sat for hours beside her son's bed during the last few days. And Luke's bed was empty, with the sheet thrown back untidily. Eleanor looked around apprehensively for a nurse.

'Hi Mum! Hi Dad!' He appeared from behind other children at the far end of the ward, a white-faced, pitifully thin, but very much alive figure, in a dressing gown which seemed to have crept up his calves since they had last seen him in it. 'I've had a cheese sandwich. And some ice cream. You going to ask them when I can come home? They won't tell me anything.'

Eleanor was fighting back tears of happiness, struggling so hard for control that she could say nothing. It was Bert Hook who had to say, 'Steady on, son! You've been pretty ill, you know.'

'I know. Susie told me they were worried I might die at one time.' He grinned, trying hard to look modest in the face of this celebrity status.

'And who's Susie?' Eleanor managed to speak at last.

'She's the nurse who's my friend, Mum. We have laughs together, when she's taking my pulse and my temperature and things like that.'

Eleanor diagnosed an early case of hospital infatuation. She was so consumed with delight at this animated son that she jumped a little when a voice at her side said, 'He's doing well, isn't he?' and she turned to meet a smiling, curvaceous nurse, who looked impossibly young in her uniform and proved to be the favoured Susie. 'He'll need to get back into bed now and control his excitement. Luke doesn't realize that he needs to build up his strength again.'

Luke climbed into bed immediately and lay down with a happy smile. 'I wish he was as amenable to orders as that at home!' said Eleanor.

'He's a good lad, our Luke,' said Susie in a

northern accent the parents could not quite pin down. 'But he mustn't try to go too far too fast, or he'll have me to contend with.'

Luke snuggled down and smiled blissfully, a willing subject to this princess of the wards. But she was right: there was something febrile about his excitement, something brittle still in his recovery. In two minutes his eyelids fluttered, then shut. Sixty seconds later, he was fast asleep, despite the bustle of noise and movement from parents and children in the busy ward.

'I think I should leave him now. He's ready to sleep the clock round,' said Susie, who had reappeared beside them after attending to a patient several beds away. 'You should probably try to do the same yourselves, you know, after what you've been through this week.'

She's half my age and mothering me, thought Eleanor Hook, without a crumb of resentment. They agreed with Nurse Susie, thanked her for her efforts, and left the ward, with a final fond look from the doorway at their sleeping child.

They congratulated each other breathlessly in the car park outside, agreed with each other that the National Health Service was still a wonderful thing whenever there was a real emergency. Not many words then passed between them in the car on the way home. But now it was the easy, companionable silence of content. People who were at ease with each other and the world at large did not need words to express their delight in life.

They were almost home when Bert said, 'He's growing taller, isn't he? I don't think that it's just because he's thin and weedy after the illness.' They exchanged a few more meaningless phrases. Then, as the familiar house came into view, Bert smiled shyly and said, 'I think he'll need a new cricket bat by the time the season starts next year.'

It was the first time in five days that either of them had dared to consider a future for their son.

Watson knew they were watching him, studying his every move. He'd dealt with the police in many different countries, plenty of them less controlled and less predictable than those in Britain. He knew that here it did not really matter how things looked until they had evidence. The important thing was what you said in answer to their probings. Anthony David Watson would be very careful about what he said to these two senior representatives of the law.

The older and more senior one looked unhurriedly round the neat, rather sterile décor of the luxury flat, taking in the absence of photographs, of paintings, of anything which would give this man an identity and a personality. Watson had switched off the stainless steel standard lamp and put on the strong central light of the room when he led them into it, so that Lambert and Rushton were sitting with their faces powerfully illuminated. They were in comfortable chairs, but it felt almost like the interview room situation with which they were familiar, with them the subjects of interrogation rather than the man they had come to see.

Lambert hastened to correct that. 'We are conducting an investigation into the murder of Mr Robin Durkin.'

Watson showed not a vestige of emotion. He did not register with even a flicker of facial movement whether he knew the name. Nor did he show to them the exultation and relief he felt in the knowledge that this was not going to be about his actions earlier in the day. The local plods were obviously baffled by the man shot dead through the head outside the club he owned in Birmingham; give it another forty-eight hours, and he'd be confident that they wouldn't even come looking for him. He said calmly to these country coppers from eighty miles away, 'You're wasting your time here, then,' and gave them one of his empty, confident smiles.

Lambert did not smile back at him. His grey, unblinking eyes continued to study the unrevealing figure opposite him. He showed neither irritation nor the revulsion he always felt pulsing within him when he confronted a contract killer. 'We know you murder for a living. We know that you were in the area at the time, Mr Watson.'

His slight, unstressed inflection of distaste turned his use of the title into an insult. Watson gave him a small, calculated shrug. 'Free country, Mr Lambert.' He echoed the superintendent's slight stress on the title, enjoying the little fencing game they had embarked upon. 'Or so they tell me. I have my doubts, nowadays. Policemen seem to be everywhere except where they're needed. Even in the homes of innocent citizens at eight o'clock on a Friday night.'

DI Rushton was more nettled by the man than his chief appeared to be. He said sternly, 'Mr Durkin was killed in the early hours of last Sunday morning. You were in the area at the time.'

There was no need to deny it. Watson said, 'And so were thousands of other innocent citizens. I hope you're not planning to harass all of them.'

'Not all of them are contract killers. Not all of them had a commission to eliminate Mr Durkin.'

Watson's inscrutability was his friend again. This was an uncompromising accusation, and he wondered exactly how much they did know, what precisely it was that had brought them to his home at this hour on a Friday night. But he showed not even a hint of alarm.

He said, 'Your information is false, I'm afraid, Inspector Rushton.' It threw the pigs sometimes when you remembered their ranks and their names. It showed them how calm you were, when they wanted you to panic. 'I certainly had no such commission. The idea that anyone would pay me to kill people is quite absurd. I am an innocent accountant. Some would say that I belong to a profession dedicated to the boring and mundane aspects of life. We certainly do not deal with anything as melodramatic as murder.'

It was a statement he had used before, but he delivered it well, with just that slight hint of contempt to underline the irony. It ruffled Rushton, who was used to dealing with rougher and less confident criminals than this man. Like an over-eager dog, the DI made the mistake of following up the bone of diversion which Watson had thrown for him. 'What are your qualifications in accountancy?'

'Not your business, as far as I'm aware. But I know enough to get by. I expect it's a phrase privileged men like you despise, Inspector, but you could say I've learned in the university of life.'

'In other words, you haven't got proper

qualifications.' Rushton, trying to sound triumphant, emerged as merely petty.

Watson smiled sardonically, enjoying watching this handsome young police high-flier losing his composure. 'People seem prepared to employ me.'

It was Lambert who said sharply, 'But not always as an accountant. We know that. What were you doing in the Ross-on-Wye area on the night of Saturday the ninth of July?'

'Visiting friends.' Watson was beginning to enjoy this. He told himself sharply that he had better be careful: you couldn't indulge in enjoyment with the fuzz. You were one man against a big organization and you had much better not forget that.

'We'd better have their names.' Rushton, anxious to reassert himself, produced a notebook with a disbelieving sneer.

'I don't think I'll give you names. I'm under no obligation to answer your questions, as you know. Unless you propose to charge me with any offence, in which case I'll let my brief tell me what I should answer.'

'You could be charged with hindering the police in the course of their enquiries.'

Another mistake. Watson gave the younger man a bland, mirthless smile. 'Not a charge that's brought very often, that, is it? I think I might take a chance on it. Especially as I've nothing useful to tell you.'

Chris Rushton wanted to glance sideways at Lambert, to search for advice on how to play this. But he didn't do so: that would have been a sign of weakness. Chris didn't have the unthinking, complementary relationship with the chief which DS Bert Hook enjoyed, despite his superior rank; not for the first time, he found himself unexpectedly envying that unremarkable-looking man.

DI Rushton decided that he needed to play his trump card. 'Money was paid into your bank account in connection with this visit to Herefordshire.'

For the first time since they had begun this, Watson felt a little shaft of fear. That was a necessary thing, though, in this business, a safety-mechanism you had to have. Like pain, fear gave you a warning, reminded you that you had to give your full attention to what you were about. He broadened his smile, looked hard into the almost-unlined, intense face opposite him. 'Invasion of privacy, I'd call that. That's if I choose to believe you. What right have you to go prying into my affairs?'

Lambert, sensing uncertainty for the first time in this coldly alert man, came in quickly. 'We know about the account you use for these transactions. There was a payment of four thousand pounds into that account, five days before you ventured south for the weekend. There was a further payment of eight thousand pounds, on Wednesday last.'

How the hell had they discovered that? He was tired of telling everyone who used him that it didn't pay to underestimate these people. The professional thing was never to underrate your enemy, however much on top of him you might feel. But some of these gangsters were amateurs: they were making big money, while their luck held, but their carelessness would catch them out, sooner or later. They paid well, but they could put you in danger when they got too confident. You had to watch your back, whoever you worked for.

Watson forced all the assurance he could muster into his voice as he said stuffily, 'You've no right to nose your way into people's financial affairs. And those in charge of personal finances should not give away information.'

'So change your banker.' Lambert let his antipathy for the man and his trade snap out for the first time in the contemptuous phrase. He noticed that Watson had not denied the facts they had thrown at him. 'And in the meantime, tell us how you came by this money.'

'Payment for past services rendered. Accountancy services.'

'In two instalments?'

'Not everyone can muster large sums at short notice. Not everyone has the salary of a chief superintendent.' But behind the insults, his brain was working fast, asking how much more they knew, what they were going to come up with next.

Now it was Lambert who indulged in the mirthless smile, as if wishing to mirror and return this man's derision in the earlier part of the interview. 'Our information is that you are unusual among contract killers, in that you do not operate upon a fifty-fifty payment basis. That you operate on a one third in advance, two thirds on completion basis. Very trusting of you, when you're dealing with the criminals who use your services. No doubt you're very confident that you can deliver.'

Watson almost made the mistake of accepting the compliment, almost acceded to the idea that this was indeed a mark of his competence. But he thought before he spoke, as always, and protected himself from such a gaffe. 'You seem to be very well informed. I would be quite impressed, if I did not know that this was an elaborate fiction.'

'You deny the facts of your bank account?'

'I neither confirm nor deny them, Chief Superintendent Lambert. I have no need to do so, as an innocent citizen.'

'So you're refusing to tell us the real reason for your visit to Herefordshire last weekend, and also refusing to explain the coincidence of the arrival of these large sums in your bank account.'

'Of course I am. Furthermore, as an innocent citizen, I resent your unwarranted intrusion into my private affairs.'

Watson was striving hard to conceal from them how shaken he felt by the extent of their information. They knew he had been commissioned to kill Durkin. They knew both his movements and the details of the payments he had received. It was something he had not anticipated and had never had to contend with before, but you put yourself in the hands of other people when you accepted work for them. He told himself firmly that the big thing was that they seemed to know nothing about this afternoon's incident, that he was in the clear for that cold and ruthless killing amidst the grimy buildings of the sweltering city.

In the last analysis, he did not fear their questioning about this week-old killing in that very different setting by the banks of the Wye. It was better to keep their attention on that. He said as casually as he could, 'How did this man in Herefordshire, this Durkin fellow, die?'

Lambert looked at him steadily for two long seconds. 'I think you already know that. He was garrotted with a piece of cable, taken from behind and killed in less than half a minute.'

'Not the method I'd have used. I was a

fighting soldier, as you no doubt know. In the entirely hypothetical event of my killing a man, it would have been with a rifle or a pistol. Firearms are what I'm used to: I'm sure your diligent researchers have discovered that for you. I should say what I *was* used to, in the increasingly distant days when I lived the military life.'

'You're a professional killer. Offered a means of murder which was swift and silent, you'd have taken it.'

'But I didn't. That's the only flaw in the beautiful little scenario you've constructed for yourselves. And there's not a court in the land which would accept that I did.'

Lambert stood up. 'Not yet, perhaps. But one of the virtues of the police machine is persistence. Unlike you, we have to work within the law. It takes us longer to achieve our ends, but we get there in the end. When dangerous men are uncooperative, we become more determined to see justice served.'

They left without the false courtesies of farewells on either side. During what remained of his evening, Watson spent much time reviewing his actions of the previous weekend, wondering where the police information had come from. Someone had known of his presence in Herefordshire last Saturday and Sunday; someone had followed most of his movements on those days.

It would be ironic if he got away with what he had done this afternoon, and ended up in court for a murder he had not committed.

Twenty-One

Andy Lennox quite enjoyed hard physical labour. When you were a student, you took whatever work you could get during the summer holidays: there was plenty of competition for it nowadays. Stacking shelves in supermarkets wasn't glamorous, but it paid surprisingly well, if you didn't mind unsocial hours. At the end of an academic year when he had run up more debt than he had planned, he was glad to take all the hours they offered him, within reason.

It kept you independent, too; it reminded Mum and Dad that you were an adult now, able to fend for yourself and make your own decisions. Andy was their only child, the son produced when Ron Lennox was forty-two and Rosemary was forty-one. They had been delighted, of course. For twenty years now, they had doted on him and been very good to him, but their love could sometimes be suffocating, for a young man anxious to discover his own paths through life. Andy sometimes wondered what it would be like to be part of a large family, or to have parents twenty years younger than his sensible and indulgent ones.

When your dad was a teacher and your mum a pillar of the local community, it made you all the more anxious to kick over the establishment traces and fend for yourself. Andy was pleased to have found this job on his doorstep in Cambridge, so that he hadn't had to move from his university digs. He had explored various methods of making money during his time as a student, and some of them had been very definite mistakes. But that was all part of the learning process, he told himself firmly, as he lifted the final carton of baked beans on to his trolley and pushed it carefully into the almost deserted store.

It was still only seven thirty-five. Andy Lennox liked this time of the day, before the floor became thronged with shoppers and the strains of replenishing the larders and fridges of the city began to tell on the tempers of the customers. It was a little cooler this morning, with a light breeze from the west. The forecast had said that the heat wave was almost at an end. He wouldn't be sorry about that. The sun was all very well when you were lounging with girls on the lawns of the ancient university after exams, but when you were involved in work like this, it was better to have it cooler.

He had been working for an hour and a half already. He found the steady, physically demanding work of lifting and stacking a welcome change from being a student in what all his tutors told him confidently was the greatest university in the world. You developed a rhythm, and you didn't have to tax your brain. After a year when your brain and the way you used it had been all that seemed to matter, manual work was a positive relief.

And the news of that death last week had been a huge, unexpected bonus.

There was little room for differences of opinion about how you stacked supermarket shelves. You noted where the deficiencies were on the shelves as the public denuded them, went to the stores and collected the tins and the packets which would replenish them. When you were a strong young man of six feet, with broad shoulders and a body full of energy anxious for outlets, you didn't need to skive. And the supervisors soon got to know the skivers and the willing workers. You became quite popular with the powers that be when you were reliable.

He'd get time and a half for this stint today, double time for the five hours he'd just agreed to take on for the morrow. Quite a lucrative return on a weekend he would otherwise have wasted. After the very different demands of revision and exams, it was a relief to have your working day planned for you by someone else. Having a supervisor who told you exactly how many packets of cereal were required was a welcome change from the challenges set for him last week by the white-haired don who had discussed his dissertation on Adam Smith. Next year, his Economics degree would get him on to the first rungs of the executive ladder. In the meantime, Andy Lennox was very content to remind himself how the other half lived.

Andy saw the police car come into the car park, wondered idly which of the thin stream of customers had been unfortunate enough to excite the attention of the law. As he trundled his heavily-laden truck towards the spot where he would unload his unremarkable cargo, he noticed the two uniformed officers, who looked no older than he was, going into the supervisor's office. The management had got rid of one of the temporary workers for pilfering last week, but he didn't think the store had reported the woman to the police.

He was surprised when the two uniformed figures came towards him, even more surprised when the woman officer said to him, 'Are you Andrew Edward Lennox?'

Andy said, 'I am indeed,' and smiled at her, to show how unthreatened he felt.

It was the fresh-faced young man beside her who said importantly, 'We need to ask you some questions, sir. In connection with the investigation of a serious crime in Herefordshire.'

A hundred and fifty miles away from where Andy Lennox laboured in the supermarket store, the mother whose love he found it so difficult to cope with had problems of her own.

Rosemary Lennox was renowned for her effectiveness. Members of half a dozen local committees could testify to that. Only this week, she had been instrumental in saving her local branch library, after it had been threatened with closure by a local authority intent upon economies. She was a doughty fighter, a polite woman who could be unexpectedly feisty and determined when a cause excited her.

There was nothing subtle or devious about her methods. Her natural instinct was to be straightforward and honest. Subterfuges were not her natural method: Rosemary preferred to state her arguments forcibly and use the logic of them to take on the opposition face to face. It was a strategy which had worked well for her over the years: there were not many occasions when she had failed to deliver.

But her natural integrity meant that she

was not at all happy with the tactics she was having to employ today. It was not straight-forward, this. She knew it was necessary, but it involved secrecy, deceit, even dishonesty, which were wholly foreign to her nature.

Rosemary waited until she had the house to herself. Ron eventually went off to the gardening club hut to buy his fertilizers and sprays at members' rates. Before he went, he discussed with her exactly what they should buy, what they would need to accelerate the translation of the refuse from their back garden into useful compost, exactly how much lime she thought they should apply to the thick clay of their new front garden this year. Rosemary tried to be patient, to respond to his queries with interest and her usual logic, but she ended up wanting to scream at him to make his own decisions and get out of the house.

She told herself that it wasn't the first time she had lost her patience with this hair-splitting perfectionist of a husband, and that it no doubt would not be the last. But a small voice at the back of Rosemary Lennox's brain kept insisting that the issue here was far more important than any involved in the previous thirty-seven years of their marriage.

Ron was gone, at last. She watched his car until it disappeared from Gurney Close, took a deep breath, and made herself climb the stairs deliberately, rather than race up

310

them two at a time as she felt inclined to do. She gathered things from the drawer where she had hidden them and stowed them swiftly into the black, anonymous dustbin bag, making sure that nothing went in which could identify the source of this package. No more than five minutes after Ronald Lennox had left the close, his wife's black Fiesta followed more swiftly after him.

John Lambert was working hard in his very different and well-established garden, anxious to do as much as he could before the sun rose too high in the sky. The soil was very dry, but there were signs of a change in the weather after the hot, dry spell. The blue sky was still unstreaked with cloud, but there was a cooling breeze from the west and a forecast that there would be rain coming in from the Atlantic later in the day.

Christine Lambert glanced down the garden from the kitchen window, viewing her husband's labours with a wife's experienced eye. It told her that he was working hard and methodically, making a deliberate effort to banish thoughts of the case he was working on and the events of the previous evening. In his first, intense years in CID, when detection had become an obsession and John had shut her out of his working world completely, their marriage had almost been wrecked. The union which everyone nowadays regarded as so secure had almost foundered. The police service was an occupation which saw many relationships washed on to the rocks; those who now saw the Lamberts' marriage as a model for others would have been amazed to hear of the problems they had fought through in those times.

In those days, John had told her nothing of what went on, had preserved the secrets of his working life in an almost monk-like mystery, as if his efficiency would be damaged by any whisper of his activities to a wife. The children had kept them together, but only just. Now those unconscious bonds were adults themselves, with toddlers and cares of their own.

Christine looked at her husband's sinewy arms beneath the short-sleeved shirt as he reached out for his mid-morning cup of coffee in the conservatory. She said, 'Caroline's coming over tomorrow – bringing the children.'

He nodded. 'I should be here. Unless something comes up in this Durkin murder case.'

She smiled. It was as though once his daughter had been introduced, he could mention the case on which he was engaged. But that was probably just her imagination, a hangover from their troubles of years ago. She said, 'You were late back last night. And very tired.'

He smiled, acknowledging the marital diplomacy; Christine was really saying that he hadn't had a word for the cat when he had arrived home in the last light of the long summer day. 'The traffic was heavy on the M5 on the way back from Birmingham. But I was enraged rather than exhausted, if you really want to know. Contract killers have that effect on me. I usually feel they're laughing at me, without my being able to do anything about it.'

He picked up a ginger biscuit and bit into it with a savage energy, feeling resentment dropping upon him with the recollection of Anthony David Watson's cool insolence on the previous evening. 'Chris Rushton was as frustrated as I was – quite rattled by the man, in fact. But he handles it better afterwards than I do, throws it off more quickly. Chris doesn't take it home with him as I do.'

They were both silent for a moment, with John thinking of his deficiencies as a husband and Christine speculating on the lonely life the divorced Chris Rushton went back to in his bachelor flat. She said tentatively, still feeling she was on dangerous ground, 'Is he your killer then, this hitman you went to see?'

John Lambert took an unhurried pull at his coffee, forcing himself to talk, to allow her into the specialized field of his work. Even now, when he was determined to do that, he was conscious of having to make a deliberate effort. 'No, I don't think he is, as a matter of fact. He was playing games with us last night, and I think he's too professional a killer to indulge in things like that if he'd really killed Durkin. We know that he was in this area at the time of the death. I think it's quite possible that he was commissioned to kill Durkin, but that someone else got there before him. The victim was certainly a man not short of enemies.'

She refilled his cup and tried not to sound too eager. 'So let's hear about the other candidates.'

He smiled. They both knew what was going on here, knew that he was being tested. But they both knew also that their tensions over stuff like this were far behind them, that whether or not he revealed his thinking to her now was not crucial to their relationship any more. He was deliberately low key as he said, 'The wife's always a suspect, of course. Just remember that when you plan to dispatch me. This one had used scissors on a previous partner. Ally Durkin also had ample reason to wish her man in hell. He'd pressurized her into an abortion, at the same time as he was supporting a child he'd fathered by another woman. He'd also had an affair ten years earlier with a woman who had just moved into the house beside them: we're still not sure whether his wife knew about that or not.'

'He sounds a real charmer.'

'You haven't heard the half of it. He was involved in illegal drugs in quite a big way. We've found getting on for a million pounds in accounts deriving from that. He was probably getting a bit too big for his boots and treading on the toes of the real barons of the drug trade.' Lambert found himself rattling off the clichés, as he strove against his nature to discuss this with Christine.

'Hence the contract killer.'

'We think so. But, as I said, my own feeling is that it wasn't the hired man who took him out. In some respects, it would be simpler for us if it had been.'

'So who else is involved, then, apart from the wife?' Absurdly, Christine found herself avoiding the phrase 'in the frame', since that seemed to her a police expression, and thus off limits for her.

'There's the woman who organized the party at which he was killed.'

'And thus set up the situation where he died.' Christine said it slowly, unconsciously emphasizing her role as an amateur looking in on this from the outside.

'Yes. Rosemary Lennox is a pillar of the local community. But we questioned her son this morning and found that Durkin had recruited him as a pusher in the drugs' trade.

The parents must have known about it, but neither of them has mentioned it to us. The boy's a student, about to enter his final year at Cambridge. The Drugs Squad are satisfied that he only worked for Durkin for a short time. But he had a lot to lose if Durkin had chosen to drop the information that he'd been involved.'

'And was he the sort of man to do that?'

'He certainly was. Durkin was a black-mailer at the same time as he was developing a drugs empire. And like a lot of black-mailers, he enjoyed having a hold over people as much as or even more than the money it brought him. So Rosemary Lennox probably wasn't paying money to Durkin, but as the boy's mother she must certainly have been aware of the damage he could do to her only son whenever he chose to. Dur-kin might even have taunted her with that thought.'

'She somehow doesn't sound like a likely candidate for murder.'

'No. Rosemary Lennox is a woman in her early sixties, with an unblemished reputation as an unpaid force for good in a lot of local enterprises. But people become desperate and act out of character when blackmailers threaten them. And women do extraordinary things when they're seeking to protect their children.'

Christine smiled, preferring not to recall

some of the embarrassing things she'd done in her time to defend her daughters against a hostile world. 'Presumably the lady has a husband?'

'She does indeed. A man who is amusing and irritating by turns. Ronald Lennox has just retired as a teacher. He taught Robin Durkin at the comprehensive and didn't like him, even then. He initially gave us the impression that Durkin was little more than a high-spirited, mischievous lad who had to be controlled. But I thought at the time that his antipathy went further than that, and he's now admitted it. Lennox is the man who first told us about both Durkin's reputation as a blackmailer and his first steps into supplying illegal drugs. He's rather drip-fed us the information over the last few days. Lennox is both a pedant and a gossip: rather a ridiculous figure in many respects. But I'm certain his dislike of Durkin runs deeper than he cares to admit. And I'm sure he's the kind of man who will be immensely proud of his son's being at Cambridge. He might be prepared to go to extraordinary lengths to preserve it.'

'What a can of worms you've opened in a quiet close of new houses!'

'Oh, there's more to come yet. Much more! I mentioned that Durkin's mistress of ten years ago, Carol Smart, had moved into the close beside him. Her own husband is a man who apparently finds it difficult to keep his wedding tackle in his trousers for very long, but Carol seems genuinely, touchingly, fond of him. The Smarts have daughters of eighteen and twenty, both working in Yorkshire. Carol was quite desperate that neither they nor Phil Smart should find out anything about her affair with Robin Durkin.'

'So she might have shut him up for good.'

'It's possible. Durkin was enjoying the secret, and it's difficult to think that a man like him wouldn't have used it to hurt someone, sooner or later.'

'What about this woman's husband?'

'Phil Smart? He's a serial philanderer who yet seems genuinely fond of his wife, as she does of him. He was also one of Durkin's blackmail victims. He'd done something irregular at work years ago – transferred some sales figures to himself from someone who'd left the firm – and Durkin found out about it. Durkin had screwed a certain amount of money from this knowledge, but by the time of his death he seems to have preferred just to taunt Smart with the knowledge that he could expose and disgrace him at any time.'

'This Phil Smart sounds like a man desperate enough to commit murder.' To Christine Lambert, he sounded the most likely suspect so far, but she was too intelligent a woman to voice the thought.

Lambert smiled grimly. 'So do a couple of other people. There's a very personable divorcee of thirty-nine in the first house in the close. Lisa Holt, a woman whose then husband was ruined by Robin Durkin, according to her, a process which also finished what she claims had been a happy marriage.'

'Does she have children?'

'A son of nine. She has also recently acquired a toy boy. I don't know how serious their relationship is, but he was close enough to her to be invited as her partner to the party which was the prelude to Robin Durkin's death. He's a gardener and small builder. We also know now that he was involved in dealing drugs for Durkin a few years ago. He concealed it at first – naturally enough, as it could lead to criminal charges.'

'What sort of a man is he?'

Lambert paused, striving to be objective. 'Jason Ritchie is tough. And no angel: you can see how he got involved with Durkin in some pretty unsavoury stuff a few years ago. He also has a conviction for Grievous Bodily Harm, which could easily have been manslaughter or even murder, if the cards had fallen differently and he'd done more damage with the knife he was carrying. He claims he'd have been kicked to death in a brawl outside a pub if he hadn't drawn the knife in self-defence. He seems to have kept out of trouble over the last few years, but he clearly has a capacity for violence. He's also more intelligent than this background would suggest.'

Christine Lambert's innate feeling for the underdog had her wishing fervently that this young man, who sounded to her both an interesting character and the police favourite for this crime, hadn't committed the murder. The lad didn't seem to have a lot going for him amongst these largely middle-class people. She couldn't dismiss the thought that if an older woman hadn't taken him into her bed, Jason Ritchie wouldn't have been a leading suspect in this case at all. But she had far too much common sense to voice any such unobjective views.

Almost as if he was reading her thoughts, John said, 'Chris Rushton thinks Jason Ritchie is the likeliest killer. The copper's instinct is always to go for people with a bit of previous. And very often that instinct proves correct.'

Christine said rather waspishly, 'You said the wife had a bit of previous, as well as this young man.'

'Indeed. Ally Durkin is very much in our thoughts. Remember that, when you are tempted to garrotte me, will you?'

John Lambert stood up, anxious to get back to his labours in the garden. He could not remember giving as much detail to his wife about any case he'd been involved in before. But as he picked up his fork and went to the vegetable plot, he decided it must have helped to clarify his own thoughts.

For the first time, he thought he probably knew who had killed Robin Durkin.

Twenty-Two

It was something Jack Hook had never had to tackle before. When you were a thirteen-year-old, every week brought some new experience, but Jack hadn't realized this yet. As the elder of the two, he was used to playing the worldly-wise and experienced mentor to his tiresome younger brother. To have to greet this vexatious creature home from hospital after a near-death experience was something Jack had never envisaged.

He had not seen his brother for almost a week, and he was astonished how white and frail he looked when he walked into the house from their Dad's car. His mum seemed to think there was nothing wrong with Luke, even to be pleased to find him walking in like this. Jack couldn't understand how she could be so unobservant: the boy was patently very sick, to his mind.

Jack took a deep breath and said, 'You can have the latest Harry Potter. I'll finish it later.' He had never known that being a saint would sit so uneasily on his shoulders. He felt sainthood pressing on his back, like a very heavy rucksack.

The thin head with its wispy strands of fair hair shook as though it belonged to an old man. 'I'm not up to reading much just yet, bro. You finish it. Let me have it then. Let me know what you think of it.' Luke smiled wanly, feeling the determined, unnatural politeness towards Jack dropping stiffly from him. Everything felt strange and new, including this elder brother he had not seen all week. He stood, awkward and gawky as a new-born foal, in the hall of the house which he had inhabited for all but the last week of his twelve years.

Eleanor Hook had to control an impulse to burst into peals of laughter as she watched this strange little tableau. She wanted to put the boy into his own bed, to bring him whatever he needed, even to lie down beside him and feel the living, vibrant warmth of him. She did nothing of the sort, of course. She said carefully, 'Perhaps you should go and sit down with the telly for a while, Luke. Watch the cricket and build up your strength.'

She had no idea whether there was any

cricket on. But her luck held. It was the third day of the test match, and Luke allowed himself to be led, docile as an old dog, to the armchair, which was much too big for him. When Eleanor Hook brought him a sandwich with the crusts cut off five minutes later, the small white face was staring intently at the winking screen.

It was a full hour later before the parents heard the first argument about switching channels, the first sounds of their boys' voices rising in querulous debate. They looked at each and smiled the congratulations they could neither voice nor understand, while the dispute in the adjoining room grew shriller as its ritual was played out.

Normal family service had been resumed.

On Saturday afternoon, the first clouds in almost a fortnight drifted over Gurney Close.

Jason Ritchie, who had needed a pick to break up the baked and compacted ground he was levelling behind the first house in the little cul-de-sac, looked up at the sky with the practised eye of the outdoor worker. He calculated that he had probably no more than an hour before the rain coming in from the Atlantic would stop work for the day and bring the first, welcome downpour to the rudimentary gardens of the new community. He worked hard and methodically, turning the clay swiftly and expertly with a fork, calculating that he could complete the rectangle that he had planned before the rain came, using the steady rhythm of the labour to distract him from other, more disturbing concerns. He caught sight of Lisa Holt's face at the window, but she turned quickly away, embarrassed as she would never have been a week ago to be caught watching him. For his part, he carried on with his work without a flicker, refusing to acknowledge that he had ever been aware of her attention.

Twenty minutes later, Lisa brought out two big beakers of tea and stood awkwardly beside him. She did not want to go back into the house without a conversation, yet she was wondering how to summon the will and the words to sustain one. Feeling how ridiculous this estrangement was between them, she eventually sat herself down firmly on one of the garden chairs beside the plot. Jason went on working determinedly, until she said, 'You should sit down to drink your tea. You've earned a rest.'

He hesitated, then came and sat down beside her, very carefully, as if they were patients who did not know each other in a doctor's waiting room. After a moment he said, 'You'll need compost of some kind. Some farmyard manure would be ideal. Most of the topsoil seems to have disappeared, and the builder's vehicles have made this clay like concrete.'

It was the kind of language he would have used with strangers who were employing him to make a garden, not to Lisa. He was sure in any case that he had already given her this advice when he had last worked in her garden, when they had been open and easy and humorous with each other. When Robin Durkin had watched them from that other house in the close.

Jason sat and looked at his handiwork, trying to think of other and better words as he sipped the hot tea. He did not want to look into Lisa's face. Instead, he looked down at her thighs and the slim, delicate, vulnerable feet beneath the aluminium frame of the chair. He was conscious without looking at her of the curl of her hair against the nape of her neck, of the soft curve of her breast a foot from his arm. He wanted her, with a simple, uncomplicated lust that had nothing to do with love. A week ago, he would have suggested quite simply that they went inside the house and made love. At this moment, he felt that nothing between them would ever be simple again.

Jason said the only thing he could think of to say. 'The police gave me quite a going-over on Thursday. That Detective Sergeant Hook and a woman sergeant I'd never seen before. They knew all about my dealing drugs; about the hold Durkin had over me;

about his threats to land me in trouble with the law.'

Lisa Holt could no more look into his face than he into hers. She stared hard at the big lumps of dry clay he had not yet broken up with the fork, watching a robin hopping nearer and nearer to where they sat. She said dully, 'We've all been having our secrets picked over by the police in the last few days.'

'Yes. Someone shopped me to them, I think.'

'That was me, Jason.' It was a relief to have it out. She had been wondering how to tell him. But the words of explanation which would normally have come easily to her were elusive now. She said clumsily, 'They warned me we couldn't keep any secrets from them. That we'd be suspected of murder if we held anything back.'

'So you sent them after me. Thought you'd get them off your back by sending them after a man who already had a criminal record.'

'It wasn't like that. And I'm sure they knew all about your criminal record and would have followed it up without any prompting from me.'

He found himself nodding when he hadn't intended to. 'I quite like that Hook bloke. But perhaps that's what they intend. Perhaps that's the way the CID operate.' He looked up at the sky, seeing the last big tract of blue

326

giving way to the approaching cloud. 'I thought it might be you who'd put them on to me.'

'I have a child, Jason. I couldn't afford to leave him without a mother.' It sounded melodramatic, unreal. That was natural enough, Lisa thought ruefully, since that was exactly what it was: she hadn't really thought she was avoiding arrest by implicating Jason.

Jason said, 'He's a good lad, George. Your divorce doesn't seem to have affected him much.' It had seemed a safe thing to say, but he could think of nothing to continue the thought, to bring him back closer to the boy's mother.

'Martin was always a good father. We didn't fall out on that score. I bet he's spoiling George somewhere at this very moment. I'm not going to make any difficulties about him having access.'

Jason was silent for a moment, considering this other part of her life which was closed to him. Then he said quietly, 'Do you think I killed Durkin?'

'No, of course I don't.' But there had been just enough pause before she replied to tell him about the nightmare scenario that started to dance in her imagination earlier in the week. 'It's just that we were all under pressure, all trying to protect ourselves.' He didn't reply, didn't say anything conciliatory as she'd hoped. She forced herself to say the words she had never intended. 'Didn't just a little bit of you think that *I* might have killed him?'

He smiled slowly, still without looking at her, and shrugged those big, familiar shoulders. 'More than a little bit of me, at times! I knew how bitter you felt about what he'd done to Martin and about the way he wrecked your marriage.'

It was his smile, not what he said, that broke the invisible barrier between them. She let a few seconds go by before she said. 'We've been a bit silly this week, haven't we?'

He nodded happily and drained his beaker. 'Throws things out of perspective, murder does.'

She inched a little nearer to him on her chair, then put her small hand on top of his much broader one. 'We could go inside, if you want to, Tiger.'

Now Jason Ritchie turned to look at her full in the face, for the first time in days, and they grinned at each other, ruefully and happily. It was the first time she had used that pet name since the murder. He reached out awkwardly and put his hand round her slim shoulders, pulling her briefly and perilously against him as the lightweight chairs threatened to collapse. She thought he was going to kiss her, but he said, 'I'd better finish this job first, before the rain comes. Don't want my mistress saying I neglected duty for pleasure, do I?'

Lisa Holt picked up the beakers and took them back into the house. She paused at the door and bestowed upon him a look which held promise of delights to come. 'I like a man who's full of surprises!' she said.

In the second house in Gurney Close, neither of the occupants was concerned with the garden.

Philip Smart was sitting in an armchair and wondering how he could convince his wife of the seriousness of his determination to reform. He was a much chastened man. Like most libertines, he had made numerous vows over the years to mend his ways. Yet he had never been so resolved upon amendment as he was on this sunny Saturday, sitting in the conservatory of the house which was still so new that it felt strange. He just hoped it wasn't too late.

'They think I did it, Carol,' he said to his wife nervously. And when she said nothing, he followed up nervously with, 'Killed our next-door neighbour, I mean. Killed Robin Durkin.'

He was looking for reassurance: Carol Smart saw that. And paradoxically, it was because she read him so well that she could not give him that reassurance. Perhaps that was part of being a wife, she thought wryly: you saw things so clearly in a long-term partner that you also saw the comfort they wanted you to offer as banal, even hypocritical. Or perhaps it was merely that when words were obvious and expected, it was not easy for you to offer them. A waspish impulse took her by surprise and she said, 'And did you do it, Phil?'

'No, of course I didn't!' He essayed a little laugh to show how ridiculous the idea was. It emerged as a strangled groan, a most peculiar sound, without a hint of hilarity in it. 'But I wish that I hadn't tried to conceal things from them in the first place. I feel they don't trust anything I say now, that they feel I'm trying to deceive them even when I'm telling the truth.'

'You're not good at concealing things, Phil. You never were.' Despite the harshness of the thought, she found herself speaking for the first time in hours with real affection.

They had sat up far into the night, engaging in the drama, the agonies and the reliefs of confession. Phil had wept as he had not done since he was a boy, seemingly as much at the shame of his own revelations as at the pain of hers. Now he said, 'You saw through a lot of my lies, didn't you, even at the time?' His sad shake of the head took in the paucity of his efforts, the pathos of human sexual aspiration, and the feebleness of men's attempts to conceal it.

She nodded. 'I saw through most of them,

I think.' She had almost said 'all of them', but something told her that that might be a foolish and pointless boast.

'Whereas I hadn't a clue about you. I'd no idea you'd been carrying on with Rob Durkin.' Phil's comfortable, florid, fifty-one-year-old face creased anew with pain; he was not at this moment sure whether that pain came from the images of his wife rolling in bed with a hated younger man, or from the thought of his own crassness in being unaware of it.

Carol didn't like that 'carrying on', but to protest that her feelings had been more serious or aspirational would only hurt him more. And she had hurt him quite enough last night. It was curious how her one serious transgression had been more shocking and much more hurtful to him than his long trail of rather desperate womanizing had been to her.

At least he had not come up with the old line about monogamy not being a natural state for men, though she had an awful feeling that she might have agreed with him if he had. Now she threw him an old line herself, realizing as she delivered it that she was anxious to get it out before Phil came up with it. 'It's best to have things on the table. Perhaps our marriage will be all the better for these things, in the long run.'

'Yes.' He paused, remembering his tears in

331

the garden behind their house when he had gone out there alone in the small, impossibly silent, hours of the morning. So quiet had it been that he had been able to hear the movements of unseen creatures in the waters of the invisible River Wye, eighty yards away behind the high, still trees. Then he said with more conviction, 'I really want it to work, you know. And not just because of the girls. I want you, Carol. I told you everything there was to know about my women last night.'

Carol smiled, looking unseeingly at the picture she had never really liked upon their wall. He probably thought he had made a full confession to her, though she'd stopped him from delivering the gory details of his womanizing as soon as she could. And he probably really believed now that his contrition was all that was necessary for their union to be restored to a full vigour. His naïvety was quite touching in one of his years; she felt a warmth for that quality in him, a warmth which was possibly going to be a great help in the years to come.

She was fairly confident now that there were going to be years together in their future. She had been surprised in the various crises which had beset them in the last week to find how much she cared for this venal, ridiculous figure who sat alongside her. She might even prevent him from turning into the ridiculous old roué he had promised to become and turn him into a dull and affectionate husband, if she worked hard at it. And she realized now with a little, not unpleasant, shock of self-knowledge that she wanted to work at it. She said, 'The police suspected me too, you know. Probably still do, for that matter. I don't think they found me fully convincing when they spoke to me at the school last night.'

'But you didn't do it.'

Carol hoped it was a statement, not a question. Perhaps she should have been insulted. Instead, she found herself merely anxious to reassure this blundering husband, who seemed to have learned so little about life during all his pathetic attempts to find love in strange places. 'No, I didn't do it, Phil. But there were times when I'd have liked to kill Rob Durkin. And when I found he was dead last Sunday, I felt no real sorrow, just an overwhelming relief.'

He smiled. That at any rate was an assurance that she had no longer felt anything for the man. 'So did I. He won't be here to worry us any more. So it's up to us to pick up the pieces and get on with our lives.'

Phil wasn't going to stop thinking and talking in clichés, Carol thought. But so long as the clichés expressed the right sentiments and were genuinely felt, she didn't give a damn. She said as casually as she could, 'I think you'd better move back into the main bedroom tonight, don't you?'

Philip Smart could think of nothing to say. Eventually he managed, 'If you want me to, I will.'

'I do want you to. Be such a pity if you didn't have proper access to our wonderful new en suite bathroom, you see.'

Carol Smart knew that it was up to her to produce the little joke Phil would never have managed, to pretend that the most deeply serious things in life were really quite trivial. Humour was the only way you could cope, sometimes, when the things at stake were so tremendous.

In the third house in Gurney Close, the one where Robin Durkin had died, his wife was determinedly getting on with her life.

Ally Durkin refused all invitations from others and made herself an excellent casserole, which would do for her evening meal today and tomorrow. At six o'clock, she would open a good bottle of red wine; but not before six, because there was no way she was going to run the risk of becoming an old soak.

At four o'clock, she was speaking to her sister on the phone. 'No, I shall be staying here ... Quite definitely made my mind up, yes. This was the house I wanted, the one I worked on with the builders at the planning stage, and I don't see why Rob's death should alter that ... No, apparently I shouldn't have any worries about money. He was a lot better off than he cared to declare to anyone, apparently ... I don't know where most of it came from – it certainly wasn't the garage – and maybe I shouldn't ask too much about that ... Actually, I don't need to worry about funeral arrangements for the moment. They can't release the body for cremation yet. A nice young woman police officer came round and explained it all to me on Thursday. Apparently when they make an arrest and charge someone, the accused will have a right to a second, independent post-mortem ... No, that doesn't really upset me at all. Our marriage was over and it's a relief now to be able to admit it ... I suppose I might be in shock, yes. Just a little. They told me I could have counselling, but I don't feel I need it. I'll come and see you though, in a week or two ... I think I'll quite enjoy it here, when everything's calmed down again. I like my neighbours, and I'm sure we're going to get on very well in the years to come ... No, you're not to worry about me at all. I'll ring you in a couple of days and let you know when I can come over.'

She put the phone down and sat contentedly in her chair, looking out not at the back garden and the spot where Rob had fallen, but at the small patch in front which she would need to work on. It seemed to her impossible that any of these nice neighbours could possibly have committed murder.

That was the thought in her mind as she saw the now-familiar police car appear at the corner. It moved slowly past the three houses and turned into the drive of the single bungalow at the end of Gurney Close.

Twenty-Three

'It's the CID again. They say they want to speak to you, Ron.' Rosemary Lennox did not trust herself to say any more as she led in Chief Superintendent Lambert and Detective Sergeant Hook.

Ron Lennox was in an old green leisure shirt with the top button missing. He looked up from the sports section of the *Times* and gestured towards the sofa opposite his armchair. 'Do take a pew, gentlemen. And please excuse my dress: I was working in the garden earlier in the day.'

He pushed himself a little further back into his chair, anxious to convince them that he was thoroughly relaxed and unthreatened. His sparse hair was dishevelled from his efforts at clearing brambles at the back of the garden, emphasizing the high dome of his forehead and the narrowness of the head behind it. He clasped his arms across his chest and then unclasped them immediately, in a gesture which was obviously habitual and gave him comfort. Then he grasped the wood at the end of the arms of his chair firmly in his lean fingers, as if the action was necessary to immobilize his hands.

Lennox's shabby gardening trousers had ridden up high as he sat back, so that an inch of very white leg showed between socks and trousers. The forearms which protruded too far from his short-sleeved shirt were sinewy without any great sign of strength. There was a smear of blood on the back of his left hand where a bramble had scratched him, another and fainter smear on his cheek where he had dragged that hand across it.

Despite the spurious confidence of his greeting, Ronald Lennox now looked watchful, frail and very vulnerable.

He said primly, 'I trust you are making progress, Mr Lambert. I'm only too anxious to help, of course, but I can't think that I can possibly be of any further help to you.'

Lambert didn't hurry. He knew he held all the cards now. But a confession was always helpful. He said quietly, 'Your son spoke to a CID inspector in Cambridge this morning.'

'So I understand. The boy spoke to his mother on the telephone whilst I was in the garden. I realize that neither you nor Detective Sergeant Hook was personally involved, but I feel I must protest at his arrest. It won't do Andrew any good with his employers you know – even if they are only supermarket executives.' He could not conceal his distaste for his son's choice of temporary employment. 'An arrest is hardly appropriate treatment, you know, for a putative Cambridge graduate.'

'Your son wasn't arrested, Mr Lennox. He was asked to help the Cambridge police with their enquiries, which they were pursuing on our behalf.'

'I'm glad to hear it. Nevertheless, this heavy-handed—'

'Andrew could have been arrested, however. Indeed, I'd say he's lucky that he wasn't both arrested and charged, in the past. Lucky not to be carrying a criminal record into the final year of his studies for his putative degree, in fact.'

'To me, this is amazing and quite ridiculous.' Lennox decided not to be irritated by the superintendent's ironic repetition of his word 'putative'. He clasped his thin hands together in his lap, wrung them against each other for a few seconds, and then returned them to the arms of his chair. 'But I make a point of never commenting upon things which I do not understand, so I shall hold my peace.'

It was impossible to tell whether Ron Lennox was shaken or not. Lambert realized in that moment that the man had prepared this reaction for them, probably at the moment an hour or two earlier when he had learned of his son's being questioned. 'I'm speaking of the time when he was dealing drugs for Robin Durkin. When he was a pusher for him, a junior in the ranks of his drugs operation.'

'You may think that you have the facts of the matter, Superintendent. I could not possibly comment.' Ron remembered the actor Ian Richardson saying something like that, in a play on television. *House of Cards*, he thought it was. Not Shakespeare, by any means, but an appealing enough melodramatic trifle. People had sometimes compared him to Ian Richardson, and he was flattered by the thought, since he liked the actor. He had rather taken to imitating his thin-lipped, acerbic delivery since two or three people at school had mentioned the likeness.

It was Rosemary Lennox, sitting with drawn face on an upright chair at the back of the room, who now said, 'Andy left all that behind him long ago. I hope no one is going to charge him with dealing at this stage of his life.'

Lambert turned his head for a moment and looked at her steadily. 'That is out of our hands, Mrs Lennox. But I don't think it is likely there will be charges; I gather that your son has so far been fully cooperative.'

Ron Lennox should have been relieved by this diversion. Instead, he felt a little piqued that he should not even for an instant be the centre of attention here. He said querulously, 'I can't see that Andrew's evidence has anything to offer that could possibly be relevant to—'

'Not evidence, Mr Lennox. Not as yet. Andrew has merely being cooperating with a police investigation. Helping us with our enquiries into the murder of Mr Robin Durkin.'

'Andrew has nothing to say about this. He hadn't even spoken to Durkin for years.'

'Nevertheless, he is central to this case. He is the reason why you decided that you had to silence Robin Durkin.'

Lambert had expected gasps of astonishment, or shrieks of protest. Instead, there was absolute silence, so that the raucous cry of a seagull, drifting inland before the approaching rain, rang unnaturally loud through the open window. Rosemary Lennox sat as still as a well-dressed statue on her chair at the back of the room, and Lambert sensed in that moment that she already knew exactly what her husband had done. Ronald Lennox had scarcely blinked at the words from the superintendent. He sat with his knuckles whitening with the fierceness of his grip on the arms of his chair, wondering whether to accept or deny the accusation.

It was Bert Hook, sensing as usual the moment when an intervention from him would be most telling, who now said softly, 'You hated Rob Durkin a lot more than you admitted to us, even back in his school days, didn't you, Mr Lennox?'

Ron turned eagerly to the ruddy, experienced face, sensing a chance for self-justification rather than the invitation to incriminate himself. 'He was disruptive and malicious throughout his time in the sixth form. He was a dreadful influence upon his peers, even then. And among the staff, he singled me out particularly for his contempt and his derision. I don't think I would be exaggerating if I say that even all those years ago he was vicious.'

He weighed the word for a moment and nodded slowly, demonstrating to them that even in this context it was important for him to be accurate in his vocabulary. Hook nodded sympathetically, as if Lennox was now making things much clearer for him. 'And after Durkin had left school, things only got worse, didn't they?'

Ron nodded eagerly, careless of the implications for himself of what he was saying, anxious only to make clear the nature of the evil he had been fighting. 'I breathed a huge sigh of relief when Rob Durkin walked through the school gates for the last time. But things got worse, rather than better. I would see him in his car outside the school gates, smiling at me, letting me know that he was still around, still making mischief.'

Rosemary Lennox leaned forward on her chair, the first, minimal movement she had made since she had taken up her post on the edge of this dramatic tableau. 'You don't have to say this, Ron. You should keep quiet, you know. You should wait for a lawyer's advice.'

'Lawyers!' His contempt for a whole profession was crammed into two syllables. 'They're no more efficient and no less grasping today than when Dickens laid into them in *Bleak House*. I'm not here to make fat fees for lawyers. I brought more justice to the world than a thousand lawyers when I killed Rob Durkin!'

His admission stunned all four of them for a second or two. Then Bert Hook glanced at Lambert and stepped forward to the man who sat so tense and still in the armchair. He informed Ronald Lennox calmly that he was being arrested on suspicion of the murder of Robin Durkin, that he did not need to say anything, but that it might harm his defence if he failed to mention when questioned something which he might later rely on in court.

Lennox scarcely listened to him, appearing only anxious to speak. He said right on the heels of Hook's last word, 'The world is well rid of Robin Durkin. I shall be proud to justify that to anyone who will listen.'

Lambert saw that Lennox was transforming himself from murderer to martyr, that this would be the image he would use to sustain him through the long years in prison. He said quietly, 'You are an intelligent man, Mr Lennox. You know better than most that we cannot allow people to take justice into their own hands.'

Lennox looked as if he would like to engage his nemesis in a philosophical discussion about the defects of the law. Then he nodded, and said, 'That way anarchy lies. That way civilization disappears. You're right, Chief Superintendent Lambert, of course you are, in general. But the system falls down with men like Durkin. The system isn't efficient enough to deal with them. He'd have come to grief eventually, no doubt, but a lot of better people than him would have suffered at his hands before the law got to him.'

'People like your only son.'

'He said he'd ruin Andrew. Said he'd be delighted to expose his dealing in drugs at the right time, when he'd graduated from Cambridge and was embarking upon a career. Said it would be the crowning victory in the campaign he'd waged against me since he was at school. I've got things he gave to me to show what he could do to us. Photographs of Andy when he was dealing, photocopies of orders my son sent to his supplier for illegal drugs. Cocaine, heroin, LSD, as well as lots of cannabis. Lists with Andrew's name on them, but nothing to implicate Durkin. He was much higher up the chain by then. Durkin said he'd drop them anonymously into a police station when he thought the time was right.'

Lambert doubted whether he would ever have done that: there would have been too great a danger of the mud spreading wider and smearing him as well, too great a danger of the action implicating other and more dangerous people in that vicious industry. But everyone said that Durkin had enjoyed threatening people, enjoyed exercising power over their lives and making them suffer. And his feud with this hyperactive, sententious man went back to his days at school, when Ronald Lennox had been the one exercising the power.

Lambert said, 'You had better let us have these things. They may be used as mitigating evidence by the lawyers you so despise.'

Rosemary Lennox spoke unexpectedly

from the back of the room. 'They are no longer available. I have disposed of them. I took them away this morning.' She spoke in the even monotone of one in a trance.

Lennox whirled upon her, his thin frame bristling with rage at the interference. 'Why did you do that? You've just heard that they might be produced as evidence in my defence.'

'They were also the evidence that could have convicted you of murder! You kept a drawer full of items which showed that you had a motive to kill the man! I didn't know you were going to boast about your killing like this, did I, you stupid, stupid man!' All the frustration of this woman who was normally such a model of quiet control and efficiency came out as her voice rose towards a scream of frustration. She glared her resentment at this pedant of a husband, who had erred so disastrously when he tried to become a man of action.

Lennox looked at her in astonishment for a moment. Then he turned his back on her very deliberately and said to Lambert, 'How did you realize that I was the man you wanted?' He spoke as if their discovery of his crime had merely wounded his vanity in some small matter.

Lambert wasn't going to admit how recently things had fallen into place, what a close-run thing it had been. Nor would he

345

point out at this stage that Rosemary Lennox, pillar of the local community, had made herself an accessory after the fact in a murder case. It wouldn't be his decision as to whether that charge should be pursued; probably, if Lennox pleaded guilty, as everything now indicated he would, there would be no charges brought against his wife.

Lambert said calmly, 'Small things, Mr Lennox. Small but significant. The fact that you carefully omitted to mention your own son's school career, even though he did very well and you had every reason to be very proud of him. The fact that Andrew's picture was on display in a position of honour here when we first visited you on Tuesday, but had been removed when we came back on Wednesday. That made us feel that your son might be significant in the case: that he should be questioned about his own relationship with Robin Durkin.'

Ron Lennox nodded, digesting this account, apparently finding it satisfied him. He might have been listening patiently to a bright sixth-form student propounding a theory about history. He said, 'He's a fine boy, Andrew. A fine young man, I should say now. Since he has been rid of the baleful influence of Rob Durkin, he's never looked back. He'll graduate from Cambridge next year. Possibly with a First. And he'll have a fine career, whatever option he chooses to pursue. I couldn't let scum like Lennox interfere with that. I don't expect you to admit it, but I'm sure that as an intelligent man you can see the logic of my actions.'

For the first time that day, he gave that small, surprising cackle of laughter which they had heard from him on their previous visits. It rang eerily round the room, shocking the detectives, his wife, even the man himself. For a moment, no one knew how to follow this startling sound, and in the silence which followed, the first flash of lightning flared in the darkening sky, the first distant rumble of thunder rolled along the ridge of the invisible Welsh hills to the west.

Eighty miles away in Birmingham, the hitman Anthony David Watson watched the beginning of the investigation into his gangland killing; it would drag on for months and end in failure. The professional killer would as usual escape arrest, and be free to carry on with his calling.

In rural Herefordshire, the detectives took the Lennoxes out to the car under an umbrella as the rain fell suddenly and heavily from a pewter sky. As if to call attention to a dramatic scene which was unwitnessed, the oaks between the close and the Wye tossed in a violent gust of wind. The lights were switched on now in the three houses of Gurney Close, even at five o'clock on this July afternoon.

Only the single bungalow where the most elderly of the new residents had dwelled remained obstinately without light, as the rain pelted harder and the evening stretched into night.